Confessions of a domestic failure

BUNMI LADITAN

Confessions of a domestic failure

mira

mira

ISBN-13: 978-0-7783-3068-4

Confessions of a Domestic Failure

For questions and comments about the quality of this book, please contact us at CustomerService@Harlequin.com.

www.BookClubbish.com

Printed in U.S.A.

Recycling programs for this product may not exist in your area.

To my hearts: M, T and F.

Monday, January 21, 5 A.M.

Aubrey's ear-piercing cry rattled over the baby monitor, yanking me out of a deep sleep.

My eyes fluttered open. I looked at my phone's clock. No, no, no, no, no.

I'd dreamt I had a full staff: a nanny, butler, housekeeper and full-time masseuse. The laundry mountain of shame that lives permanently on my living room couch had vanished, and in its place, eighty-one bottles of delicious exercise wine. What's exercise wine? It's a wine that, when consumed, stimulates your muscles, resulting in rock-hard abs. While my nanny, who wasn't hot enough to be a threat, played with Aubrey on the floor, I enjoyed sip after mouthwatering sip and watched my kangaroo-pouch stomach tighten into a washboard.

Another scream over the monitor.

I don't know whose grandmother I dropkicked into a well in a previous life to have an eight-month-old who regularly wakes up before the sun, but I wanted to apologize. I glanced at my darling husband, David, who was sleeping soundly.

I watched him breathe deeply and suppressed the urge to smother him with a pillow. How was it that he could hear me adjusting the thermostat from two rooms away but could sleep through the ear-stabbing howls of our eight-month-old every morning?

"I know you're faking," I whispered, trying to call his bluff. No movement.

I threw my legs over the side of the bed and bent down to find my trusty black stretch pants. They're the same ones I'd been wearing for the past two, three, maybe six days. They didn't smell bad, they smelled…rich with character.

After making my way to the bathroom, I splashed a bit of water on my face, hoping the H_2O would magically fade the dark circles around my eyes. I glanced into the mirror and was surprised to see Medusa staring back at me, but instead of snakes coming out of my head, there was just a ratty ponytail. I ran my fingers through the mess and cringed. If my hair got any greasier, I'd be able to stand outside on a hot day and cook breakfast on it.

I was exhausted. My back hurt. My head hurt. My eyelashes hurt.

I tried to remember when my last good night's sleep was. It had to be when I was six months pregnant. That's when the heartburn kicked in. Did I say heartburn? I meant boiling hot lava. Flaming acid rain. Whatever it was, it meant I had to sleep sitting up in bed while Aubrey Riverdanced on my bladder. If there was any justice on Earth, women would take the first twenty-week shift of pregnancy and men would take over for the last four-and-a-half months. But based on how a common head cold transformed my husband from a thirty-five-year-old man to a ninety-six-year-old granny with malaria, I wasn't sure he'd make it through one day with child.

Another angry scream shot through the baby monitor.

"I'm coming. I'm coming," I whispered, dabbing at my face with a towel. I stared at my tired reflection in the mirror.

When Aubrey was finally born, every ounce of throat-searing bile was (mostly) forgotten as I looked into her adorable little face covered in that weird, white marsh scum★ infants are born with. I wish someone had warned me about the vernix situation. Maybe then I wouldn't have screamed, "IS SHE A LEPER?" in front of two nurses, the doctor and a team of horrified interns. David teased me for weeks. Every time I'd hand her to him, he'd make a cross with his fingers and yell, "Unclean!"

She really was a beautiful baby. Or I thought she was. Everyone thinks their newborn is a looker when the truth is, 99.99 percent of them look like Groucho Marx.

I looked down and noticed that the pants I had slipped on in the dark featured a large hole in the crotch. A custom air vent, I rationalized.

It was almost impossible to believe that two years ago my mornings started with a ridiculously long shower as I got ready for work at Weber & Associates. I was a rising superstar in the marketing world. Back then, my mornings revolved around my intricately detailed makeup routine, dressing in trendy but professional skirt suits, and the vanilla latte and egg, cheese and ham croissant that I'd devour on my commute. Now breakfast consisted of whatever finger-food scraps Aubrey doesn't eat and peanut butter on a spoon while standing up with my face in the pantry. This wasn't how I pictured motherhood at all.

In my motherhood fantasy, I'd wake up at 7 a.m. and float into my still-sleeping baby's designer periwinkle-and-slate nursery (with a plum accent wall—like in *Real Simple*'s Fall

---

★ When you think about it, my uterus was kind of like a marsh: it was wet, dark, warm. All that was missing were the alligators.

issue). Everything in the spotless, clutter-free baby sanctuary would be made by obscure Etsy artists living in the woods in Oregon, Italian designers or handmade by yours truly. You'd be able to feel the oak knots in the crib. They'd tell a story.

While my baby slept, I'd sit in her custom-made organic bamboo-and-pine rocking chair and write her a poem every day. She'd treasure these poems for her entire life and eventually turn them into songs. She'd win armfuls of Grammy Awards while I, an old but hot grandma, cheered her on from the star-studded audience. I can already see the award show camera go from her, in a beautiful gown on stage giving her acceptance speech, to me, tearfully clapping for my baby girl. She'd blow me a kiss, I'd catch it, and people around the world would be inspired by our mother-daughter connection. "How did she raise such an amazing young woman?" they'd ask themselves.

I'd wear stylish but casual clothing: white sundresses and practical but fabulous strappy Bohemian wedges. I'd save the skinny jeans for playdates.

Speaking of playdates, I'd be invited to so many of them that I'd be turning them down. "Sarah, I'd love to pop by, but I'm making organic applesauce and canning tomatoes from my garden today, sorry!"

I'd have one of those cute planners to keep all of my events straight—a pink leather-bound agenda with a matching pen that I'd keep in my fantastic diaper bag. The fantastic diaper bag that I'd never forget at home.

Aubrey would wear nothing but 100 percent organic cotton matching separates, lots of delicate vintage lace and those $60-a-pop suede booties in every color. I'd visit the farmers' market daily and sniff loads of fresh fruit, vegetables and local honey before selecting the items that would become the rustic, delicious dinners that I would Instagram to the delight of my hundreds of thousands of followers.

My meals would be beautiful and epic. People on Facebook would stare in admiration at the photos of my homemade Bolognese with handmade pasta. I'd definitely have one of those countertop pasta-drying things that look like they're for hanging miniature laundry.

Obviously, I'd cook while wearing seasonally themed aprons with Aubrey warm and cozy in the baby wrap I got at my shower a year ago and that I have yet to learn how to put on. David would brag to all his friends about how naturally I took to motherhood and how he always knew I'd be a great mom.

My reality? Aubrey screams me awake at 5 a.m. every morning and I'm about six months behind on the laundry that's taking over my living room like some kind of poisonous mold.

Forget about all of the cute outfits I thought I'd be putting my firstborn in. Every day my daughter wears one of four pairs of footie pajamas. She can't even walk and the feet are getting worn out from use. Two of them are stained: one from a diaper blowout (since when does infant poop stain?) and another from red wine (don't judge me). I wear the same three pairs of black yoga pants and a rotating army of stretched-out tank tops that can barely contain my jiggly muffin top.

Two weeks ago in the grocery store, an elderly woman looked us up and down, shook her head and handed me $20. I wanted to yell, "We're not homeless. I'm just too tired to care!" but she'd already turned down the baked goods aisle.

My thoughts were interrupted by another howl over the baby monitor as I hurried to pee. I finished up and washed my hands more slowly than I should have, savoring the last few moments of my day alone.

Before having Aubrey, I thought I'd be an amazing mom. I

thought I'd be Emily Walker. Yes, THAT Emily Walker, the mom *everyone* wants to be; the famous mom blogger turned media darling who went from sharing her perfect family (including five children) and their perfect life with an audience of millions of mediocre moms to getting her own morning television show where she tells moms everywhere how to knit, craft and bake their way to a better life, all while getting to yoga class on time.

Not that I go to a yoga class. And let's not even talk about my body. I refuse to let David see me naked. The few—and I mean few—times we've found ourselves in a *compromising position* since Aubrey was born, I insisted that the lights remained off and as much of me stayed under the covers as possible. Yeah, I'm a regular vixen.

But Emily Walker has five kids and looks incredible naked. I know because on her blog are gorgeous photos from her vacation in the Bahamas (sponsored by a sunscreen company, of course). In one of them, she's lying on a huge yacht in a bikini that looks like a piece of dental floss. She doesn't have a single stretchmark on her toned, tight abdomen. Not one. I only have one kid and not only can I tuck my stomach into my pants, but it also looks like a bear clawed its way down my doughy center. But who's keeping score? Okay, I am.

Motherhood has done a number on my body. My hair has somehow become an oil slick and bone-dry at the same time. My skin is always broken out from the hormonal roller coaster I can't seem to get off of. Last week I cried during a commercial for yeast infection cream. David looked at me like I was insane. In my defense, the mother and daughter bonding over their shared vaginal fungus really touched me.

I thought being a stay-at-home mom would be easier. But the house is a disaster. David doesn't say anything, but I can tell by the judge-y way he looks around when he gets home that he's noticed we currently live in an upscale rattlesnake's nest. I'm not exactly the best home chef, either. My idea of cooking is flipping through takeout menus with a spoonful of Nutella in my mouth or throwing something together at the last minute as if I'm on one of those "race against time" cooking shows. The result is usually spaghetti or quesadillas—you know, the kind of food fourth graders eat for lunch. Basically, I'm failing.

Don't get me wrong, I have no regrets. I love Aubrey. I just didn't think I'd get pregnant so fast after David and I got married. I know how babies are made, but getting knocked up on the first try was a surprise. I was equally surprised to get laid off while on maternity leave. I guess that's what happens when a company has to tighten its belt after the CEO is caught embezzling money. I never even got to ride on his yacht. Pity. So, here I am, an accidental stay-at-home mom.

In two short years I went from being a professional thirty-two-year-old semifashionable woman who ordered cranberry martinis during happy hour and spent Friday nights hopping from fusion restaurants to invite-only "what's the password" bars, to a thirty-four-year-old lumpy, bone-tired, hormonal mom who lives in semiclean activewear and spends Friday nights passing out at 7:48 p.m.—three minutes after I get Aubrey to sleep.

Just when I was really starting to feel sorry for myself, another impatient yelp boomed through the baby monitor. I peeked out of the bathroom into the bedroom where David had turned onto his side.

"Still pretending to be asleep, huh?" I spoke directly at him. Still nothing.

I shook my head but let him off the hook. In an hour he'd be off to work, fighting to make a name for the advertising agency he'd left his job to start four months before I decided not to find another job. I knew he was under a lot of pressure to make his company successful. If his sales skills were half as good as his early-morning acting skills, he'd have no problem at all. But in all seriousness, I was proud of him for fighting for his dream. I just wished he'd get up with the baby once in a while.

"I'm coming. I'm coming," I said, as I walked toward my daughter's bedroom. She was standing up, full of more energy than anyone should have before dawn. Her smile was contagious and I found myself cracking a slight one as I scooped her into my arms. If there was anything more delicious than a baby in footed pajamas I didn't know what it was. I mean, ham and cheese croissants came close, but she was still cuter. Before having Aubrey I thought it was horrifying when people talked about wanting to eat up their babies, but now I totally got it.

She babbled enthusiastically as I nuzzled her cheek. My heart dissolved into warm fuzzies as she pawed at my shirt. I looked down at her sweet face and tried to memorize every curve and dimple. I may not be the world's best mom, but gosh, how I love this little girl.

"Just so you know, when you're ready to talk, it's perfectly fine to call for Daddy in the morning," I said, as we made our way downstairs and into the kitchen. I flipped the switch and blinked as the light burned my eyes. It was too early.

Coffee. Must ingest caffeine. Before becoming a mom, I loved coffee, but now I needed it to function. My body went on autopilot as I fumbled with the coffeemaker with one hand. Aubrey cooed to herself on my hip. I pressed the Start button and the machine began to gurgle.

In a few hours, my ex-coworkers would be in the main conference room brainstorming PR campaigns for a new sugar-free energy drink or sparkly nail polish over a catered breakfast, while I was still sitting in my living room trying to stay awake.

I grabbed my coffee and walked with Aubrey, still happily on my hip, into the living room. I plopped her down on the enormous play mat that dominated the room and she quickly got to work finding her favorite toys. I flipped on the television and found a comfortable spot on the couch, cradling my coffee mug in my hands. Sensing my comfort, Aubrey began to squawk angrily. I picked her up and sat her on my lap for snuggles. She immediately dove for the hot coffee in my hand. I managed to take a few urgent sips before placing it on the end table and out of her sight. I looked longingly at my warm cup of daily motivation. I'd finish it when Aubrey napped. Of course, it'd be stone-cold by then, but that's what microwaves are for.

I heard a familiar voice on the television.

It was Emily Walker, mom blogger turned media superstar, on her highly acclaimed morning show, aptly titled *The Emily Walker Show*, doing a cooking segment with her latest celebrity guest.

Emily, impeccably dressed in a canary yellow ensemble, stood next to the redheaded bombshell and looked into the camera.

"Your kids are absolutely going to LOVE these butternut squash date scones!" Emily said, waving her hands enthusiastically.

"Which kids would love those? Human ones?" I said to Aubrey, as if she could understand anything I said. She blinked.

Emily held up a book. "Don't forget to pick up Alicia Winter's new wheat-free, sugar-free, dairy-free, fat-free dessert cookbook! It's in stores now!"

"I'll get right on that," I said sarcastically to Aubrey, who was now happily chewing on a runaway strand of my hair.

I really needed to get some friends. Surely they'd appreciate my witty commentary more than an eight-month-old could.

Truth be told, I'd love to be the kind of mom who showed up to playdates with a tray of delicious, homemade treats: baby carrots cut up to look like snakes, baskets of muffins made with beet puree, and hand-churned yogurt in mini glass mason jars topped with fruit I preserved myself. The other moms would watch in astonishment as their children devoured my domestic creations. But so far I've been invited to exactly zero playdates. Even if I were asked, I'd probably bring a few bags of drive-through fries. Fries are a vegetable, right? They're also vegan.

I stole another sip of my coffee and turned up the volume.

Emily was now sitting on her trademark pink EW-logoed interviewer couch, having what she called a Mama Heart to Mama Heart. It's how she ended every episode of her show—with a few words of her own brand of wisdom.

"My mission for *The Emily Walker Show* has always been to inspire mothers." The camera zoomed in tight. "I see you there, mama. You're tired, frumpy, exhausted..."

I looked down at my stained purple sweatshirt and holey pants and glanced around the room. Were there cameras in here?

Emily narrowed her eyes dramatically. "Every day I get hundreds of emails and letters asking me how I raise my five beautiful children while running my empire, and I'm thrilled to announce that my book, *Motherhood Better*, comes out today. In it you will find the keys to my success and your own. Are you ready to be the mom you've always known you can be? Are you ready to truly enjoy motherhood?"

I found myself staring at the camera, hypnotized. She was saying all of the right things. It's true. I had always wondered how Emily's social media accounts were constantly full of gorgeous meals and perfectly groomed children, and boasted of her latest ventures, when the only thing I'd accomplished last week was moving my laundry pile from the bedroom floor to the recliner. I'd also figured out that a spoon half full of Nutella and half full of peanut butter dipped in powdered sugar tastes like a Reese's cup.

"My new book, *Motherhood Better*, will take you from frumpy to fabulous, struggling to spectacular. It's time to become the mother you've always known you could be."

This was exactly what I needed. With that realization, I practically flew off the couch, startling Aubrey, and grabbed my computer from the dining room table. Within minutes I'd purchased the book from BookSpot, a local store downtown and opted for same day pickup. This was an emergency, after all.

I was almost shaking with excitement. This was my moment. This is exactly what I'd been waiting for. That, and I was running out of places to hide laundry.

I opened my email and was excited to see a confirmation message waiting for me.

You purchased Motherhood Better by Emily Walker.

I looked at my phone. Only four hours until the store opened. Today I will become a mother, better. A better mother? Anyway—I'll get the book today is what I'm saying.

2 P.M.

I'd finally gotten Aubrey down for a nap and was lounging on my bed, trying not to let the two sinks full of dishes distract me from my well-deserved break. The day had been one for the record books. Everything that could have gone wrong had, and I learned some important lessons.

Lesson #1: If you forget the diaper bag at home and your

baby needs changing at a bookstore, remember that you CAN-NOT, in fact, craft a diaper out of an old ziplock freezer bag that you found in the trunk of your car and a pair of emergency period panties from your glove compartment.

Lesson #2: When you arrive at home and see that your mother-in-law, Gloria, has popped in for a surprise visit with one of her classic six-cheese casseroles because she thinks (knows) you can't cook and doesn't want her David "starving to death," don't forget about your ziplock bag/period-panty diaper monstrosity and hand the baby to her.

Lesson #3: When your mother-in-law gasps and recoils in horror upon changing the baby and seeing your ziplock bag/period-panty diaper debacle (complete with a stained merlot mosaic of periods past), think of something clever and blasé to say rather than just standing there with your mouth open. Don't manically yell "Yolo!" She'll just ask what "yolo" means and you'll sound like an idiot explaining it. Also, don't try to cover your tracks and say that yolo is an ancient Tibetan prayer, because even though your mother-in-law doesn't know how to call before she visits, she does know how to Google.

Lesson #4: Be more prepared. Keep the diaper bag by the door. You should be better at this by now.

What kind of people "just pop by" anyway? Perhaps my dear husband casually let his mom in on the not-so-secret secret that I'm not taking to motherhood as naturally as I thought I would. In my defense, Aubrey is only eight months old. Eight months into any job isn't really enough time to become an expert.*

Despite my sweet mother-in-law going on and on about how motherhood is an instinct, I can't be the only newish mom having a bit of a time finding her groove.

---

* Not that I'm calling motherhood a job. It's a blessing. Really, it is. Such a blessing. I'm blessed. Truly. #soblessed

To be fair, I had very little preparation for this whole motherhood thing. Before Aubrey, the only newborns I'd ever held were my sister Joy's kids, the last of whom, my niece, was born just a month before I joined #TeamMom. That's a day I'll never forget, and not just because my niece was so adorable. Joy had just dropped the enormous bomb that she was giving her baby girl the name we'd both loved, I mean LOVED, as in we'd named every doll and teddy bear Ella since we were four and seven. When we found out that we were both pregnant, we even met at a coffee shop and decided that neither of us would take the name. So when the nurse said, "Isn't Ella darling?" I almost hit the ground.

"Don't be childish, Ashley," was Joy's response as she lay looking like a freaking goddess in her hospital bed. She was probably the first woman there to give birth in a $200 custom nursing gown. It was gorgeous. Pink apple print with cute little yellow blossoms.

It wasn't just the gown. Joy always looked fantastic. Her hair was even prettily tousled like she'd been boating all day rather than pushing six pounds and seven ounces of person out of her vagina.

When I told her I wasn't being childish and brought up the conversation in the café, Mom chimed in to defend her like she always does.

"Stop it, Ashley. Your sister just had a baby, for goodness sake. And she really does look like an Ella."

I had Aubrey one month later.

I love Ella and, of course, her brother, my three-year-old nephew, George, but I'd be lying if I said it didn't sting a little every time I hear her name.

"Aubrey is a gorgeous name," Joy gushed when she came to visit me in the birthing center. Joy and Mom were dead against my giving birth to my first outside of a hospital. In our typical Easton style, they never actually told me this. They just sent me every birthing center/natural-birth-gone-wrong horror story ever published while I was pregnant.

So maybe I did feel a little smug when Aubrey was born all warm and perfect in my hippie den aka birthing center. That is, until Joy spoke.

"You really are brave, Ashley. I never could have rolled the dice with my baby."

Once again, Mom backed her up. "Yes, Ashley, you're very lucky."

Lucky? They acted like I'd run blindfolded across six lanes of traffic while balancing my baby on my head rather than just given birth in the #1 birthing center in the nation, directly across the street from a top-rated, fully equipped hospital.

Before Aubrey was born I'd decided that I'd be one of those all-natural moms who made their own peanut butter, wore their baby 24/7 in one of those slings and breast-fed well into toddlerhood. Giving birth to Aubrey in a birthing center was just what I needed to catapult me into my new, organic lifestyle.

But my earth-mother adrenaline rush lasted until about four days after Aubrey was born, when my milk didn't come in. After Aubrey lost two pounds, even my "fight the man" midwife had to admit that something was very wrong.

"You might just be one of those women," she said to me in a hushed whisper, as if we were undercover spies trading government secrets. "One of those women who don't make milk."

"BUT YOU SAID THEY WERE ONE IN FIVE MILLION!" I cried, pushing my raw nipple into Aubrey's screaming mouth. "I HAD A NATURAL BIRTH!"

Two lactation consultants, bloodwork, a dozen delicious but ineffective lactation cookies, two boxes of lactation tea and a rented breast pump later, I gave in and bought my first tin of failure powder. That's what a mom from my online breast-feeding forum calls formula. Failure powder. For failures like me. Did I mention that Emily Walker made so much breast milk for her last baby, Sage, that she donated gallons to her local milk bank?

Joy was as helpful as she always is. "I'd totally pump for Aubrey, but I'm making just enough for Ella as it is. Sorry." I could tell she really was sorry, but it didn't help with the feeling of crushing disappointment. The studies that go around Facebook every fifteen minutes about how babies who aren't breast-fed grow up with dragon scales covering their entire bodies didn't help.

Eight months later I still hate myself just a little every time I scoop that white powder into the bottle. Formula. I'm a formula mom. This wasn't how I saw it all happening. It's not that I think formula is evil; I just always pictured myself breastfeeding under a willow at the park, its leaves gently swaying in the warm breeze, onlookers stealing admiring glances at me. Ask me how many admiring glances I get whipping out a nine-ounce bottle at Starbucks. ZERO. One mom even asked—with tears in her eyes, no less—if she could breastfeed my baby for me. As if Aubrey is some malnourished third-world baby on television with flies buzzing around her emaciated body. I may have lied and said that she's allergic to human milk.

Oh, and we stopped using the million-dollar-a-can organic formula blend when Aubrey was three months old. Now she's on the cheap brand stuff. She's the only eight-month-old I know with zero teeth—probably from all of the trace minerals she's missing from my malfunctioning mammary glands. Formula. When she drops out of community college, we'll all know why.

Yesterday, Emily Walker posted a photo of herself breast-feeding her eighteen-month-old in front of the Eiffel Tower.

She's doing her show live from Paris for her *Motherhood Better* book tour, and I'm sitting in funky pajamas trying to remember the last time I shaved my armpits.

Back to the lessons I learned today. So in all of the "confusion" (shorthand for poopy-diaper-ziplock-bag-period-panty-replacement among us moms) I left my copy of *Motherhood Better* in the bookstore bathroom. I called and they said my copy had been thrown away (an employee complained that its proximity to the baby changing area was unhygienic) but they're giving me another one free of charge. David is picking it up on his way home from work. I asked him to pick up dinner, too. I'm exhausted from a day thinking about all the ways I'm screwing up his child, and the fridge is practically empty other than chardonnay, string cheese and almost-rotten produce.

It's not that I don't want to run to the store for groceries when Aubrey wakes up, it's just that leaving the house feels like more trouble than it's worth.

If I could ask the entire world one question, it would be: Why does it seem like people hate moms so much? Before anyone could accuse me of overreacting, I'd point out my first piece of evidence: the size of parking spots. Last time I was at the grocery store, as I squeezed my eight-months-postpartum body between millimeters of steel like a human panini, I had to wonder whether whoever paints those lines either...

Has never seen a human family before.

—or—

Despises mothers with the heat of a thousand diaper rashes.

How hard would it be to paint the white lines two inches farther apart? Would these mom-hater paint despots rather we go around scraping their BMW two-seaters with our mini-van doors?

Is it deliberate fat shaming? Yes, I've only lost seven pounds of baby weight (which is weird, because the baby weighed eight pounds, two ounces), but we can't all be celebrity moms who go straight from hospital gowns to string bikinis.

And unlike those magical Hollywood moms, I didn't have a personal chef on call to make me macrobiotic, paleo, organic, fat-free, sugar-free, carb-free (taste-free?) meals every day.

It probably doesn't help that the closest thing I get to doing sit-ups is lying on the living room floor lifting my head for sips of Shiraz, but a girl's gotta live a little. And there's no way I could quit gluten. Do they know how many carbs it takes to stay awake when you have a baby who sleeps about fourteen minutes a night? A lot. Cutting carbs would make me a bad mother and I have to put my child first.

I got up and made my way into the kitchen, savoring the silence of nap time. I browsed the pantry for a few seconds before grabbing a jar of chunky peanut butter. After selecting a spoon from the dishwasher, I helped myself to a heaping mountain of peanut-buttery delight.

"I really should exercise," I said to no one in particular, my mouth full of sticky goodness.

Last week Emily had a celebrity trainer on her show. She showed the audience how to lie on their backs and bench press their babies while wearing a hot pink sports bra and matching designer leggings. I was tempted to get on my living room carpet and give it a shot, but I had a premonition of Aubrey puking partially digested milk into my hair. I smelled bad enough without being doused in baby vinaigrette.

I took another spoonful of peanut butter. Peanuts have protein, right? Protein is important.

Back to the ridiculous parking spaces. Every time I parked and had to squeeze my jiggly post-baby stomach between vehicles it was just another reminder that I'm not where I should be, body-wise. It's hard enough getting out of the house with an eight-month-old who only poops when we're in stores.

Which led me to...

Piece of Evidence That The World Hates Moms #2: Public Changing Tables.

Nobody's asking for a Four Seasons-inspired changing room with baby bidets and Egyptian cotton, rosewater-scented wipes individually handed to me by a gloved bathroom attendant, but three days ago I almost gagged changing Aubrey on a sticky, crusty monstrosity with broken straps, soiled with what I HOPED was dried prune baby food. I did my best to clean the biohazard with wipes and hand sanitizer, but really?

Sometimes it feels like moms are supposed to be invisible in society. Seen but not heard. We're supposed to quietly and quickly go about our task of raising perfectly mannered, groomed Gap babies who speak four languages before they're six without distracting the rest of the world from their important work.

I took one more heaping spoonful of peanut butter before replacing the lid and closing the pantry door. How nice would it be to live in a world that actually considers mothers? In Sweden, everyone takes care of everyone else's babies. Seriously. I read somewhere that when parents go to cafés or restaurants, they just leave their strollers outside by the door on the sidewalk, knowing that if the baby cries or needs help, passersby will jump right in and breastfeed or whatever. That sure beats feeling like every peep your baby makes in public is a capital crime.

I've watched way too many episodes of *Law & Justice* to put my faith in a stranger on the street, but it kind of sounds like paradise. The last (and only) time we took Aubrey out to eat, I ended up standing outside the restaurant bouncing her around while she screamed and tried to buck out of my arms like a wild pony. I ended up eating my cold eggplant parm out of a Styrofoam box in the kitchen at midnight. Good times.

My train of thought was interrupted by a baby yell. Was that Aubrey? I listened again. Nothing. Lately, I'd been experiencing phantom cries—thinking I heard Aubrey make noise when she hadn't. David thinks I'm losing it. He's not wrong.

Oh, wait, there was that sound again. Definitely Aubrey. I guess the dishes will have to wait.

9:30 P.M.

I was lying in bed next to David, who was sleeping soundly. Instead of joining him in dreamland, I had Emily's book propped open with one hand, and my phone's flashlight in the other, illuminating the page.

So far, the book was everything I expected. It only took half a chapter to make me feel like crap. Inspired crap, but crap.

Motherhood can be a joyful experience if you allow it to be. Too many moms spend their days in tense anger or regret, which is then energetically transmitted to their children.

Good to know. I've been frying Aubrey's heart via my toxic gamma rays.

As a mother, you are the gatekeeper of your child's health. It's up to you whether their bodies are filled with preservatives and chemicals, or nourished with home-made broths and fresh-from-the-oven grain-free breads.

I ran downstairs, flipped on the light and grabbed the Funny O's that Aubrey gobbles up from her high chair every morning. I turned the box around to read the label.

Whole grain oats. That's good. Oats grow in fields under sunlight and in the fresh air.

Modified corn starch. Okay, well corn is a vegetable. Modified. I tried not to picture Aubrey growing an extra hand out of her forehead.

Sugar. Salt.

Are babies supposed to eat this? I vowed to myself to spend the extra dollar on the organic ones next time. I guess the book was working. Sitting down on the couch I continued reading.

Motherhood and meal preparation go together like peanut butter and jelly.

Note to self, I thought. *Learn to love cooking.*

If June Cleaver were to enter my kitchen right now, she'd wonder two things...

How does someone with such poor culinary skills make such a terrible mess?

—and—

Where is that smell coming from?

To address the first query, people who have well-below-average cooking skills make bigger messes because, much like intoxicated folks, they are confused and disoriented. For example, last month I felt ambitious after watching a FoodTV episode about Eastern cooking and tried to make curry. I remember hearing that in India, they always stir-fry the spices to bring out the flavors. My interpretation of this step involved burning the spices in oil until they were a greasy, black, charred mess that not even cubed chicken, chickpeas and coconut basmati rice could save.

It was a very sad, very bitter stew.

David did his classic, head-cocked-to-one-side smile-frown before saying, "No, no, it's good, just...strong." He choked down another bite before gulping his entire glass of water in eight seconds. I think he was starting to sense how close to the edge I was, and was afraid to hurt my feelings lest I dissolve into a puddle of tears. Good. He'd always been good about picking up on my feelings. Needless to say, he didn't pack the leftovers for lunch the next day.

Three hours after my disastrous curry dinner, the kitchen still looked like a culinary crime scene. Almost every pot, mixing bowl and wooden spoon was out, vegetable trimmings were still on the counters and the sink was overflowing with dishes.

It's tragic that such chaos birthed such bland food, and it's a downright crime and shame that cooking must always be followed by cleaning.

Now, to answer the second question. What's that smell?

The odor June would have taken exception to is coming from under the counter. Six weeks ago, when I was feeling particularly roosty and productive, I joined a Facebook group of homesteaders. These are people who don't believe in grocery stores and try to live off the land as much as possible, in case civilization collapses. I just wanted to learn how to make bread.

One of the members told me about how she grows potatoes in her crawlspace. Despite the fact that I am barely able to nurture a human child, I decided to try this form of indoor gardening in the darkness of a floor-level kitchen cabinet.

The result was a gallon of rotten potato goo. My "starter spuds" melted into slop and seeped into the wood. I've tried bleach and vinegar, and I aired out the cabinet for weeks but the putrid smell still lingers. Would it have killed the potatoes to at least turn into vodka?

Earlier this afternoon, I made the mistake of hopping onto

Emily Walker's Instagram to get a bit of dinner inspiration. Do you know what she made for her family tonight? Roasted rosemary organic chicken on a bed of garlic mashed potatoes with a side of sautéed baby spinach and crushed cashews. The photo looked like it was pulled right out of a gourmet cooking magazine. Even her tablecloth was fancy. My heart sank a little. There was no way I could do that with Aubrey crying on my hip, clawing at my neck like a gremlin. How did Emily do it? I consider grilled cheese with sliced red bell peppers a gourmet meal.

I let out a sigh and looked around the dark living room, as if help was in one of the corners cluttered with Aubrey's toys. Sensing no woodland fairy was going to pop out of nowhere and fix my life, I sat down on the couch and my hand settled on something hard. My laptop. I went onto Emily Walker's website, hoping to find an easier recipe for tomorrow, but instead saw a teaser link to a "special announcement" on the homepage.

Are you ready, mommies? the teaser read. I clicked the link.

To celebrate her book, she was launching a program called the Motherhood Better Bootcamp. Twelve moms would be chosen to be personally mentored by Emily herself, and—get this—at the end of the five-week transformation period the whole group would get flown out to Emily's home in Napa Valley, California, for three days of wine, rest and relaxation.

I continued to read. There was more.

The mom who had the biggest transformation would win $100,000.

One hundred thousand dollars.

One thousand dollars, one hundred times.

I was totally doing it. Not just for me, but for Aubrey. She deserved a great mom. A happy mom. A capable mom. She was too young to care that I had no idea what I was doing now, but what about when she was six or seven? By then she'd be old enough to compare me to the squash-scone-making moms of all her friends. I needed to change before that happened.

Fingers and toes crossed.

I clicked through to the Motherhood Better Bootcamp application. I filled in the basic information and then began tackling the harder questions.

"Why do you want to be accepted?" I resisted the urge to write, "Because I suck at being a mom," and wrote "To become the mom I know I can be in my heart." That sounded like something Emily would say.

It was almost midnight when I finally finished. My hand trembled a little as I pressed the green Submit button.

A message screen opened.

Thank you for applying to the Motherhood Better Bootcamp. The chosen participants will be announced next week. Have a beautiful day and don't forget to sparkle.

I looked at my phone. It was 12:14 a.m. Yeah, I'll sparkle tomorrow. Like a zombie dipped in glitter.

Tuesday, January 22, 5 A.M.

Aubrey woke up extra early this morning. #SoBlessed. I'd planned on doing a few leg lifts but of course I had to check Facebook and fell right down the rabbit hole.

What's Facebook? It's where moms like me post about how much we love the husbands who annoy the living bejesus out of us, and share expertly edited photos of our kids* and generally talk about our lives like we're living in an enchanted fairy tale blessed by rainbow angel unicorns. In short, it's for lying. But I'm addicted.

Joy (Easton) Thompson
Status: Ella is LOVING her new BabyBGo Stroller!

Below the status update was a photo of my dear sister in fitted black yoga gear—the expensive kind, not the cheapies

---

* Joy will never admit to this, but I know for a fact that she thickens her kids' eyelashes in Photoshop—I caught her in the act once.

I wear—pushing my adorable niece in a brand-new stroller that cost as much as my laptop. Her cleavage was perfect (nursing). "How is she so tiny?" I wondered, trying to blow up the photo. Maybe I should have tried those post-baby waist cincher things she swears by, but forcing myself into a corset while I was still bleeding post birth felt like a little much. Anyway, what is this, the Renaissance? She looked great, though. I hated her.

Uncle Grover (yes, her husband, my brother-in-law, was named after a Muppet) must be doing really well. He's an actuary. I have no idea what that means, and when he talks about his work during family functions I usually picture him dancing on *Sesame Street* hand in hand with Elmo.

Note to self: Look up how much actuaries make. I'm super proud that my David is finally pursuing his dream and starting his own advertising agency and all, but it'd be nice to have some extra money for sexy yoga clothes and fancy strollers.

But my sweet niece, Ella, really is beautiful. She looks just like her mom: dimpled cheeks, almond eyes, jet-black hair and a toothy smile. (Aubrey has yet to pop even one tooth.) Aubrey looks so much like David that I get asked constantly if I'm the babysitter. If I were the babysitter, wouldn't I be better dressed and have time to put on some makeup?

This is exactly why I hate Facebook. I know it's just a website, but I truly believe from the bottom of my sleep-deprived heart that it has created absolute monsters out of the lot of us. If we're not bragging and showing people (people we barely care about) our Pinterest projects (I'll tackle this cold sore of a website later), we're comparing our lives with everyone else's. I hate it. I hate it for making me jealous of Suzy Wexler, someone I haven't seen since high school graduation sixteen years ago, but somehow know way too much about—including, but not limited to, the fact that her husband buys her flowers every single Friday.

Every Friday.

Did I mention that she lives in a gorgeous waterfront home in Malibu and is now a television executive? She and her husband, who looks like a silver-haired former Abercrombie model, have three kids plus two dogs that resemble tampons on legs. Somehow Suzy still looks like she could grace the cover of *Self*. As if I needed another reason to think I suck at life, Suzy's three-kid body looks about five hundred times better than my slashed-with-stretch-marks-like-I've-been-in-a-naked-knife-fight, pizza-dough-belly, one-kid body. David tells me I'm beautiful, but it's while he's pawing me in the dark, obviously trying to butter me up for some action.

In short, I did NOT need to wake up to a photo of Suzy Wexler's thin, beautiful form lying on a beach chair in front of her backyard pool. Not when I'm still wearing maternity tops.

Of course, I accidentally clicked Like on said photo, which prompted an almost immediate, Thanks Ashley! How are you? from my ever-polite old high school friend.

It should be illegal to be gorgeous and sweet. It's not fair. Just pick one. You cannot be a good person and hot. Hot and evil, yes. Homely and sweet, that's okay, too. Pick a lane.

I told her how much I'm loving motherhood, not being able to lose my baby weight and feeling like I'm losing my mind. Okay, maybe I left out the last couple of things.

It ended with Suzy saying, We have to catch up sometime!

Of course, Suzy. I'll just jump on a plane to Malibu with Aubrey and put on my ratty pregnancy swimsuit with the full skirt to hide my grizzly-bear bikini line while we chat and drink mimosas. You can tell me what it's like to be successful and meet celebrities every day, and I can tell you about the Target bill that I'm currently hiding on top of the microwave until I can explain to my better half how I spent $2,000 on miscellaneous goods.

I hate having to explain my purchases to him, like I'm a child, just because he's the breadwinner.

Note: I'm doing my best to get my spending under control but it's hard when (1) Target is life and (2) spending money is my love language.

I'm planning on deactivating my Facebook account just as soon as I upload some photos of Aubrey in a dandelion field from last weekend.

11 P.M.

> Motherhood is a gift that keeps on giving. When your child whines, they're telling you they love you. Learn to hear their nighttime cries as a heavenly song composed by your little angel.
>
> —Emily Walker, *Motherhood Better*

Aubrey just woke up. Her new thing is to go directly from REM to a level-ten scream. It's awful, and I'm considering calling for an old priest and a young priest. I settled her down, but now I'm wide awake and exhausted at the same time.

David always says, "Just lie down, you'll fall asleep eventually." Yeah, after my mind picks apart every mistake I've ever made since I was three, every possible bad thing that could ever happen to Aubrey in her entire life and then tosses around the "What am I going to make for dinner tomorrow?" query. It's so easy for men to fall asleep. Scientists should study whatever enzyme it is that they produce that helps them turn off their brains at night and drift into that deep, annoying I-can't-hear-the-baby-crying slumber. They could turn it into a sleeping pill that women can take.

But good for him for being able to snore it up while I can't even remember what it feels like to sleep through an entire night. Great for him. I'm happy. He needs the sleep. He works outside of the home, right? He has to fight traffic. All I have to fight is the 1 p.m. urge to inhale my weight in cheesy puffs. But, I mean, isn't raising a child a job, too? Yeah, I do it at home, but it isn't exactly a cakewalk. It's not like I lounge on the couch painting my nails, eating bonbons all day.

I'd give blood plasma for a night nanny. It's not fair that only celebrities who are already rich, famous and beautiful also get to be rested while I'm lying here in stretch pants covered in mysterious stains trying to remember the last time I took a shower. The other day I thought I smelled curdled milk. It was me. I smell like a yogurt factory.

I guessed I should try to sleep again, even though I knew the moment I lay down she'd start crying.

Help.

Wednesday, January 23, 10 A.M.

Coffee is a crutch for stressed-out, joyless moms. To stay energized, I start each morning with positive affirmations and loose-leaf hibiscus-beet tea sweetened with honey from my family's own hive.

—Emily Walker, *Motherhood Better*

Impossible Goal of the Day: Stay awake.

It was not even noon and I was a complete zombie. I didn't end up falling asleep until 4 a.m. and Aubrey was up by 5. When David kissed me on the cheek and jetted out of the house, I would've held on to the hem of his jacket and panic-whispered, "Take me with you!" if I didn't think I'd look like a complete lunatic. Instead, I gave him a very quick peck and felt guilty for an hour afterward. It wasn't his fault I was struggling with this whole motherhood thing. Note to self: Be a sweeter wife and ask how business is going.

I was on my fourth cup of coffee, so while my body felt

dead, my mind was racing. I felt like a coked-out sloth. Can sloths do cocaine? It's made from a jungle plant, right? What if sloths figured out the recipe and started making it? We'd have an epidemic of drug-addicted sloths. We'd have to change their name from sloths to fasts. We'd also have to invent sloth rehabilitation centers complete with beautiful waterfalls and sloth sharing circles of trust.

I pulled out my phone. How was it only 10 a.m.? It was as if time was moving slowly to punish me for staying up too late. It was then I remembered. The Motherhood Better application. Emily was probably reading it right now in her massive Los Angeles kitchen, sitting at the counter with her five perfectly dressed children. She was most likely wearing a bone-white cardigan over a pink, lace-trimmed sundress and strappy flats. I bet she drinks her organic teas out of real china. I looked down at the plastic, lidless sippy cup I was slurping my vanilla-flavored coffee in.

I needed to win this.

Aubrey brought me back to earth by throwing a handful of Funny O's at me. One landed in my coffee.

We had to get out of the house or I was going to fall asleep right then and there. Wait—would that be bad? Yes, time to go.

3 P.M.

I tiptoed out of Aubrey's dark room toward the door. Turning back, I took a moment to admire her little body, splayed out on her back in the green-and-yellow pajamas she lived in these days. I closed the door slowly, stopping before it was completely shut. I'd learned the hard way that the smallest click of the door closing woke Aubrey up. Nobody tells you that babies hear like dogs.

Today turned out to be better than I'd ever imagined it

could be on so little sleep. I'd made a friend! This was huge, because I was just reading about how Emily Walker believes creating your mama village is an essential part of happy motherhood. Of course, the mom friends who show up on her blog all look like freelance models, but who cares? We were all the same on the inside. Of course, their insides probably had no cellulite but that's neither here nor there, either.

Here's how it happened. I was sleep-shopping at BabyOutlet (spending money helps me stay awake) and the sweetest-looking mom with her four-year-old son in tow approached me out of nowhere and asked how old Aubrey was. Everyone knows that inquiring about the age of a baby is how moms break the ice. I must have been letting off some seriously positive vibes because we talked right there in the six-to-twelve-months girls' section for fifteen minutes and exchanged phone numbers! She raved over Aubrey and said that her cousin's best friend's stepsister's daughter didn't get her first baby tooth until ten months and that it's totally normal. Her name was Isabel and I loved her.

Get this. She's already texted me and invited me to a playdate for the following day. I was practically giddy and would have done a cartwheel if I'd had the energy. I was only two chapters into *Motherhood Better* and was already about to meet my group of probably lifelong mom friends. My own mama village—as Emily called it.

I could already imagine how we'd spend afternoons together drinking tea (wine), laughing, baking bread, making double casseroles so we could trade, gardening, telling secrets…and then when our kids grew up and married each other we'd all go on epic road trips in between meet-ups with our grandchildren who were practically all related. Okay, maybe that last part was a little creepy, but I was excited.

As I was walking down the stairs, being careful to avoid the two that creak, my phone buzzed in my pocket.

It was Isabel.

Just wanted to let you know you can bring friends tomorrow!

How sweet! If I'd had any other friends, I certainly would have. I texted back that I'd ask around, which I did. I asked around the living room. There was no need to tip her off that I was a loner.

I curled up on the couch and flipped on the TV. Soaps. Soaps. And more soaps.

It didn't matter, though. Within thirty seconds I was asleep.

9 P.M.

David was brushing his teeth in the bathroom when Isabel texted me to let me know that there would be gifts at the party tomorrow.

My shoulders did a little dance as I sat in bed. Gifts? Maybe this was her circle's way of welcoming me into the fold. I was going to bring my famous Lemon Poppyseed Cake. Technically, it was Joy's famous Lemon Poppyseed Cake, but nobody needed to know that I stole the recipe off my sister's computer after she stole my baby name.

David stepped out of the bathroom in his blue-and-white striped pajama pants and white tee and saw me grinning.

"You met this woman where, again?" he asked, sliding into bed next to me.

I frowned. "David. This is how moms meet," I said, trying to sound like I'd done this before. "If I get any weird vibes or if she sacrifices a lamb on the front lawn, I'll get right out of there. I'll go back for Aubrey the next day," I teased.

David smiled and slithered his way up the bed toward me

like a crocodile. He was in a great mood today after winning a bid to handle the PR for LuxSpecs, a high-end line of sunglasses.

He reached for me and wrapped his arms around me, massaging my back.

My danger alarm went off, and I gave him a quick shoulder squeeze.

"Watcha doing there, buddy?" I asked.

He purred in my neck. I knew exactly what he was doing, but seeing as how I'd just gotten Aubrey to bed fifteen minutes ago and hadn't had a chance to shower since…she was born, not to mention spending a day being drooled and spit up on, I felt about as sexy as an ingrown toenail. We really should have sex soon, it had been too long. Just not tonight.

"David, David," I said, backing away from his neck nuzzles. "I haven't showered in forever. I feel like a moldy dishcloth. Rain check?" I felt terrible. Minus-twenty wife points.

"Awwww," he said, and kissed me tenderly. His lips were so soft. Those lips. I loved them the minute I first kissed him, all those years ago in the rain outside of our office building. We'd been friends for three years and neither of us knew that the other had been harboring feelings until that kiss.

I kissed him back and sighed, remembering the simpler days when my hair was clean and we could spend an entire Saturday morning snuggling in bed.

He pulled me into a spooning position and began exploring my body with his hands. I yelped self-consciously when they grazed my stomach. I still couldn't bear him feeling the loose kangaroo pouch Aubrey had left me with. Hot shame shot down my spine and I covered my abdomen with my hands, protecting it from his.

He sensed my discomfort and placed his hands over mine. "Hey," he said, in the most gentle voice I've ever heard him use. He touched my face and whispered into my ear. "You're beautiful. All of you."

Butterflies danced around my stomach and I felt so moved, tears welled up in my eyes. I loved this man. I turned toward his warm body, gazed into his brown eyes. He meant it. He really did think I was beautiful. I kissed him and almost heard the rain from that evening so many years ago hitting the pavement.

Thirty seconds later we were breaking our dry streak. It was fantastic—it always is, even with me insisting that the lights stay off lest my jiggles be seen. Afterward he hugged me tight, as if afraid to lose me again to the world of mother.

"I miss you," he whispered into my ear. Tears sprang into my eyes again. Dang hormones. I missed me, too.

I wished I could promise him that I'd be this person, this loving, giving, sexy person again tomorrow night or the next night, but I couldn't. I tried to squash the feelings of guilt swirling around my psyche.

I kissed his cheek. "I know."

He turned over and fell fast asleep. Normally I would, too, but I couldn't quit my thoughts.

I tried to think about something else. My very first playdate. Tomorrow.

I decided to dress Aubrey in her pale pink jumper and heather-gray top with the matching gray booties. She looked like a baby model in that ensemble. It was made by some fancy Italian designer. Joy gave it to me as her way of apologizing for #BabyNameGate.

I'd actually tried to invite Joy. After all, Emily Walker wouldn't be worried about Joy stealing her friends. Emily Walker would be secure in her friend-getting abilities and say, "The more the merrier!"

But, of course, Joy had to get all weird. "You met this woman while discount shopping and are going to her house?"

You'd think I was taking Aubrey to an abandoned meat warehouse at midnight. Classic Joy. She decided against coming, which was fine by me. Anyway, she had tons of friends from her scrapbooking club, book club and cookie swap. I'd asked if I could join the cookie club once, but all of the cookies have to be homemade so it wasn't a good fit.

I wiggled in bed a little, getting myself comfortable.

I was almost asleep when I heard David say, "Do you smell yogurt?"

Thursday, January 24, 9 A.M.

Isabel's party was in an hour and we were ready.

I texted Isabel and told her that though I'd invited my sister she couldn't make it and I'd be coming alone. She's so sweet, she offered to talk to Joy directly but I let her know it'd be a lost cause.

Aubrey looked absolutely adorable! I need to submit her photo to modeling agencies, seriously. I showered, brushed my teeth, and put on foundation, mascara AND lipstick. I was wearing a dress that fit like a (slightly tight) glove and I felt incredible. I should do this every day! I didn't have time to make the Lemon Poppyseed Cake, so I would be picking up a dozen doughnuts on the way there. Wish me luck!

11 P.M.

Well.

I'm not even sure where to start.

Aubrey and I arrived at 10:15, just a bit late. There was a long line at the drive-through for the doughnuts.

When I got to Isabel's house I rang the doorbell and was greeted by a woman with red hair holding a clipboard. She asked if I was Ashley, scribbled something down and gave me a name tag with my name already on it. That didn't immediately strike me as odd. I'd never been on a playdate. Maybe there are so many moms that they wear name tags when getting to know one another.

She led me to the living room where eight other moms with babies in their laps and toddlers walking around aimlessly were watching a video on the large flatscreen. The woman showed me to the only seat left available. At that point, I wondered what we were doing, but I saw Isabel smiling at me from the left of the television screen and figured this was some kind of chick flick movie time.

Then the film started. Wait no, the INFOMERCIAL started.

A woman in a bikini wearing some kind of linen girdle popped up on the screen. "Are you ready to feel sexy again?"

That's when I started to feel like an idiot.

"In just three hours you'll feel the YES Wrap start to shrink your belly fat and trim your waistline! Get ready for a lean, mean tummy! I love my YES Wraps and you will, too!"

I watched in stunned horror for the next twenty minutes as women mummified their abdomens while animated fat cells floated out of their bodies. Finally the video went to black and Isabel walked to the front of the room holding a green and white box with YES Wrap emblazoned on the sides.

"Does anyone have any questions?"

I knew I shouldn't have raised my hand, but I couldn't help it.

"Is this the playdate?" I asked.

Isabel fake smiled at me. "Absolutely! I've invited all of you here to make some friends and learn about a product that has helped moms around the world lose weight naturally."

I went on. "Right. So you invited me—no, targeted me—because you think I'm fat?"

The fake smile didn't fade but her eyes flickered.

She shifted her weight from one foot to the other. "I didn't *target* you. I shop at BabyOutlet all the time with my nephew."

At this point I may have snapped. "HE'S NOT EVEN YOUR SON? YOU'RE NOT EVEN A MOM?"

I don't know what came over me. The humiliation turned into hot, searing anger.

"I MAY NOT HAVE A TIGHT STOMACH BUT AT LEAST I'M NOT A LIAR. YOU CAN STICK YOUR WRAPS UP YOUR—" then I noticed the kids in the room "—BUTT!"

Isabitch started to speak but I ripped off my name tag and a patch of my dress at the same time, grabbed Aubrey's car seat and stormed out, but not before scooping up my box of doughnuts. I ate five of them this afternoon and another two after dinner. So much for a lean, mean tummy.

Joy texted to ask how the playdate went. I said it was a blast. She wants to come to the next one.

Just my luck that when a (fake) mom wants to get to know me it's because she thinks I could stand to lose a few pounds and she wants to make a few bucks off me in the process.

FML.

Friday, January 25, 10 A.M.

Visualize what you want out of your mommy life. Just because you've had kids doesn't mean you can't live the reality of your dreams. My five children, beautiful husband and I take two tropical beach vacations a year thanks to the power of intention.

—Emily Walker, *Motherhood Better*

I was shaking off the predatory playdate. I needed to move on. I needed to put my energy elsewhere.

Wishes For My Fairy Godmother.
- Take 25lbs off of my body. Not boobs or butt, please, and not via some playdate marketing scam
- Give them to Suzy Wexler (kidding)
- Make sure Aubrey grows up to be happy, healthy and safe (move that to the top)
- Make me a great housewife
- World peace (move that to second place)

- End famine (move this up, too)
- Delete Facebook.com
- Pass a law that all boxes of diapers should be accompanied with a Buy One Get One Free coupon for a bottle of wine
- Make me a nicer wife
- Remove all calories from wine but keep taste intact
- Organize my house

Impossible Goal of the Day: Improve my grocery shopping.

Speaking of the power of intention, I ran to the market today and actually took a list with me.

Grocery List
   Kale (For Emily Walker's famous kale, quinoa, and fat-free feta salad with pomegranate vinaigrette.)
   Quinoa.
   Fat-free feta (Even though fat-free cheese should be illegal.)
   One pomegranate.
   Blueberries.
   Radishes.
   Organic milk (In *Motherhood Better*, Emily says regular milk can cause toddlers to go through puberty.)
   Eggs.
   Flour.
   Butter.
   Cream of tartar (For baking, because I'm going to start doing this any minute now.)
   Cherries.
   Apples.
   Celery.
   Chicken.

Oats.
Toilet paper.
Cheese.
Tomatoes.
Onions.
Red peppers.

Here's what I bought:
Kale (For rotting in the fridge. Let's be real—I'm never going to make that salad.)
Quinoa (I have no idea how to cook this. Is it rice? Is it pasta? Nobody knows.)
A pomegranate (For watching dry out in the fruit bowl over the next several weeks.)
I didn't buy the fat-free feta. It felt wrong.
Organic milk.
Eggs.
Cookie dough.
Honey Nut Cinnamon Crunch cereal.
A pound cake.
Toilet paper.
Gum.
Sugar-free fake strawberry poison liquid drink mix (for weight loss.)
6-pack glazed doughnuts.
Hot dogs (for snacking.)
Frozen Tater Tots.
Apples.
Cherries.
Strawberries.
Frozen onion rings.
Tortilla chips (for unexpected guests.)
Nacho cheese dip (also for guests.)

3 tank tops.
2 pairs black pants.
Running shoes.
Workout DVD.
Water bottle.
Ice cream.

Someone told me they named it "pound cake" because it contains a pound of butter. I prefer to think it's just honest labeling: you gain a pound per slice. But on the bright side, butter contains milk, which contains calcium, so in a small way, pound cake is helping fortify my bones. I also always eat pound cake with strawberries, which contain minerals and vitamin C.

Confession: I hadn't showered in four days and I was kind of okay with it. That's what deodorant is for, right? Right now, I had six layers of Lady Smells Bad antiperspirant on my underarms. It's strong enough for a man but pH balanced for a mom who can't find the time to wash her privates.

I smelled like a cross between sheets that were put away wet and very expensive cheese.

I checked my bank statement after this "grocery" shop, and do you know what stood out? Every third line was either for vanilla lattes or Burger Central. The only two food groups I consumed were caffeine and fast food. It wasn't my fault, though. Junk food and caffeine were all that were keeping me going. I needed these treats to make it through the day. I didn't get to sleep anymore, there was no "me" time, I didn't have friends—the value menu, sweet caffeinated beverages and wine were currently pleasure central and I would not apologize for it. My pants might, though, because they were stretched to capacity.

PS: Emily would announce the twelve Motherhood Better Bootcamp winners on her show in a couple of days. She said they received over 7,000 entries. Please fairy godmother, come through for me.

11 P.M.

> Motherhood is an ashram; our religion is love, diaper changes and sleepless nights. This begins with pregnancy. Speak to and dance with your unborn baby every day—preferably to music that features either harps or Tibetan gongs.
>
> —Emily Walker, *Motherhood Better*

Fun fact: Did you know that some women take their placenta home with them after giving birth? Some send it away to be freeze-dried into capsules and others eat it raw, like sashimi...supposedly it helps balance out the hormones and make you feel like a normal person again faster.

I was on the Mommy Chat online message board complaining about how tired and emotional I always am, as one does on a Friday night post baby, and someone asked if I'd eaten mine. I said no, and she responded with, "That explains everything."

Really? So motherhood would be easier for me if I'd just cooked up the afterbirth like Bolognese and served it over linguini with a side of garlic bread?

Joy's neighbor buried her placenta in their backyard under a tree. If you bury a placenta under an apple tree, are the fruits then an apple/placenta hybrid? If you bury it in a vineyard, would the wine have hints of afterbirth?

Sommelier in a fancy restaurant: "This full-bodied pinot grigio hails from Napa Valley. It was aged in maple oak barrels. You'll notice hints of elderberry and subtle notes of the placenta of a seven-pound six-ounce child."

Maybe I should have kept my placenta. The birthing center

offered, but between figuring out how to install the car seat, heal my broken vagina and oh, yeah, trying to wrap my mind around the fact that a human baby was coming home with me, I'd felt like I had enough on my plate (no pun intended).

I was fascinated by the thing, though.

It was way bigger than I thought it would be. In my mind I imagined a pork chop but it was more like a blobby T-bone steak. It had all kinds of veins on it. An old high school friend on Facebook dipped her wet, bloody placenta into red paint and threw it against a canvas. The art now hangs in her family room.

No comment.

If I had taken my placenta, what would I have brought it home in? A freezer bag? Do they put it in a to-go box like restaurant leftovers? Wrap it in foil or maybe drop it into a Styrofoam box complete with utensils, and salt and pepper packets?

Mom to nurse: "Can I have this wrapped up? I'm taking it with me."

There was a whole section of the Mommy Chat website, I was discovering now, dedicated to placenta recipes. Smoothies, cakes, even stir fry. STIR FRY. Bok choy, onions, bean sprouts and thinly sliced placenta. Maybe a little Chianti on the side?

This was way too much for me. I should go to bed.

The contestants chosen for the Motherhood Better Bootcamp program would be announced tomorrow live on the show. If I hear my name I am going to absolutely freak.

Saturday, January 26, 10 A.M.

Of course Emily had to keep everyone on their toes until the last sixty seconds of her show. Well, I didn't make it into the Motherhood Better Bootcamp, but I wasn't going to let it get to me. Emily said something on her show today that really struck me. "I wasn't born a good mom, I willed myself into one." All I needed to do was try harder. I needed to put the same energy that I once put into my job into motherhood.

I had Emily's book. I could do this on my own. I decided to embark on a mission called Ashley the Perfect-ish Mom. First thing in the morning I was going to join a gym (or at least research gyms), eat healthy and be the best, most attentive mom ever.

It was time for me to stop living in dirty sweats and move up to the fancy $10 stretch pants from ShopMart. I was going to start dressing up Aubrey like a human and not a *Les Misérables* extra. I was browsing Etsy right then, picking out some bows. She needed them. I'm not saying she looked like a boy, but I swear she could be sitting in a pink stroller, wearing a pink and purple dress, with a fluorescent flashing sign that read, I'M FEMALE, and people would still ask "How old is your son?"

Anyway, maybe I'd even start juicing once I figured out exactly what that was and if mix-ins like tequila were allowed (tequila is from a plant).

I had this.

Impossible Goal of the Day: Get accepted into a group of mom friends, or at least make one awesome best friend sometime this century.

I joined three local mom Facebook groups but hadn't posted yet.

What would I even say?

Hey guys, friendless mom looking for a new bestie. Need someone to share secrets with? I'm your gal!

Maybe something a little more subtle.

Lonely, unemployed, reluctant stay-at-home mom looking for 2–3 moms for my mama bear pack. Must be cool, love complaining, not be a YES Wrap representative and be imperfect. Must NOT have a Pinterest account.

I know the last part sounds harsh, but I don't need a crafter in my life. You know why? Because it'll only be a matter of time before I've spent $500 on yarn, crotchet needles, puff paints and a glass-etching kit in a sad, futile attempt to become her. I'm too easily influenced to have these bad seeds in my emotional space. I need another sister in failure. Someone who not only fails to achieve resolutions but forgets she even made them. Yeah. Someone like that. A leader.

Being a new mom is like being a freshman in high school. You have just a few days to find your clique and commit to the corresponding lifestyle. So far, the available groups are:

1. Crunchy Moms
2. Stay-at-Home Moms
3. Working, Executive-Type Ambitious Moms
4. Moms Who Hate Their Jobs But Do Them Anyway
5. Wine Moms
6. Hot Moms

There's a bit of overlap here and there, but so far I haven't found one that I identify with and, therefore, still have exactly zero friends. It's getting a little old walking Aubrey through the park alone, especially when it seems like there are groups of moms gathered all over the place, laughing, smiling, being best friends and sharing stories about their kids. I want to share stories about kids. Someone should invent a match.com just for moms who want to find their life mom-mate.

It seems like once you're an adult, if you don't already have your friends picked out, you're screwed. Nobody makes new friends after twenty-seven.

I miss my office friends, but since I had Aubrey, they've all vanished. I don't blame them. Given the choice, who would want to spend an afternoon at the park with me and Aubrey when they could be getting manicures? I just wish they would have kept in touch more than the occasional "She's so cute!" Facebook comment.

All I want is one mom friend I can talk to about life. Is that too much to ask? In fourth grade my best friend was Ruthie Miller. We did everything together. We ate lunch every day in the cafeteria side by side, we played at recess, we even sat together on the bus. I was never lonely because she was always there. She was my default person. I need a Mom Ruthie.

Hospitals and birthing centers should assign every woman a mom friend the second they give birth. Then we wouldn't have to spend afternoons alone on the living room floor wishing we had someone other than people in mail delivery to chat with.

How amazing would it be to have a best friend who lived across the street? We'd talk about everything. How David has been working twelve-hour days, but I feel bad complaining because he's the only one bringing in an income right now and seems super stressed-out, even though I'm also super stressed-out. I'd tell her about how I feel like being a stay-at-home mom is amazing because I get to watch Aubrey grow right in front of my eyes and, while my heart is so full of love for her that it feels like it's going to explode, how I'd do anything for just one good nap. I'd also tell her that I feel like I matter less to David since having her. How I feel like he sees me as some kind of maid/caretaker to his child and not the woman he pined for desperately for years. I can't remember the last time he asked me how I am.

I'd listen to her rants, too, of course. Friendship, especially one based on complaining, is a two-way street.

David had worked through the last few weekends but took today off so we could all go to the FunsieLand play center together. Before becoming a mom I avoided places like FunsieLand like the plague. Every once in a while I'd get invited to a coworker's child's birthday party and would always make a point of sending a huge gift in lieu of my actual presence. The last thing I wanted to do was spend five hours in a loud, rave-like, plastic ball and E. coli petri dish, but since there aren't many places where parents feel 100 percent okay letting their kids be kids, that's where we were headed to this morning.

It'd be nice to do something as a family. David had been so busy lately. Every time I asked him how Keller & Associates was going, he would close up. I wanted to support him, but talking about work just stressed him out even more. A day of bonding as a family was just what we needed.

9 P.M.

I need three shots of vodka, a hot shower and a shot of penicillin. To think, for my entire adult life I've avoided play centers because of the kids, when the real monsters lurking in those places were the moms.

We made it to the play center at 10 a.m., and even though it'd just opened, it was already so loud that David and I had to scream in order to be heard.

"LET'S SET UP BY THE BABY AREA!" I yelled, one hand over Aubrey's ear as I carried her through the center that was packed with shrieking, running and crying children. Above us, a twisted spiral of tubes was filled with children, crawling like rats through plumbing.

I motioned to David, who had both hands over his ears and whose eyes were wide with terror.

"WHAT?" he yelled back. A five-year-old crashed into his legs and fell to the floor, laughing hysterically.

"THE BABY AREA!" I motioned toward the back of the sprawling center.

We navigated carefully around birthday parties, children who seemed jacked up on Mountain Dew and rock cocaine, and seemingly millions of small multicolored balls that were everywhere.

From atop a small stage, a band of large furry animals sang a song about a big blue boat. The music boomed across the entire arena.

We finally made our way toward a door in front of a clear Plexiglas wall. On the other side of it was a smaller version of a play center: a carpeted room featuring a small jungle gym. It was littered with stuffed toys and babies crawling around their parents.

David pulled the door open and I hurried through with Aubrey. As soon as it was shut there was silence. We took off our shoes (Shoes Off in Babyland, Please!) and let out a deep sigh of relief, as if we'd just narrowly escaped with our lives. David pointed back toward the chaos that was now a muted version of insanity. "We are NEVER having Aubrey's birthday party there."

"I agree."

We scoured the sides of the Baby Room and found a section of wall without a diaper bag leaning against it.

David and I sat cross-legged on the floor and placed Aubrey in front of us.

I bent down to her. "Okay, Aubrey, go! Play."

She sat up and stared out into the play area where other children were flailing on their backs and older babies were struggling to make their way up the small slide stairs.

She instantly burst into tears.

"Awww, Aubs," David reached out his arms and pulled Aubrey into them. "Don't cry, honey." He pulled her close and pressed her face into his chest with his hand.

My heart fluttered as I watched the two great loves of my life embrace. Nobody can prepare you for the magic that is watching the man you love become a father. I found myself swooning every time I caught him gazing at Aubrey, feeding her or just cradling her in his arms.

A woman's high-pitched voice cut through the moment. "She doesn't socialize much, does she?"

I turned to the mom on my left. She was in her mid-thirties and was wearing dark blue jeans and a pink sweater. Her hair was pulled back in a tight bun.

"What?" I said, looking around.

The mom crossed her arms. "Your daughter. She doesn't spend much time with other kids, does she?"

My mouth hung open. I didn't even know what to say.

"She doesn't have many friends or coworkers, no…" I said slowly.

The woman smiled tightly. "Funny. But it's not going to be funny when she's eighteen and still living in your basement. Let me guess, stay-at-home mommy?"

I tried to smile back. "…Yes."

The mom examined her nails. "I can tell. You're really going to want to get her socialized ASAP."

David, who had been listening quietly, cut in. "She's a baby, not a dog."

"David," I whispered, trying to calm him down.

The woman pursed her lips. "I was just trying to help." She collected her bag and walked away.

"The nerve of that woman," David said when she walked away.

"David," I hissed. "We're here to have fun."

"I know but—" He motioned in the direction of the woman.

I gave him a look before picking Aubrey up and carrying her over to the center of the room where several babies were playing with the communal toys.

Aubrey and I sat down with the other moms. I could feel myself starting to sweat. Hanging out with other moms always made me nervous. I was terrified of coming off as a parenting noob and highly conscious of how desperately I wanted the friendship of even just one of these women.

I sat Aubrey down and pushed a blinking jack-in-the-box toward her. Aubrey smiled and began tapping the buttons with her hands.

"Is that fun, baby?" Aubrey pressed another button and a rabbit popped out of one of the toy's hidden doors. She screamed with delight.

I looked up at the other moms. Surely people were taking

notice of me and my adorable child having a Hallmark moment. Then, out of nowhere, Aubrey began to cry. I looked down just in time to see an eighteen-month-old little boy wearing a pair of brown cotton shorts and a red shirt toddling away with the toy she had been squealing over.

I scooped the hysterical Aubrey up and followed the boy to where he sat down to play. He was seated next to a young mom with blond curly hair wearing a flowing burnt-orange dress.

"Excuse me," I said, kneeling down next to her. "My daughter was playing with that toy when your son came over and grabbed it."

She stared at me blankly before pushing a stray hair out of her face. "I'm sorry?"

Her son was now happily playing with the toy Aubrey had had earlier while Aubrey sobbed.

"Your son, he grabbed that toy out of my daughter's hands." I pointed to the little boy sticking his tongue out at me.

The mom held up a hand defensively, "Please do not point at River. We point at places, not people."

"Okay..." I said, lowering my hand.

"And I'm sorry your daughter is having a shadow experience today, but we do not force River to share."

"You *what* now?" I asked, puzzled.

"We do not force River to share. River makes his own decisions. It's part of his journey," she said, smiling serenely.

"What? Lady—"

"Please do not gender me," the woman said, shaking her head.

"My daughter is going to need that toy back," I said flatly.

"Please do not gender your child," she said, staring at me.

"Okay, that's quite enough." I reached down and pulled the toy away from River. He let out a squeal.

The woman was livid. "How dare you?"

A play center supervisor wearing a white shirt with the center's logo on it walked over. "Is there a problem here?"

River's mom stood up and put her hands on her hips. "This woman just snatched a toy out of my child's hands!"

I struggled to stand while holding Aubrey. "Only after he took it from mine."

David popped up. "What's going on, Ashley?"

The employee, a man in his early twenties with a crew cut, spoke up. "It appears as if your wife took a toy from a baby."

David looked at me, startled. "Is this true?"

"Yes, but no, he took it from Aubrey first…"

David could barely speak. "Took a toy from a baby?"

The employee put a hand on my elbow, "Ma'am, we're going to have to ask you to leave."

"Fine. We don't want to be here with this kind of lawlessness anyway." I turned to River's mom. "This isn't over."

I took a step forward and felt my foot sink into something mushy.

"What the—" I looked down and saw that I was four toes deep in a soft turd.

"I eliminated, Mama," said River.

David laughed all the way home, and eventually even I had to giggle after replaying how I hopped through the play center on one foot to the public bathroom to wash off River's elimination.

"You do realize we can never go back there again, right?" said David, struggling to hold back hysterical laughter.

"Do you think there's a photo of me by the cash register?" I said, a smile playing on my lips.

"Hopefully it's not scratch and sniff," he said, dissolving into hysterics.

He reached over and took my hand. Our fingers intertwined as Aubrey slept in the backseat.

As we turned off of the freeway I stared at David. It felt so good to laugh again together. I studied his profile as he drove: his strong jaw, five o'clock shadow…he really was incredibly handsome. This is what I wanted when I found out we were pregnant—to just enjoy being together as a family. Sure, there was less foreign kid feces in my fantasy, but all in all, I considered the day a success. A poop-covered success.

Sunday, January 27, 4:30 P.M.

I spend every Sunday morning doing a deep clean of my home. My littles love to help with age-appropriate jobs like wiping down silk flowers, stirring the compost and watering our bonsai trees.

—Emily Walker, *Motherhood Better*

Impossible Goal of the Day: Declutter everything.

My closet is no longer a closet. It is a mini-secondhand store/storage space for all of Aubrey's things. How can a baby so small have so much stuff? I know it's my fault, but girl clothes are so cute. How am I supposed to not spend every last dime buying clothes I never put her in? I know for a fact that her wardrobe is worth more than mine. All of the money I used to spend on myself, I now spend on her.

My postpartum body doesn't exactly say DRESS ME UP! If it could talk, it'd probably say something like, STOP WITH

ALL THE CHOCOLATE, or COVER ME WITH A BUR-
LAP SACK.

In my closet are no less than four sizes of clothing that
serve as a living monument to the old me, the pregnant me,
the postpartum me and the postpartum-PMS-bloated me. I
read in *AllWomen* magazine that your closet is a metaphor for
your subconscious. If that's true, then my subconscious is a
mess and needs to be taken out back and put out of its misery.

Confession: I hate cleaning.

Does anyone else find it entirely unreasonable that a human
being should be required to cook AND clean on the same
day? I woke up determined to get my kitchen in a state that
doesn't make me shrink with shame. David ended up having
to go into the office so I spent Aubrey's afternoon nap wearing ill-fitting rubber gloves scouring the stove top, washing
dishes, organizing cabinets, sweeping, mopping, etc.

Ridiculous Things I Found In Our Pantry:
5 partially consumed boxes of cereal
3 cans of fortified shakes for pregnant women (I drank one.
Don't judge me; it was chocolate.)
7 boxes of cake mix (I made a cake.)
3 tubs of frosting (I frosted the cake. See? I'm baking.)
3 one-pound bags of cashews from when I wanted to make
my own cashew butter (Homesteaders. Don't ask.)

When I was done my kitchen sparkled like it never had
before. Aubrey woke up and I honestly felt like an amazing
woman and mom until I realized something. I had to start dinner. In an hour, the kitchen would be destroyed. It seemed like
a waste of my hard work so I ordered Chinese food, instead.

As I bounced a cranky post-nap Aubrey on my hip while
watching television in the living room, I couldn't help but wish

David were home. It was Sunday, after all. I glanced around the room trying to think of something to do while waiting for the food to be delivered.

I wished parenting books talked about how utterly boring motherhood could be. I felt guilty for feeling it, but...I was bored. I tried to set Aubrey down on her foam mat, but as soon as her tiny feet grazed the floor, she let out a banshee scream. Like a good servant, I picked her right back up and headed into the kitchen to eat my feelings. Yes, food was coming any minute, but I needed calories to deal with my emotions.

I grabbed a clean spoon out of the dishwasher and made my way toward the pantry. It only took a few seconds to pop the top off of the industrial-sized tub of peanut butter and dip my spoon into its creamy goodness. It was like therapy for my mouth.

"Ah! Ah!" Aubrey begged for a taste. If she hadn't already had peanut butter at Gloria's house (even though I'd asked her not to give her any high-allergy foods—apparently peanut butter cookies don't count), I would have hesitated. I watched, amused, as Aubrey worked the Tic Tac-sized piece of peanut butter around her mouth.

"Pretty good, isn't it? One day you'll eat your feelings, too, honey," I said, closing the pantry and sitting with Aubrey on my lap at the kitchen table. I sighed. I pulled out my cell phone and considered texting David just for a little conversation. No, he was probably busy. I put the phone back into my pocket.

I don't think he will ever fully understand what my life is like. I'm with Aubrey pretty much every waking minute. Yes, he and I are equal parents in the sense that we share equal DNA with the kid, but I'm with her *all the time*. I just want to talk to someone who doesn't crap her pants every three hours.

I'd kill for some adult conversation. Last Wednesday I tried to spark up a convo with a barista at the café. I think she could sense my desperation because she nodded and smiled as if speaking to a child bragging about how old they were.

The other day the FedEx guy said, "How is everything?" and I went into a three-minute monologue about Aubrey's sleep situation before the weird look on his face told me he was just being polite and not applying to be my therapist.

I get the feeling that sometimes David thinks I'm being dramatic about how exhausting this all is. "Just get more organized." That's like telling someone who's drowning to simply learn the backstroke.

No, I'm not digging trenches all day, but motherhood is draining. I can't nail down exactly why it's so hard. Changing a diaper in itself isn't difficult. Neither is feeding Aubrey or taking her on a walk.

I think what makes being a mom so hard is that it never stops. It just keeps going in perpetual motion. It's a cycle with no end. The days of the week don't mean anything to me. I don't punch out. I'm never "off." David comes home at the end of a hard day and has a sense of completion. He kicks off his shoes, throws his socks anywhere but the laundry basket, opens a beer, and sits on his recliner and plays with Aubrey. I never have that moment because I'm never done. Even when Aubrey goes down for the night, I stay on alert. She could wake up at any time for any reason. Teething. A cold. A wet diaper. I'm always in a heightened state of awareness.

There's no paycheck as a sign of a job well done. No pats on the back from a manager. It just keeps going on and on, twenty-four hours a day, seven days a week.

I pulled out my phone again and couldn't resist sending a quick text to David. Almost done?

A few seconds later my phone beeped with a new message. PR crisis with the Loeman account. Don't wait up. Love u.

No problem. Love u too, I texted back, before returning my phone to my pocket.

I felt my eyes start to well up with unexpected tears. "What's wrong with me?" I asked, brushing them away.

I thought about calling Joy, but remembered that Sunday night is her book—i.e., wine and chatting—club. Even if I had a babysitter, her friends are the organized, always dressed perfectly, "Oh, look, I made organic blueberry muffins" type, and I don't need that kind of negativity in my life.

I'd call Mom but she's an hour and a half away, and hearing my tone would just worry her.

The idea popped into my head before I had a chance to stop it.

Gloria?

Was I desperate enough for company that I'd call the mother-in-law who once referred to my three-bean casserole as a "cute experiment"?

Yes. Yes, I was.

I stood up and switched Aubrey to the other hip. She squawked in protest.

Dialing the number, I tried not to notice that my fingers were shaking. I held the phone to my ear.

Ring. Ring. Ring. Okay, she's not there, I should just hang—

"Hello?" Gloria's voice caught me off guard.

"Gloria. Hi. Hi. Um. It's me, Ashley. Hi. Um…"

"Ashley? Is that you?"

I tried to remember why I was calling.

"Hi, Gloria. Yes, it's me. I'm just calling because… I just wanted… I wanted to see if you were free to pop by for dinner?" I bit my lip.

The line was silent.

"Tonight? Ashley, I…"

"If you're busy, I totally understand. I just ordered Chinese food, David's working, Aubrey won't let me put her down and..."

To my horror a lump started to rise in my throat blocking my words. New tears flooded down my cheeks without warning. I let out a heaving sob.

"Ashley? Dear, are you crying? What's wrong?" Gloria sounded more alarmed than I'd ever heard her.

"I'm just tired. And a little lonely. I'm so sorry..."

Gloria's voice was steady. "I'll be there in ten minutes."

She must have flown down the highway because eight minutes later there was a knock at the door. I'd had just enough time to splash some water on my face and pull my hair into a ponytail.

I opened it, and to my absolute surprise there was Gloria, in full makeup and hair with a black evening gown under an unbuttoned black faux-fur coat.

I gasped. She looked amazing. "Gloria! I..."

Gloria walked into the house and closed the door behind her. "I was getting ready to go to the theater with some friends from the community center but clearly you need me here."

"I had no idea! I wish you hadn't..."

Gloria waved in front of her face.

"Nonsense. I know a breakdown when I hear one. Tell me what's going on, at once."

In one sweeping motion, Gloria draped her coat over a dining room chair and took Aubrey from me. It was such a glorious relief to have my arms free. It was then I noticed that she was holding a bottle of red wine. My heart soared.

Gloria stared at me. "Well? Are you going to get us a couple of glasses?"

Ten minutes later we were sitting at the kitchen table surrounded by takeout boxes. Gloria placed a chunk of white rice in Aubrey's waiting mouth. I took a sip of my wine.

She cleared her throat. "So, if I understand correctly, you're exhausted, tired of being alone with Aubrey all of the time, you miss David, wish he'd help you more and want to lose twenty pounds but are unwilling to exercise."

I stared at the ceiling trying to remember if I'd missed anything.

"That's about it, yes." I nodded furiously, taking another long sip. "It's just that, I thought motherhood would be more fulfilling. I'm here with Aubrey every day, watching her scoot around on the floor or holding her all over the house—and there's nowhere I'd rather be—but I'm bored. I have no one to talk to. David is busy with work. I'm just…"

"You're just a mom," cut in Gloria. "You feel useless and essential at the same time. You feel like everyone is doing a better job than you and that nobody understands what you're going through."

I stared at Gloria with my mouth agape.

"Yes," I said quietly.

Gloria reached her chopsticks into the Kung Pao chicken and popped a bite into her mouth.

"Dear. We all felt like that." She sipped her wine. "David was the first baby I'd ever held. I remember being so surprised when the nurse let us take him home after I had him. I was terrified. Back then, dads made the money and moms did all of the child raising, so I was completely on my own. Then, when David Senior passed away when the kids were just ten and eight…well…I was really on my own."

I looked into my wine. I tried to imagine what that must have been like, raising two children on your own while navigating your own personal tragedy and theirs.

Gloria coughed. "But do you know how I got through it?"

I took a sip of wine. "You pulled yourself up by your boot-straps?"

Gloria scoffed. "No. Vodka. One shot every day at 5 p.m. on the dot."

We dissolved into laughter. I couldn't believe I was actually bonding with my mother-in-law, who only an hour earlier I thought didn't much care for me.

Gloria picked up a stringy piece of chicken with her fingers and placed it in Aubrey's waiting mouth. "Ashley, there's no way around it. Motherhood is hard. And you young moms put more pressure on yourselves than we ever did, with your crafts and your activities. Do you know what we called crafts when David was young? Chores. We didn't play with our kids, we sent them outside. All day. They'd only come back in when the streetlights came on. You moms have it different. You're expected to be on 24/7 and look good doing it. My advice is this. Stop being so hard on yourself. And drink more vodka."

I giggled again, this time with a mouthful of noodles.

Gloria and I watched as Aubrey gummed the chicken.

"When are you going to get some teeth, baby girl?" Gloria teased.

I shrugged.

Aubrey began to fuss and I realized it was almost her bath time.

I stood up. "I should get her ready for bed. Feel free to keep eating. I'll bring her out after her bath."

Gloria stood and held Aubrey close. "Absolutely not. This is your time. Put your feet up and eat your dinner. I'll put her down to bed tonight."

I was speechless. I blinked back the wetness that was rapidly rising behind my eyes.

"Thank you, Gloria. For everything. Thank you for coming tonight."

Gloria smiled and squeezed my shoulder. "You're welcome. I know I'm not your mom, and I know you wish she lived closer, but I'm here for you. Remember what I said. Stop putting so much pressure on yourself, and don't forget…"

"The vodka," we said together.

Gloria kept her word and didn't leave until Aubrey was breathing heavily, her chest rising steadily. We stood together, mother-in-law and daughter-in-law in the darkened doorway, and just watched her, splayed out in her pink bunny sleeper.

I peeked over at Gloria, and for the first time wondered if I'd gotten her all wrong. She had come through for me.

As we walked down the stairs I felt the need to say something. I needed to cement this moment in history as the turning point in our relationship.

She was putting on her coat when I cleared my throat.

"Gloria, I just wanted to say thank you…thank you for coming tonight. It means a lot."

"Think nothing of it," she said, slipping her arm into her enormous fur coat. "I'm actually glad you called. From now on, whenever David is working late, I'll be right here with you."

What?

She continued. "Don't worry, I'll get David's schedule directly from him so you don't even need to call next time. I'll pop right over."

I tried to keep my mouth affixed in smile formation. "That's…great, Gloria. Okay. Thank you."

What had I gotten myself into?

When Gloria left, I sank onto the couch and opened up my phone, hoping to see a text from David. It was already 8 p.m.

Nothing. I clicked through to Instagram and pulled up Emily Walker's page.

She'd just posted a photo of herself with the twelve moms

in Motherhood Better Bootcamp and their kids. They were standing in the lobby of her New York office, a gaggle of excited mothers, babies in strollers and a few older children. I've seen her office plenty of times on her Instagram; it's baby pink and white, and has silver accents. She calls the lobby "the Pavilion" and has posted loads of photos of her two youngest children, Sage and Willow, eighteen months and three years, crawling around on the Shibori Jasmine wood floors next to celebrities, chefs and athletes. The moms all looked so happy in their pink shirts monogramed with Emily's EW logo in white calligraphy.

I wasn't jealous at all. No really, good for them.

Maybe I should make myself a T-shirt for Operation Perfect-ish Mom. No, that's just pathetic. And it means more laundry.

I sat on the couch and pulled out *Motherhood Better*.

Too many moms depend on alcohol to relax and let off steam. I prefer yoga and sunbathing.

I took a long sip of wine. I was about to turn the page when the home phone rang.

"Dang!" I hissed, running toward the kitchen receiver. I'd forgotten to put it on silent for the night. What if it woke up Aubrey?

I skidded into the kitchen and breathlessly picked up the phone.

"Hello?" I said, annoyed.

"Is this Ashley Keller?" a woman's voice asked.

Oh, no, was this about my credit card?

"Um, no… I'm…her nanny…may I take a message?"

"Yes, this is Rebecca Anderson, assistant to Emily Walker."

I dropped the phone. Or threw it, rather. Rebecca Anderson? Emily Walker? I had to be dreaming. This was a dream.

I ran over to the sink where I'd thrown the phone and picked it up.

"I'm so sorry. Um, Ashley actually just walked through the door. Let me get her. One moment, please." I put the phone down on the counter, and with my heart beating out of my chest, tiptoed over to the kitchen table. I then stomped over to the counter, pretending I was just entering the room.

"Hello? Ashley Keller speaking," I said, trying to sound casual even though my voice cracked.

At this point, my heart was pounding so loudly I was afraid she could hear it.

"Hello, Ashley. This is Rebecca Anderson, assistant to Emily Walker of *The Emily Walker Show*. I'll get right to the point. I'm calling you today because a spot in the Motherhood Better Bootcamp just opened up and you are next on the list."

I think I passed out. She kept talking but I didn't hear anything she said. At one point the line went quiet.

"Hello? Are you there? Can you do it?"

"YES, YES, I CAN DO IT. YES, PLEASE!" I scream-whispered into the receiver.

I still can't believe any of this happened. Turns out, one of the moms was a "dog mommy" and didn't have a human child, which got her disqualified.

I'm in. I'm actually in. I missed the kick-off party at Emily Walker's studios, but the program officially starts tomorrow so I didn't miss anything!

I slid down to the kitchen floor. It was happening. I was in.

"Hello? Are you there?" Rebecca's voice spoke through the receiver.

"Yes, yes, I'm here," I said, struggling to compose myself.

"As a member of the Motherhood Better Bootcamp, you're

required to attend weekly video chats with Emily Walker and the rest of the team. You missed the introductory one, but the first real chat is tomorrow morning at 10 a.m."

"Uh-huh," I responded, brilliantly. I felt like I was in a dream. Could I be dreaming? I looked around the kitchen at the empty takeout boxes. No, if I were dreaming my kitchen would be cleaner.

Rebecca kept talking. "In six weeks, you'll be flown out to the gorgeous Napa Valley in northern California for the closing reception and a special taping of *The Emily Walker Show*. The $100,000 grand prize winner will be announced live. Is all of this something you can do?"

"Yes. I can do this," I said, trying not to float away.

"Great. I'll send the details to your email shortly."

"Okay, thank you, Rebecca. Please hug Emily for me." Did I just say that?

"I, um, okay. Goodbye." The phone clicked off.

I sat there on the living room floor trying to make sense of what had just happened.

Tomorrow I would talk to Emily Walker face-to-face. Tomorrow was the first day of my new life.

Thank you, fairy godmother.

Monday, January 28,
NOON

The first video conference was this morning at 10 a.m.

I showered, even though no one would be able to smell me, and even did my hair and makeup. What to wear was a harder decision. My daily hoodie didn't seem right. It was my first time meeting Emily Walker, so looking like a slob wasn't an option. I settled on a long-sleeved purple cotton T-shirt.

I was searching through the laundry pile on my bedroom floor for pants and clean underwear when I realized the call started in three minutes. I plopped Aubrey in her bouncy chair and grabbed the only remaining piece of clean underwear from my drawer, which just happened to be my wedding night white lace thong. It wasn't like anyone was going to be seeing me from the waist down. Maybe I'd keep them on and surprise David tonight. Maybe.

All of the participants were already logged on to the Motherhood Better portal before I signed in. With a little beep my name and face popped up in a pink-outlined square on the screen next to eleven other faces. It was almost like the Brady Brunch opener.

The other moms were so lovely—they were all smiles and excited waving. It was like being part of an exclusive club. It was, in fact, an exclusive club. We were all better mothers. Or, at least, we would be.

The moment Emily Walker's face illuminated the screen was pure magic. I couldn't get over the fact that Emily Walker, blogger turned media darling, could see me. Sure, I was just one of twelve little faces at the bottom of the screen with the other moms, but she could *see* me. She was just as beautiful in video conference as she was on Instagram. Her makeup was that "natural" style that I can never get quite right—the kind that looks like you aren't wearing any at all but are just blessed by the gods with a flawless, dewy complexion and soft, tinted lips.

In the V of her plush, white (moms can wear white?) cashmere V-neck sweater was a gold heart pendant held by a thin platinum chain. Emily's jet-black hair was in an immaculate topknot and her face was framed by sparkly diamond earrings. She looked like a princess. There was something about her that almost looked like an oil painting come to life.

"Hello, mommies!" Her voice was like a bell ringing. "Welcome to the first of six Motherhood Better Bootcamp video chats. Who's ready to change their life?"

There it was. The dazzling Emily Walker smile. Two rows of perfect white teeth. We all cheered! Aubrey stirred a little in her bouncy seat from the noise but didn't wake up.

"As you know, the Motherhood Better Bootcamp program is divided into six challenges. Every Monday, we'll discuss the week's challenge via video chat. Last week's challenge was to reflect on the mom you've been versus the mom you want to be. The next five challenges are as follows. Week two, create a physical fitness regimen. Week three, find a hobby you truly love. Week four, put the spice back in your marriage. Week five, find your village of moms. And week six, turn your house into a home.

"Okay, does everyone have their copy of *Motherhood Better* with them?" Emily asked, holding up her book.

I did. So prepared. I felt like a Girl Scout. Minus the pants.

"This week's challenge is to shake off the shackles of baby weight and find a fitness routine that works for you. Please open it up to the first chapter, 'Your Mommy Body: Your Mommy Temple.' Who's ready to get in shape?"

The cheering was noticeably quieter this time, but everyone was still all smiles.

Emily lifted a transparent water bottle monogrammed in black calligraphy with her initials.

"If you follow me on Instagram, which I hope you do, you already know that every day I drink no less than seventy ounces of water infused with lemon, stevia and fresh-pressed ginger. I call it my 'mommy tonic' and it's what helps me stay on top of my five kids and bustling business!"

Emily took a dramatic sip from the bottle.

"Yummy! The recipe is on the *Motherhood Better* online communication portal. By the way, don't forget to check into the forums daily and let us know how you're doing!"

I made a note to myself to buy a cute water bottle and make some mommy tonic. Hopefully it tasted something like a gin and tonic.

Emily put the bottle down. "Okay, this week, your challenge is to focus on your health by adopting a fitness routine that works for you. Every morning, I spend forty-five minutes with my personal trainer, Sven, and we..."

My mind wandered. Oh, we all knew about Sven. He was the Norwegian Hercules who graced Emily's blog regularly, and always in some kind of graceful but intimidating yoga pose. Most of the time he donned only a pair of skintight elastic short shorts. The way his skin glistened in Emily's photos, it looked like he'd been freshly oiled up for a body building competition. All of Emily's followers were obsessed with him, and posts featuring her trainer always were flooded with comments.

Is he available for sessions out of state?

What are his rates?

I snapped myself back to reality.

"Sven and I prefer to exercise in nature and barefoot. It promotes a mind/body/Earth connection. Look, ladies, if I can get my body back after birthing five littles, so can you!" Emily continued. "Now, I'd like to hear from some of you. What are your personal body goals?"

A mom with long, wavy brown hair, a glittery tank top and expensive-looking sunglasses perched on her head spoke up. "Yeah, hi. I'm Kimmie from Los Angeles." She popped her chewing gum. "My personal body goal is to lose the last one-and-a-half pounds of baby weight and complete the last abdominal skin laser treatments from my plastic surgeon. It's painful, but I know I'm worth it."

Emily smiled sweetly into her camera. "Those are all very good goals, Kimmie. Would anyone else like to share?"

Two more women shared their goals. Fiona, a mom with two dark brown braids that hit just past her armpits, said she wanted to start every day with yoga. A woman named Lillian with a short blond bob talked about joining some kind of stroller exercise club.

"These are all so fantastic," Emily said, clapping her hands.

"I just know this week will be a turning point. Remember, it's not about being a size two, it's about having the confidence of a size two."

The call ended in a way that I couldn't have ever imagined.

"Before we go, I'd like to introduce the group to our new member, Ashley Keller. She's replacing Mellie."

She said "Mellie" like the name tasted bitter in her mouth.

"We're so excited to have you, Ashley! You do have a human child, right?" she asked, with a slightly annoyed giggle.

I was frozen with shock that Emily Walker was addressing me by name but managed to sputter out an embarrassed, "Yes."

"Tell us a little about yourself, Ashley!"

"Um, my name is Ashley…"

Duh! She just said that! I could feel my face getting hot. I rubbed my sweaty palms on my shirt. "My daughter, Aubrey, is, um…"

My mind went blank. I couldn't remember how old Aubrey was. Everyone was staring at me, Emily included. She has five kids and probably never forgets how old any of them are. How could she? She throws them massive fabulous birthday parties every year. If anything, her kids' ages are marked in AmEx bills.

"She's…less than a year old."

Less than a year? A tiny bead of sweat formed around my temple. I brushed it away with my hand.

Emily smiled warmly. "Is she there with you?"

Emily Walker wants to meet my baby. The Emily Walker. I broke out in a dopey grin.

Of course! I jumped out of my seat and bent over to pick up Aubrey. It wasn't until I heard the audible gasps that I realized I'd just mooned the entire group. Eleven people, including the woman I want to be when I grew up, had just seen my thonged, practically naked backside.

I ducked down immediately under the desk and out of frame. No. No, no, no, no. No. This wasn't happening. This couldn't be happening. Every last member of the group and Emily Walker—my mom crush, future bestie and mentor—did not just see the bottom back half of my birthday suit, including the Minnie Mouse tattoo I got when I was eighteen that only David and a handful of others know about.

No, no, no, no. I held a now-fussing Aubrey under the table for what felt like an eternity and tried to melt into the floor and wish my existence off of the planet.

"Ashley?" I heard Emily say through the speakers. "Are you there?" Behind her I could hear a muffled snicker.

I crawled back up to the chair with Aubrey.

"I'm… I'm sorry about that. I forgot I wasn't…"

A booming, confident female voice cut me off, "I'm not wearing pants, either, Minnie Mouse," said the brown-haired, burly mom who had earlier identified herself as Josie from Iowa.

Everyone broke into laughter and I sheepishly smiled, relieved. I mouthed "thank you" to Josie.

"Well then! That was exciting," continued Emily, tersely. "This must be Aubrey! She's darling! We've run out of time but I just wanted to thank all of you for your commitment to being the best moms you can be. Remember, great moms are made, not born. Good luck with the challenge!"

Before I knew it, everyone was saying goodbye and the screen went black.

Well, it could have been worse. I could have done a full frontal.

I decided not to let my peep show get me down. Yes, it was humiliating, but I had three huge things to be grateful for: I just had a meeting with Emily Walker, in six weeks I'd be going on a three-day vacation with her and I was on the path to becoming the mom Aubrey deserves. A mom who wears pants.

Now I just had to figure out how to do it.

This week's task was to exercise. I wondered if stretching to reach the candy on top of the fridge counted as Pilates.

My first step in the Fitness Challenge was to make Emily's mommy tonic. It only called for water, lemon, stevia and fresh ginger, but the only ingredient I had on hand was H_2O. I was not 100 percent sure what stevia was. Hopefully it was some kind of Russian vodka I'd never heard of. With any luck this tonic would be more of a cocktail than something I'd have to choke down all day like cough medicine.

It was already 7 p.m. when I realized I was missing two ingredients for Emily's magic elixir and David had just texted me, letting me know he was on his way home (he worked late AGAIN), so I asked him to pick them up. You would have thought I'd asked him for a pound of flesh from his passive aggressive, I'm exhausted, but sure, text. I can count on one hand the number of times I've asked him to go to the grocery store since Aubrey was born. Was I supposed to put a freshly bathed and pajamaed Aubrey in the car and take her to the store? I don't know if it's work stress or what, but asking him for anything these days results in a huge man tantrum that is starting to get on my last nerve.

I never wanted to be the type of wife that nags, but if I need something done I have to say it a minimum of six times to make it happen. The kitchen faucet was spraying me in the face from the base for two weeks before he finally fixed it. Over those fourteen days I must have brought it up twenty-eight times. If that's nagging, I guess I'm a nag. Excuse me for not wanting to look like I'm about to enter a wet T-shirt contest every time I wash my hands.

At 7:45 p.m. David walked through the door and angrily

tossed me a small shopping bag. It turns out stevia is not a Russian vodka but an all-natural sweetener that he had to go to three stores to find. I would have felt worse for him if he hadn't had such an attitude about it.

"You're welcome," he uttered sarcastically after kissing me on the cheek.

I pursed my lips and used the sing-song tone that means I'm trying not to snap.

"You're welcome, too, for me taking care of the baby all day, cleaning, changing the worst diaper I've ever seen in a six-inch by six-inch public bathroom, doing the laundry, and…" I almost said "making dinner" but stopped myself. The frozen chicken tenders, mashed potatoes from a box and canned corn waiting for him on a plate in the microwave probably wasn't a meal I wanted to brag about.

He set his briefcase on the kitchen table. "And you're welcome for my working an entire day so that we can have a house to live in and food to eat."

I took his lunch container out of his bag and placed it in the sink. "You're also very welcome for my doing everything at home so that you're free to work and interact with other adults while I sit at home all day like a hermit with only dirty dishes to talk to."

He began to walk upstairs toward the bathroom. I followed him, my plastic grocery bag still in hand.

David sat on the bed and kicked off his shoes haphazardly, knowing full well how much that annoys me.

He sighed. "If you hate being at home with Aubrey so much, why don't you get a job?"

I felt like I'd been stabbed in the chest with a jagged icicle. I walked slowly toward him. Suddenly he wasn't my husband, he was the enemy.

"First of all, I do not hate being home with Aubrey. She's

my entire life. It's hard. Every single day it's hard. Why aren't I allowed to say that? My life isn't easy."

David stood up and loosened his tie. He leaned into me. "Neither is mine."

Without another word he walked into our bathroom and shut the door. I heard the shower start. I went downstairs to clean up.

I felt conflicted. I never thought his work was easy, but if I were to be honest, it did seem more interesting and less... tedious than being a stay-at-home mom. I love Aubrey with all of my heart and wouldn't change a thing which in some ways makes it worse. How can my life be exactly how I want it to be but feel like such a daily struggle?

I turned on the microwave and set it to two minutes to warm David's gourmet meal. Hopefully he'd see it as a peace offering. A slightly overcooked peace offering with a side of ketchup.

I walked over to the kitchen counter and opened the plastic bag. It contained a small bottle of stevia, lemonade, and ginger ale. Lemonade? Ginger ale? I asked for stevia, a lemon and fresh ginger. I slammed the bag down on the counter and tried to control my rising anger.

This would have to do for the night. I mixed three drops of stevia and a splash of lemonade into a glass of ginger ale and took a big swig. Not bad.

I walked upstairs to my bedroom with my not-so-healthy elixir and settled into bed with my computer in my lap. I could still hear David in the shower.

I clicked through to the *Motherhood Better* message boards. Rebecca, Emily's assistant, had sent me login information for the portal late last night. Apparently, it was some sort of private online journal where all of the Motherhood Better Bootcamp members were supposed to update each other with their progress. Scanning the page I saw that there were already over a hundred posts.

Hello ladies! Today I jogged for six miles while pushing my three-month-old twins in their jogging stroller. I felt incredible. I'm training for a half-marathon to raise funds for a local charity.—Heather from New Jersey, mom of two

Hi moms! Oh, I have had the best day ever! Our video chat with Emily really lit a fire underneath me. I have three children three and under, but that didn't stop me from signing up for my city's intramural lacrosse team! My husband is so supportive and is bringing the kids to every game and practice.—Naomi from Wisconsin, mother of three

Gosh. The most physical thing I'd done that day was break a sweat trying to open a particularly difficult bag of potato chips during Aubrey's nap. At least I was drinking the mommy tonic. I sipped the sweet, carbonated beverage, hoping the core ingredients were melting away my cellulite.

I needed to up my game. This was a competition, after all, and Emily was probably reading all of these posts. I jumped up and checked my face in the mirror. I looked alright. Standing in the light of my bedroom next to my closet, I opened my phone's camera and held it at a flattering angle, making sure to hold up my glass of tonic. I snapped a photo.

I had dark circles under my eyes and my hair was noticeably slick, but it would have to do. I quickly uploaded it to the Motherhood Better Bootcamp portal with the caption, I'm loving the mommy tonic! I can feel my body getting detoxified already. Thanks Emily!

It was only after I was admiring my brilliant post that I noticed three loads of unwashed laundry, including my inside-out panties with the crotch section facing up, were in the background. I scrambled to delete the photo but there was no option to do so.

Typing quickly, I added, Photo taken at my best friend's house.

As my eyelids became heavy I checked Emily's Instagram one more time. I thought Bare-Butt-Gate had been long forgotten, but she'd snapped a photo of a small purple bottle of some kind of body cream on top of her Egyptian cotton sheets with the caption, Perfect for keeping arms, legs, AND BOTTOMS smooth. ☺

I fainted. Good night.

Tuesday, January 29,
12:30 P.M.

Too many mothers rely on caffeine to keep them going. What they don't know is that motherhood comes with its own natural pick-me-up: love! When your heart is wide open to the miracle that is your blessings, you'll no longer need sugary coffee drinks to make it through the day.
—Emily Walker, *Motherhood Better*

I made it to noon without a cup of coffee, but after almost falling asleep on the living room floor three times this morning while Aubrey banged a plastic octopus on my head like a judge's gavel, I knew I had to get some coffee in my body. It was in Aubrey's best interests. I'd never made it to the café that quickly—on the way, I almost ran over an elderly woman with my stroller, but if I slowed down, I risked dozing off in the street. The smoky black liquid tasted like heaven in my mouth and I downed it in less than six greedy gulps. A few minutes later I had that familiar buzz.

The café was mostly empty, except for two women chatting

together in the corner. They'd lean into each other, whisper something and then laugh raucously, as if they were sharing the most hilarious stories anyone had ever heard. I tried not to watch them.

It was a recurring theme, but ever since Gloria came over, I'd been thinking more and more about how desperately lonely motherhood is. I ran through the different times in my life, teenage years included, and had to admit I'd never been this lonely in my entire life. David could be right next to me in bed and I still felt like I was by myself. I just didn't feel like he understood me anymore. I didn't feel like anyone did.

Ever since Aubrey was born, I'd felt like I lived on a deserted island of baby television shows, chores and diapering accessories. I had one teeny finger based in reality and the rest of me was stuck in an oblivion of sleepless nights.

I loved being a mom. I loved Aubrey, but I wished I had real friends to talk to every day. I couldn't open up to David. He'd just go on and on about how I needed to start making to-do lists and getting things done while the baby slept. I wanted a friend who would just listen and complain, not make reasonable suggestions.

David was as involved as he could be, but at the end of the day he'd never know what it was like to hate his flabby stomach but love the cause of it. I knew he worked hard, but whenever he said, "I'm tired," I wanted to cut him a little bit. Tired? You get to sleep through the night. I give 100 percent of myself but still feel like I'm failing at the most important job I've ever done.

Before I knew it, it was time to take Aubrey home and put her down for a nap. Even with the cup of coffee coursing through my veins, I knew I'd probably have one, too.

Looking around at the empty tables, and longing for connection, I pulled out my phone before leaving the café and logged into the *Motherhood Better* portal.

Motherhood Better Bootcamp Journal Entry
From Ashley Keller, mom of 1
Today I enjoyed a brisk walk with my daughter to a nearby café. I really worked up a sweat. I'm still adjusting to the mommy tonic and indulged in a small coffee, but instead of my usual chocolate cookie I opted for fruit-based apple pie.

3 P.M.

When I met Sven I was like most of you: unhappy and overweight. I couldn't shake the last six ounces of baby weight. Within three weeks, he whipped my body into the best shape of my life. My high school cheerleading uniform is too big for me now.

—Emily Walker, *Motherhood Better*

I'm tackling the Exercise Challenge today. Guess what? I joined a gym. I signed the contract for a year and paid the first three months up front. The very fit personal trainer guy at the front desk asked what my fitness goals were. I don't think "general thinness" is what he was expecting so I added "muscle building" in at the last minute.

Want to hear the best part? The gym has childcare. You can drop off your baby for an hour at a time. I feel a little bad leaving Aubrey with strangers, but I checked it out and they've all been background checked, fingerprinted, have at least thirty early childhood education college units and are CPR certified. Come to think of it, they're probably more qualified for motherhood than I am.

I start tomorrow. Today I'm going to get my new fitness clothes: a few pairs of stretchy black pants, two sports bras, a new water bottle, indoor running shoes and four sporty tops should do it. Maybe I should get some of those electrolyte drinks that look like they glow in the dark. And some granola bars for energy. Peanut butter, too. I have a coupon for the new kind with swirls of chocolate. Yum!

I can't wait.

Wednesday, January 30, 2 P.M.

Always incorporate your children into your exercise routine. It's important to model healthy living. My five love to join me on my 5 a.m. walks. The baby fits snugly in my wrap and I pull my middle two in a wagon. More weight means a better workout!

—Emily Walker, *Motherhood Better*

I love the gym. Aubrey and I got there at 8:30 a.m. today and she was the first baby in the Kid's Korner (don't ask me about the double K. I'm trying to ignore it). After dropping her off I headed to the locker room and changed into my new, very cute ensemble. I felt fitter already!

Then I saw it: the hot tub. I didn't spend the entire hour soaking. Just forty-five minutes to warm up my muscles before a very brisk ten-minute speed walk on the treadmill. The machine said I burned thirty calories, which is probably half of a granola bar, but it's not just about calories burned, it's about the changes to your metabolism and muscle building. That's what I overheard a personal trainer saying. I'm learning so much.

Aubrey slept the entire time. Can't wait to go back. I'm such a gym rat already. I'm going to be such a MILF: Mom I'd Love to Feel good about. #SoFit.

Thursday, January 31, 9:30 A.M.

Salad makes a wonderful breakfast! My breakfast salad bowls include baby arugula, six organic grapes, red onions, cucumber slices, fair trade walnuts, ¼ cup of quinoa, and a generous serving of aloe and mango juice vinaigrette.

—Emily Walker, *Motherhood Better*

Not only does this gym have a hot tub, it has a steam room and free WiFi. I walked once around the track today. I did two sets of three pushups, as well. I've gained a pound but muscle is heavier than fat so I'm not worried.

After my pushups, whew! I fired up my laptop and watched two episodes of *Hillside Heights* in my nook. What's my nook, you ask? It's a private changing room where I sit with my feet up on a bench in the corner and just focus on being present, like in yoga. Naturally I use my headphones so as to not disturb anyone. It is extremely similar to yoga.

Amazing Fact: This gym has a snack bar with the most delicious creations. The Chicken Tucson wrap is to die for. It has only 300 calories without the Southwest sauce. I added the sauce, of course, but just for a bit of flavor.

I also jogged for almost six minutes. #FitnessFreak.

I took a gym selfie and sent it to David. He replied with a heart-eyes emoji. He's so incredibly proud of me, but not as proud as I am of myself.

You'll be happy to learn that I've changed my eating habits entirely. No more ice cream, only frozen yogurt. There's a new place two doors down the street and it has all kinds of mix-ins: breakfast cereals, chocolate chips, almonds (healthy), and coconut caramel flakes (also healthy). When you buy four cups you get the fifth one free. Guess who's getting a freebie tomorrow?

Friday, February 1, 11 A.M.

Don't feel pressure to lose the baby weight too quickly. After the miracle of childbirth, for me, it takes between 10–15 days.

—Emily Walker, *Motherhood Better*

Quick update: I felt bad monopolizing the changing rooms, so after I dropped Aubrey off in the gym childcare today, I watched *Hillside Heights* in my car. If I pull up right beside the back entrance the WiFi is still incredible. I didn't have time to work out, but I really do need the downtime. Aubrey is doing great in the Kid's Korner.

I think I'll come back this afternoon for another workout.

2 P.M.

We have a snitch. When I returned to the locker room today after watching two episodes of *Celebrity Style Scoop* in my car, there was an envelope tucked into my locker. Inside was an official letter.

Dear gym member,
Please be advised that the use of the Kid's Korner is for active gym members only. We require all guardians to stay inside of the fitness center while their children are being minded.
Warmly,
The Management

How dare they? My car is only a hop and a skip away from the treadmills. It's barely on the other side of the glass. They're acting like I went on a shopping spree in the next city. Relaxing one's mind is just as important as working on your body. Emily always says that. How do they know I'm not meditating in my car or doing laps around the building? How do they know I don't have a medical condition and need to give myself injections in the privacy of my vehicle? If that were true, I could probably sue for discrimination.

I am furious.

I am determined to find the source of the information leak. My top suspects right now are:

#1: The super-skinny blonde who runs the gym café. Sometimes I order a chocolate protein smoothie to go before popping off to my car.

#2: Yolanda. Yolanda is another Kid's Korner mom. She drops off her two-year-old, Jasper, at the same time I drop off Aubrey. We're usually in the changing room together. She's asked me if I'd like to weight train with her once—be spotting buddies—and I turned her down not just because I don't want to lift weights but because "spotting buddies" sounds like some kind of mutual agreement to discharge blood between periods together and that's gross.

I've seen Yolanda give me side-eye more than once as I saunter back from my car, relaxed and happy to pick up Aubrey. It's not my fault that I've figured out a way to enjoy my life while she gets sweaty and punishes herself.

Update: It's definitely Yolanda. As I tucked the letter into my bag she walked past me and gave me a half I-told-on-you smile. Wench.

Tomorrow I'm going to try some yoga if the class isn't full.

Saturday, February 2,
11 A.M.

Sven is a licensed massage therapist. I highly recommend
that mothers treat themselves to a massage once a week
to work out some of that stress.

—Emily Walker, *Motherhood Better*

Yolanda is watching me. After I dropped Aubrey off at the
Kid's Korner, I headed over to the elliptical machines and
saw her peeking at me, not once but TWICE, from the free
weights area. How childish of her to tattle on me just because
I wouldn't be her period partner.

The upside is that I burned a hundred calories, which means
I can stop by the froyo place and treat myself on the way home.

Aubrey cried a little when I dropped her off today. She
could probably sense my stress from the situation. Thanks,
Yolanda.

In more uplifting news, I signed up for a Mommy & Me
yoga class. A Bikram (that's yoga-speak for "unnecessary tor-

ture") studio a few minutes from my house has a few open-
ings and I thought, why not?

Someone on Facebook said it helped them bond with their
one-year-old and connect their souls or something. I don't
know what that means, but I'd love for my soul to be connected to Aubrey's.

I know it sounds crazy, but I'm already worried about what
her teen years will be like. If she's anything like me, she'll be
absolutely insane and risk her life twelve times before breakfast. I'm hoping that if I keep an open dialogue and attach
chains to her ankles, it won't be so bad. The yoga can't hurt,
either. Maybe by the time she's thirteen we'll have bonded so
well that she'll confide in me, come to me when she needs
advice... A mom can dream, right?

Our first class is this afternoon. Wish me luck and flex-
ibility.

10 P.M.

> The decision to move Sven into our pool house was a
> natural one. He's like a member of our family now. Our
> kids call him Uncle Sven! It's my solemn prayer that every
> mom finds a trainer and friend like him.
>
> —Emily Walker, *Motherhood Better*

How did Mommy & Me Yoga go? Thanks for asking. It
started off a little rocky. We were running late and I didn't
have time to change, so I just Febreezed my yoga pants in case
we had to sit with our legs open.

I must be doing something wrong because all of the other
babies seemed much calmer than Aubrey. She spent the entire
time crying and trying to squirm out of my arms. She wasn't
at all interested in Baby Crane or Downward Facing Puppy.

A mom in white linen pants to my left kept eyeing me like I was failing some kind of Zen-ness test.

Near the end, we were supposed to meditate "third eye to third eye," with our faces pressed against our baby's faces. I leaned into Aubrey, who was sitting on her green mat, and she head butted me. Right in the nose. Stars exploded behind my eyes and I almost blacked out. Before I could think, six or seven curse words flew out of my mouth. Loudly. Aubrey and the babies on either side of us burst into tears. White Linen Pants picked up her son and held him to her chest like I was holding a machete.

The yoga teacher tried to salvage the tattered calm vibe in the room, "Okay, accidents happen. Draw in the good air, breathe out the bad."

I'm pretty sure I was the bad.

We left shortly after that.

We weren't banned for life but I'm not going back. Aubrey can head-butt me in our living room for free.

I canceled my gym membership. I decided that I don't want to be part of an organization that discriminates based on how people choose to interpret "working out" or uses a K to spell Korner. But I am going to miss those wraps.

Fun news: I checked into the Motherhood Better Bootcamp online portal today.

Bad news: There's a thread for updating everyone with your progress, and seven of the moms have already lost weight, toned up or done things with their bodies other than stuff them with frozen yogurt and get knocked out by their infant.

I can't mess this up. Today I did ten pushups (over a three-hour period) and three sets of four sit-ups. For dinner I'm making cheese tortellini, but I'm only eating a baby bowl-sized portion with just once tiny piece of buttered French bread.

Progress.

Sunday, February 3,
9 A.M.

Not every meal you eat needs to be solid food. I replace at least two a day with juice made of vegetables from my garden. For enhanced vitality, add a teaspoon of heart-healthy colostrum.

—Emily Walker, *Motherhood Better*

Today is my last day to make some progress before the boot-camp video chat tomorrow.

I started a new diet. It's called Ship Shape Shake, and according to the infomercial, I should start seeing dramatic results in just seven days. I bought the box after the failed yoga class yesterday, and I haven't read through the literature yet but I'm excited.

Full disclosure: I may have messed up just a teeny bit. I didn't realize that each silver packet of strawberry flavored powder was supposed to be a meal REPLACEMENT. I thought it was a kind of fat-melting solution that would enter my body, bear hug the cellulite and then carry it out.

Apparently, I'm actually supposed to mix the powder with cold water to make some kind of sad watery shake and drink that instead of eating actual food.

I downed the first shake with a bowl of cereal, one hard-boiled egg and a vanilla latte with whipped cream.

I'm totally on board for lunch, though.

For dinner you're allowed to have a shake and a "reasonable dinner." The picture of the dinner in the brochure was a romaine salad, chopped tomatoes and grilled chicken but David is working tonight so I'm going to finish the last slice of pepperoni pizza in the fridge for dinner before it goes bad. People are starving all over the world and it feels wrong to waste food at a time like this.

10 A.M.

Today started out rough. I was so hungry I started eating almonds to curb the pangs. Forty-five minutes passed and I was still starving.

10:45 A.M.

I'm not sure, but I believe the diet is starting to affect my cognitive functions. As hard as I tried I couldn't remember what bagels taste like. I would've killed for a bagel and cream cheese. Okay, maybe not kill, but I would have definitely slapped someone for one.

10:50 A.M.

I ate six of Aubrey's baby cheese puff things. Not on purpose. I gave her one and then before I realized what was happening, six were in my mouth half chewed. Yes, I could have spit them out but that's insane. Who spits out food?

10:54 A.M.

I broke down and had an apple with peanut butter. It's not on the meal plan, but apples are fruit and peanut butter is just nuts which have omega 3s, I think.

11 A.M.

Took Aubrey on a walk for some cardio. Bought a low-fat mocha with no whip at the café. I would have opted for nonfat milk, but that's against everything I believe in. Have you seen nonfat milk? It's blue.

I bought a croissant but gave most of it to Aubrey to gnaw on. May have had a few bites for energy for the walk.

11:30 A.M.

I drank my second shake in less than ten seconds. I was supposed to wait for lunch, but I couldn't. My stomach felt empty and acidic. I ate twenty more almonds. If I have to see another almond in my life I will immediately barf. Unless it's a chocolate-covered almond, I love those. I wonder who discovered chocolate-covered almonds? That person should have a national holiday named in their honor.

11:45 A.M.

I kept walking in and out of the kitchen like a lost child. I ate a cherry tomato in desperation.

11:47 A.M.

Just ate a plate of sliced red onion dipped in fat-free dressing with six shakes of pepper. I pretended it was a steak. Did not work.

SUNDAY, NOON

Aubrey was having a jar of pureed butternut squash, apple and beef for lunch. Normally the dark orange mush wouldn't appeal to me, but after warming it in the microwave for twenty seconds, I tested it on my tongue. It was like heaven. I took one more mini bite. Then one more. I ate half of the jar before coming to my senses. This was a new low.

2 P.M.

CraigsPage.com
New Listing
For Sale:
Almost complete starter kit of Ship Shape Shake Meal Replacement Diet Kit.
Strawberry Flavored.
Only two pouches missing.
Note: You can't eat actual food. The shakes are the food. Just thought you should know.

11 P.M.

Aubrey just went back to sleep for the second time, so I decided, since I was up, I'd update my Motherhood Better Bootcamp online journal before tomorrow's call.

Motherhood Better Bootcamp Message Board Entry
Hello ladies and Emily! So far I've joined a gym and taken up yoga with my daughter. She's such a strong little girl. Very headstrong. She inspires me to see stars in the mundane every single day. I love her. I'm eating more consciously and really savoring my meals. Thank you for the Ship Shape Shake

recommendation. They're delicious and really changed the way I look at food. Xo Ashley

I shut the computer and sat in the dark of my bedroom next to David, who was sleeping soundly.

I was just settling into bed when I heard Aubrey wail again. She sounded wide awake. "No, no, no," I wailed internally.

Moments like this I wish I had sister wives. Surely my sister wife would hear my baby's pitiful wails from the next room and help me. She'd float in, wearing a long, modest ivory Victorian nightgown and smile sympathetically at me before picking up my baby and whisking her away. Before she left I'd pretend to protest her help, and she'd put a finger to her lips and mouth, "No. Sleep. You deserve it."

I threw my feet over the side of the bed and quickly made my way down the hall. I opened Aubrey's door to see her sitting up, sleepily. She could barely stay upright as she rubbed her eyes with a chubby hand. My heart melted.

I carefully laid her on her back and rubbed her stomach. Without warning she let out an enormous burp. She sighed, closed her eyes and within moments was breathing deeply again.

That's all it was? Gas? I stroked her fine hair.

Suddenly, a sister wife didn't seem like a brilliant idea anymore. As utterly exhausted as I was, seeing Aubrey's still face in the moonlight, I knew I wanted this moment to myself.

Monday, February 4, 11 A.M.

It's important for every mom to have a passion. Your calling is motherhood, but you must have something yours alone that lights a fire under you every day. My hobby is crafting. Whether I'm monogramming organic T-shirts for orphans in Russia or simply making sustainable and aromatic sachets for friends, creating beautiful things with my hands is what makes me excited to wake up in the morning.

—Emily Walker, *Motherhood Better*

The Motherhood Better Bootcamp video chat had started promptly at 10 a.m. Despite being jetlagged in Australia as part of her book tour, Emily looked fantastic. Her shiny black hair was pulled into a side French braid and she wore a long-sleeved cashmere shirtdress. Her eye shadow and lipstick were both a luxurious deep plum and her skin was flawless.

"Hello, mommies!" she said excitedly, her sparkling pearl-like teeth shining in her camera's light. "I've been reading all

of your online journal entries and am so proud of the progress
you made during the Fitness Challenge! Brava to each and
every one of you! Now, who's ready to get crafty?"

I sat at the kitchen table staring at my computer and bouncing Aubrey in my lap, trying to look enthusiastic. I don't exactly have the best history with crafts. Joy tried to get me on
the DIY bandwagon but quickly gave up when she realized I
didn't know my macramé from my marzipan.

Emily leaned into the camera. "Having a hobby is so important when you're a busy mama. It gives you something to
do that's just for you, nobody else. Right now I'm working
on a needlepoint of my entire family." Emily held up a thick
three by three white sheet showing a half-completed—but
clearly expert—embroidery of her family of seven.

"Oh, my freaking—" I stopped myself before I cursed aloud.

The other moms oohed and aahed.

"This week, the challenge is to flex your crafting muscles.
I want you to dig deep and get those creative juices flowing.
Does anyone have a project they're currently working on?"

Josie from Iowa raised her hand. She was a stocky woman
who wore lots of flannel. I recognized her from her journal
entry photos. As down to earth as she seemed, I'd hate to
cross her, as I was sure she could break a grown man in half.

Josie cleared her throat. "I'm building my kids a playhouse
out of reclaimed wood from the lumberyard. I'm laying the
concrete foundation later today."

Emily's face froze. "Wow, well, that's certainly a...craft, I
suppose. Anyone else?"

Kim from LA raised a finger before speaking. "I'm having
my nanny make a quilt out of Connor's old onesies. She's really good at those things."

Emily blinked. "That's wonderful, Kim, but the challenge
is to make something by yourself."

Kim's mouth hung open. "I made Connor."

Emily paused before continuing. "If you're stuck and need craft ideas, check the message board. I put a few links up to some of my more popular crafts including the papier-mâché mold of your child's hand that everybody loved a few months ago."

The ladies oohed and aahed.

I didn't manage to get in any face time with Emily during the call so I knew I'd have to knock it out of the park this week. If I couldn't get her attention, I had no chance of winning the competition.

After the call was over, I put Aubrey in her stroller for a walk to give myself time to think.

As we sauntered down the sidewalk, I made a resolution.

I decided to not only learn to craft but to learn to LOVE to craft. I always pictured myself as the kind of mom who made every sweater, spent the afternoons dipping candles and was always up to some adorable project.

So what if I almost burned the house down two years ago trying melt crayons onto canvas with a blow-dryer (RIP blow-dryer)?

Fact: Blow-dryers cannot be propped up for several minutes using a stack of paper plates while on full blast.

I've learned that crafting is a great bonding activity with children. I can't open Facebook without seeing what my high school friend turned perfect mom Penny McConnel is crafting. Today her status was, "Found a vintage olive oil bottle at the recycling center. Turned it into a fun lotion dispenser." The photo looked like something out of the Anthropologie catalog. I bet her four daughters (yes, four daughters) all wore matching aprons and made their own mini homemade coconut-oil lotion and lotion infused with freshly picked lavender. I want that for me and Aubrey.

I noticed that Aubrey had fallen asleep so I parked the

stroller at one of the patio seats outside the café. I pulled out my phone and spent a few minutes scrolling through Pinterest, and even though I hated the website from the bottom of my soul, Ashley the Perfect-ish Mom was going to learn to tolerate it. I'd feel differently once I had a few successfully pulled-off crafts under my belt.

To really impress Emily Walker, I was going to choose three crafts to master over the next few days.

Potential crafts:
1. DIY watercolor coffee mugs (Yes, they sell beautiful mugs at the store, but why would you want to buy one for $3 when you can spend $20 in supplies to make one that will stain your cuticles?)
2. DIY stain remover (All you need is a little borax, vinegar and salt, and you no longer need to be dependent on drugstore laundry products. As a bonus, you get free chemical burns.)
3. No-bake cake batter truffles (These would be wonderful for holiday gifts or eating in the kitchen in the dark.)
4. DIY mason jar etching (These are gorgeous! I could already see them filled with wildflowers and decorating my home.)
5. DIY ruffled baby romper out of a pillowcase (For Aubrey. I should really just sew all of her clothes.)

I put a shopping list together and just had to go get the supplies.

Who's a slacker? NOT ME!

3 P.M.

A Crafting Essentials starter list can be found on my website. The 67 items listed will get you started on your

crafting journey. You'll find they are more than afford-
able and add up to only around $600. My children and
I begin a new craft every morning at 7 a.m. on the dot.
We begin by changing into our matching aprons on
which I hand-embroidered our initials. We enjoy crafting by the light of the sun on a project table made from
reclaimed lumber that I sanded and stained myself over
a lazy weekend.

—Emily Walker, *Motherhood Better*

I decided to wait until Aubrey woke up from her nap to
start crafting. Yes, she's just a baby, but I was sure Laura Ingalls
Wilder's mother passed down all of her canning and quilt-
ing skills to her at a young age. I felt like it was important for
Aubrey to grow up in a homemade environment and see me
take charge of the home or something.

To get into the mood, we even wore matching aprons, just
like the ones Emily and her kids wear. Unlike Emily, though,
I didn't make them; they sell them at Michelle's, the home
base for all crafters. It's a huge chain. I'd never been in there
before today, and after I'd spent a house payment on supplies
I was still confused by the prices. Was everything supposed
to be that expensive? I actually had to double-check the cur-
rency with an employee. "I'm sorry, but what money is this
in? Turkish lira? Pesos?" Maybe everything was blessed, like
kosher food but by Martha Stewart.

Wasn't the whole point of making things to save money?
I was pretty sure Laura Ingalls Wilder wouldn't have stepped
foot in a Michelle's.

Michelle's lures you in with the promise of a better life and
then empties your checking account. It's like one of those
fraudulent emails from an overseas "prince" promising you an
inheritance you don't deserve. Michelle's has the same business model as movie theaters: offer you a good time, and once

you're trapped inside charge $12 for a small popcorn—or, in Michelle's case, $200 for an old-timey popcorn maker. I almost bought it, too. That is, until I pictured David's face when I told him that I spent a car insurance payment on the promise of buttery snacks.

There was an entire aisle just for glue. GLUE. And one for cake stands. Since when did people get too good to eat cake out of the pan it was baked in? I bought one anyway. I've decided I'm going to make Aubrey's birthday cakes every year. I also picked up some piping bags, a book about cake decorating and some fondant for snacking while I learn. Unfortunately, they didn't sell baking skills, but I have a couple months to learn.

I've already completed my first craft! After we returned from giving all of our money to the craft store, I placed Aubrey in her high chair and got to hobbying! The first craft up was the DIY watercolor mugs.

Outcome: Moderately successful.

The instructions said to fill a plastic bowl with water and gently dump in whatever colors of nail polish you'd like. Then you're supposed to swirl around the colors with a toothpick until they're "dreamy looking." Technically, I did this correctly because last time I checked, nightmares are considered dreams. Maybe I shouldn't have purchased so many blacks and blues.

After that, you carefully dip your white mugs that cost $6 each at Michelle's in the water, creating beautiful designs. I bought eight so that I could give them as gifts to the family.

You should see Joy's Pinterest profile. She has more than thirty pages and half of them are crafts she invented. I know I can't outdo her, but at least I can prove I'm not completely useless.

Back to the crafting. Maybe it was the colors I chose, but

my mugs look less "a starry night" and more "acute skin damage." They look like they're emo. I'm going to call them Mood Mugs Inspired by Xanax and hope they're not interpreted as a cry for help.

Other than that, totally nailed it.

Next I was going to try my hand at the DIY stain remover that's supposedly a staple in Emily Walker's laundry room, but Aubrey was getting fussy. I threw a handful of fruit puffs down on her high chair. She inhaled them. Like mother, like daughter. I decided we needed a break and picked her up for a little bit of play (and reality television) in the living room. Before leaving the kitchen, I looked back at the colossal mess I'd created. For a lot less money, time and effort, I could have purchased eight mugs that didn't look like they'd been in a fight. As hard as I tried, I just didn't get the point of crafting. Maybe I just had to give it some time.

After that, I put Aubrey down for her nap and felt the familiar fatigue and boredom of late afternoon setting in. I wondered what David was up to.

The phone rang three times before he answered it.

"Hi, Ashley." He sounded stressed.

"Hi, David, how's work?" I yawned, exhausted.

"It's busy. What's up?"

"Oh, nothing. Just wanted to say hi. I hit up the craft store this morning and—"

"Is that where you spent $300? I just saw it come out of the bank account."

Well wasn't he Mister On Top of the Finances.

"Yes. But David, I'm learning that it's very important for me to flex my creative muscles. Crafting is my outlet."

"Well, it's also a bit of a drain. Just don't go crazy. Things might get tight soon."

My ears perked up. "What? Why?"

"We were just underbid on two accounts I was counting on. It's a lot rougher out here than I thought."

I tried to think of some words of encouragement for my brave entrepreneur husband. "I know you can do this. You're smart."

"Yeah. Thanks, babe. I'm trying." He sighed softly. "I'd better let you go."

"Okay. What time are you coming home tonight?"

"After dinner. Sorry."

I felt a tug in the pit of my stomach.

"That's okay. Do what you have to do."

I hung up the phone and collapsed onto the couch. Even though I'd only intended to rest my eyes for a few minutes, I found myself waking up two hours later to Aubrey whining loudly.

I checked my phone. It was 4:45. Time for the second shift. Motherhood had a way of making one day feel like two. Or three.

I was just picking Aubrey up out of her bed when the doorbell rang.

"Did I order a package?" I thought to myself as I galloped downstairs with a sleepy Aubrey on my hip. David wasn't going to love that.

I could see the cheetah print through the glass window on the door and knew who it was before I even opened the door.

"Hi, Gloria!" I said, puzzled. "What are you, um…what are you doing here?"

Gloria walked past me and into the house. She was wearing a cheetah-print tracksuit. "I called David and found out he'll be working late again today. I knew you might be too shy to call me, so I figured I'd come over and help out."

I wasn't sure what to say but "can you leave?" didn't feel appropriate. It's not that I minded the company, it's just that I was looking forward to relaxing in various stages of undress for the rest of the afternoon and evening.

Gloria set her purse down on an end table and made her way into the kitchen. I followed her. It wasn't until I heard her gasp that I remembered the mug mess.

"What happened here?" she asked, her hand over her cheek as she stared at my crafty watercolor tornado.

I handed Aubrey to her. "Oh, I was just getting creative." I rushed over to the sink and started cleaning up.

I was happy I'd put the mugs in the oven to dry. I didn't want her to see her gift before I could present it to her.

"Well, you're certainly getting into it. Is this for the motherhood program you're in?"

David must have told her. I dumped a large plastic bowl of nail polish-colored water down the sink.

"Yes. It's going really well," I said convincingly.

Gloria sat at the kitchen table with Aubrey. "You young moms. Always up to one thing or another. Is this the book?"

Gloria picked up my copy of *Motherhood Better* from the kitchen table and, before I could stop her, opened it.

She put on her glasses and began reading. "Forget juice or soda, give your child kombucha." She looked up at me. "What's kombucha? Is that some kind of vaccine? Witchcraft?"

I tried to take the book away but she playfully held it away from me. "It's a type of fermented tea…" I said.

Gloria's eyes grew wide. "Rotten tea! What's wrong with milk these days?" She flipped a few pages and continued reading. "Enjoy my recipe for gluten-free beet muffins with a date-coconut oil glaze."

Gloria lowered the book. "Are you allergic to gluten?" I shook my head. "Is this Emily person allergic to gluten?" I shook my head. "Then why the hell are you avoiding it? When

I was a kid we were afraid of the hydrogen bomb. Your generation is afraid of gluten." Gloria handed me the book.

"Yes, some of the ideas are a bit radical, but Emily's actually quite amazing."

"Amazing at what? Getting moms to buy books full of half-baked ideas? Oh, I'm sorry, half-baked, gluten-free ideas with a coconut-date glaze?"

Even I had to laugh. Gloria couldn't understand. She was from a different time.

"That reminds me." Gloria stood up and handed Aubrey to me. "I have groceries in the car."

"Groceries?" I asked, confused, following her to the front door.

"Yes, groceries."

Gloria slipped out the front door and returned carrying two bags full of food.

I followed her into the kitchen.

She began pulling out ingredients. A large bag of shredded cheese. Two huge bags of corn chips. Canned corn. Sour cream. Salsa.

"What's all this?" I asked, watching more items come out.

Gloria stopped and looked me dead in the eye. "I'm going to teach you how to cook—starting with my signature recipe, Frito Pie."

Frito Pie. I knew the name because David had asked me hundreds of times to make the dish that featured the popular gas station snack, but I'd refused.

"It's David's favorite and an easy weeknight recipe. Your Emily Walker friend probably wouldn't approve, but it's a big hit at parties," Gloria said, searching for a casserole dish in the cupboard.

"What's that smell?" she asked, as she closed in on the section under the sink where my ill-fated potato farm had once grown.

"A plumbing problem," I said, handing her a casserole dish from the top shelf.

Gloria preheated the oven to 350 and began mixing cheese, chips, and globs of cream cheese. Within fifteen minutes it was ready to go into the oven.

"That was fast," I had to admit.

"What's that smell?" Gloria asked again, sniffing the air.

"It's just the plumbing," I lied again, hoping she'd finally drop it.

"No, it's something else. Something's burning."

As soon as she said that, I began smelling it, too. It was coming from…oh, no, the oven. I'd forgotten that my mugs were drying on the brand-new plastic platter I'd purchased earlier.

I practically threw Aubrey at Gloria and opened the oven. A cloud of toxic black smoke billowed out. Gobs of hot melted plastic were melting from the top rack onto the oven floor. It was a disaster.

"What IS that?" Gloria asked, backing out of the room with Aubrey. "Did you try to bake?"

I opened the back door and all of the windows, but not before the smoke alarm went off.

"It's a craft. I crafted," I shrieked.

Gloria played in the living room with Aubrey while I fanned under the smoke detector. I then poured cold water all over what looked like a radioactive mess in the oven. Thirty minutes later I was still chipping burnt plastic out of the oven with a knife. The mugs themselves weren't too damaged. Once I pried the burnt plastic off, they looked almost post-modern. I decided not to give them as gifts but to definitely keep them. They were artistic and smelled of the struggle.

Gloria walked into the kitchen.

"I put the casserole in the fridge," I said. "I'll make it when I finally get this clean. Sometime next week, I anticipate."

Gloria laughed. "Don't worry. I ordered pizza. You know, you really shouldn't use your oven as a cabinet. Even if you don't use it often."

I cringed.

I heard the front door open.

"Anybody home?" called David cheerfully.

He rounded the corner into the kitchen, and upon seeing his face Aubrey screamed happily. He kissed her on the cheek before hugging his mom. Last, but not least, he gave me a quick peck.

"What a treat to come home to all three of my girls! What's that smell?"

I was really getting tired of people asking me that.

"There was a slight problem with the oven," Gloria answered. "Ashley's still learning how they work. But it's all better now. Are you hungry? I ordered pizza!"

I bit my lip.

David looked at me sympathetically. "Rough day, hon?"

"I'm okay. How was yours?" He looked so confident standing there holding Aubrey and she looked so perfect in his arms. I stared at them, feeling like the odd person out—the obvious screwup. I shook the thought out of my head.

"Work is work," he said, but I could tell he was worried. "Just let me know before you do any more expensive craft store runs. How did it turn out?"

"It turned out!" I answered, hoping the questions would end with that.

Later that night, after David had fallen asleep, I took my phone off the bedside table and peeked into the Motherhood Better Bootcamp portal.

There were already eight journal entries in the craft challenge section.

Josie from Iowa, mom of two
I'm setting up indoor plumbing in the playhouse I put together for my kiddos today. We're inviting local foster children to spend their afternoons here.

Tanya Gregory, mom of three
In the past 24 hours, I've knitted six sets of baby booties for newborns born in my hospital's maternity ward. The mommies were so grateful when I dropped them off this afternoon. I used organic, fair-trade yarn.

I quickly shut off my phone. Who were these women? How could I ever stand out when they were all mini Marthas? Tomorrow, I'd need to bring my A game to the crafting table.

Tuesday, February 5, 11:30 A.M.

I don't use any mainstream chemical cleaners in my home. From my tabletops to my bathroom floors, every surface in my domain is gently cleansed with essential oils and natural products that ensure that babies' bodies can grow healthily. Even the rags I use to clean come from old organic-cotton T-shirts. One can never be too careful.

—Emily Walker, *Motherhood Better*

Aubrey had just gone down for her nap and I was ready to take a crack at making my first DIY natural cleaner. I took the recipe right from Emily's blog. Apparently, she uses this stuff to clean every nook and cranny of her giant home and it serves double duty as a laundry stain remover. I figured this would be a pretty simple way to show her that I'm a huge fan and therefore deserve to win the $100,000.

Supplies:
• Vinegar

- Baking soda
- Water
- Lemon essential oil
- Eucalyptus oil
- Blue dishwashing soap

The only things I didn't have were the essential oils. I feel like their title was a little presumptuous, anyway. *Essential* oils. Shouldn't they let us be the judge of that? It's like if I called myself Best Ashley. Hello, everyone, my name is Best Ashley. Nice to meet you. What's so essential about these oils? And if they are essential, why is it in their title? It screamed of insecurity. We don't say "essential sunlight" or "essential water." We don't even say "essential oxygen."

Truth be told, the whole essential oils industry bothered me. They had mobsters in Lululemon peddling the stuff with a hard sell in every city. I had one mom at the park try to convince me lavender oil would get Aubrey to sleep through the night. Of course I immediately bought six bottles. Aubrey smelled like a Bath & Body Works but she didn't sleep through the night no matter how much I put in her bottle. (Joke.) But seriously, it didn't work. The same mom sold me a Himalayan sea salt lamp, three amethyst crystals to help with my non-existent milk production (something about past life trauma affecting my confidence) and eight bamboo-cloth diapers for the low, low price of $39.99 each.

Did I mention I did a brief cloth-diapering stint? It was all fun and games until I realized that they needed to be washed. Who has time for that? I guess I got sucked into visions of beautiful multicolored diapers line-drying in the sun. And when she told me that disposable diapers took a hundred years to biodegrade it was a no-brainer. I only lasted three days before I got behind on laundry and our house started to smell like a porta-potty. I decided to use disposable diapers and off-set my carbon footprint by recycling all of my wine bottles.

I still feel bad about all of the cloth diapers I ended up buy-ing, but it just wasn't for me. I could barely stay on top of the essential laundry (note the proper use of "essential") much less deal with a wet bag overflowing with sewage-soaked nappies. I was a little jealous of those moms who have it down. Those photos of chubby babies in cloth diapers running through flower fields, their amber teething necklaces blowing in the wind, are adorable.

It took me only three minutes to put together the DIY cleaner. After mixing the ingredients (minus the essential oils) I poured them into an empty spray bottle and affixed a cute little label I'd printed off of Emily's blog to the front. There. I was officially a natural earth mother!

When I was done, I plopped down on the couch with a bag of the remaining Fritos from Gloria's casserole and logged on to the Motherhood Better Bootcamp portal. The previ-ous night I'd posted photos of my Emo Watercolor Mugs but hadn't had a chance to read the comments. I headed straight for my notifications.

Aubrey did such a great job! These will make wonderful keep-sakes for grandma and grandpa!

Wow, your little one has talent! Great job!

Beautiful work! I'm a preschool teacher and might have my kids make these for the holidays! Hats off to your budding artist!

Um… I made those. But I played along. No need to let people know that I have the creative skills of a toddler.

I polished off the bag of Fritos but was still hungry. For something sweet. Something about naptime made me want to eat the whole house. I flipped through *Motherhood Better* for an easy but impressive recipe to pass the time.

Coconut-Flour Cherry Spelt Cookies… No. I didn't even know coconuts could make flour. Does it taste like piña coladas?

Banana Quinoa Loaf with Gingerroot Lemon Glaze… No. That sounds less like dessert and more like some weird foot cream.

Date, Macadamia Nut and Dandelion Energy Bites… Never. Energy bites? Desserts are supposed to make you comfortably sleepy, not ready for a run. I'm pretty sure running and dessert are sworn enemies.

I opened up my computer and pulled up Pinterest. There it was: No Bake Chocolate Cake Batter Truffles. And I had all of the ingredients. My stomach rumbled in anticipation.

I almost ran into the kitchen and started pulling out the ingredients I'd need.

I was all set. I scanned the recipe and felt my mouth watering. This recipe was easy. Even for me. All I had to do was mix a frightening amount of butter, chocolate chips, powdered sugar and vanilla together until it formed what I think my thighs are made out of. Then I formed half of it into balls to set in the fridge and ate the other half while watching daytime talk shows.

The next step was supposed to be to melt a brick of white chocolate and dip the truffles into it with toothpicks, but I opted out of that step. "No bake" meant "no cook" in my mind, and I wanted to stay true to the heart of the recipe.

The recipe made twelve truffles, not including the handful of dough I ate while watching *30-Minute Dinners* with Robin Ray.

They were cooling in the fridge when the doorbell rang.
Guess who? Gloria and her little poodle mix, Terry. It'd been a
while since she brought him over so I didn't mind, although I
wished she had called first. I'd have to ask David to say something. I love all animals, but you'll excuse me if I can't overlook the fact that Terry looks like a rodent. A drooling rodent
who constantly yaps and barks.

I'd just gotten Aubrey to sleep, so the idea of that little rat
dog making a racket was less than ideal.

"Do you mind leaving Terry outside, Gloria?"

"Would you leave Aubrey outside?"

I held myself back from saying, "If she were an animal, yes."

As soon as we were inside, I tried to get to the bottom of
today's visit.

"So, what brings you over today?"

"Oh, nothing, I just wanted to see how my granddaughter
was doing," she answered while looking around the house,
probably searching for evidence that I'm somehow unfit to
parent her precious grandchild.

She bent over and placed Terry on the floor. He immediately started banging into walls and yapping. Five seconds later
I heard Aubrey crying in her crib over the downstairs monitor.

"Oh, good, she's awake."

Good? I wanted to strangle Gloria but she'd probably fill
Aubrey's head with all kinds of lies about me when I was in
jail. "Your mother didn't know a sieve from a strainer!" Okay,
that one is true.

I went upstairs to get Aubrey and the next thing I knew,
Gloria was screaming.

I flew down with Aubrey in my arms to see Gloria sitting
on the kitchen floor, tears running down her cheeks, with a
suspiciously quiet Terry in her lap.

"What is it? What's happening?!" I asked, shaking.

"Ch-ch-ch-chocolate," she sputtered, and then I saw the remnants of one of my truffles and several chocolate chips beside Terry.

Oh, no. I must have dropped one.

Several hours and a visit to the emergency veterinarian later, I'm happy to report that Terry is fine. Gloria caught him before he had a chance to eat all my chocolate chips. David spoke to his mom before bed. She wants me to doggy-proof the house before she comes over. Well, that would require a phone call, wouldn't it?

I pretended not to hear her yell, "I didn't even know she baked!" through the receiver.

Wednesday, February 6, 3 P.M.

My all-time favorite craft was my lake house in upstate Washington. What started off as six acres of lush wildflowers is now a gorgeous cabin that my family escapes to whenever we can. My husband, a world-renowned architect, built the home from the ground up. I planned the décor of each room by myself.

—Emily Walker, *Motherhood Better*

Today was glass-etching day. What's glass etching? It's when someone who doesn't know what a Target is uses acid to burn designs into glassware. I don't know why I tried to do this. Okay, that's a lie. I do know why. I had this vision of burning "Keller" in some swirly but respectable font onto all of my casserole dishes. Then, when I took dishes to family events and all of the potlucks I'd surely receive invitations to once I made friends, I could show them off.

"Who made your custom casserole dish, Ashley?"

"Oh, I did! I get invited to so many of these functions that I thought it would be a simple way to keep tabs on my dishes."

"Genius! I never knew you were so crafty! I mean, I knew you were a fantastic homemaker and amazing mother, but creative and skilled, as well? Can we be best friends? I'd also like to formally apply to be your intern."

It sounded simple. "Keller" going across the long side of the casserole dish with a few accent hearts. Except it wasn't.

Supplies:
- Glass dish.
- Etching cream.
- Stencils.
- Brushes.
- Tape.

In my defense, I watched three YouTube videos and read no fewer than five blog posts by annoyingly bubbly moms before starting.

Can I share something? I have a theory that crafters have conspired together to make crafting complicated. There are secrets and tips that they're not sharing because deep down, they want to see us normals fail. This shouldn't have been as hard as it was. I'm a smart person.

1. Glass Etching Mistake #1: Not wearing gloves. Don't be fooled by the word "cream" in *etching cream*. This isn't Lady Loves Her Face lotion; it's acid. I knew this going into the craft, but figured since it was sold at Michelle's that it couldn't be *that* toxic. Wrong! I'm pretty sure I burned two of my fingerprints off. So, if you're an international spy and looking for a way to burgle the royal gems from the Queen of England or whatever, get your-

self a glass-etching kit and take care of your fingerprints the old-fashioned way!

2. Glass Etching Mistake #2: Thinking that I was detail-oriented enough to pull this off. I ruined three, that's right, THREE casserole dishes in the following ways:

   - Getting distracted and leaving the etching-acid burn cream on for too long. Aubrey woke up from her morning nap earlier than she should have so I ran upstairs to settle her. Fast forward to me lying on her bedroom floor with one arm in her crib and, yes, I fell asleep. When I woke up forty minutes later, the dish broke in half when I tried to wash the cream off. I like to think it was symbolic of my broken craft dreams.
   - Focus. Wait—what? Focus. Casserole dish two out of three was ruined when I spelled my own last name wrong using the stencils. I guess I could petition David to change our last name from Keller to Keler. Why not go through the court system to make our name reflect this casserole dish that I put an hour of my life and $200 in craft supplies into? Makes sense to me.
   - Getting too excited. Casserole dish three out of three was broken due to sheer enthusiasm. I lined up the stencils just right. I left the etching cream on for just enough time. But you know what I didn't do? I didn't factor in my limited grip due to the burned-off pads of two of my fingers. During my celebration dance I dropped the dish on the kitchen floor.

The shattering casserole dish startled Aubrey, who instantly began crying. I picked her up.

"It's okay, honey. That's just the sound of Mommy being a hot mess." It was time for her afternoon nap, anyway.

I changed her diaper and, after rocking her in the glider for almost half an hour, she finally settled down and fell asleep. As I lowered her into her crib, my arms burning from fatigue, I took in her beautiful little face. I fought a cascade of tears. She really was just so gorgeous.

Does every mom get lost in their child's face like this? I wondered. I studied her eyelashes, the bow of her lips and her soft cheeks. She really did deserve the best of everything. I had to try to be the mom she needed.

I crept downstairs and cleaned up the broken glass, sweeping every corner of my destroyed kitchen. Afterward, I sat at the kitchen table with my computer and my third cup of coffee.

Scrolling through Pinterest, I stumbled across a photo of a little girl who couldn't have been more than Aubrey's age sitting in front of a window. She was wearing the most adorable little dress with ribbons on the shoulders. The sunshine poured through the window behind her, creating little flecks of light that caught in her curly hair, giving the impression of a crown. Underneath her, the text read: No-Sew Pillowcase Dress Tutorial: 30 Minutes and EASY!

That's it! I felt hot determination creep up my back. I remember Emily sharing on a blog post a few months ago how she makes pajamas for all five of her children. I'd probably learn Mandarin Chinese before I could learn to operate a sewing machine, but this dress was right up my alley.

I ran to the linen closet and found the perfect pillowcase. It was part of a bedroom set I'd purchased months ago for the guest room we'd surely have one day. The off-white satin pillowcase was decorated with little purple, pink and yellow flowers. It would make the perfect dress. I found a roll of ribbon in the garage in the Christmas supplies box.

I sat on the living room floor, hunched over the pillowcase, with the ribbon, scissors, and a needle and thread.

All I had to do was lay the pillowcase flat, cut out the head and armholes and hem them (my stiches were a little shaky but you could barely make them out and they were more rustic that way). Then I threaded the ribbon through the armhole hem. The ribbons served as the straps, ensuring a custom fit every time.

This dress will really grow with her, I thought, as I held it up, impressed with my work. It was a bit big...maybe I should have used a smaller pillowcase, but it was so pretty. Who knew, I might just be the new face of baby clothing design. Okay, maybe that's a bit of a stretch, but I'd just successfully made a piece of clothing for Aubrey and I felt great about it.

I could barely wait until Aubrey woke up, and when she finally did, we did a small (big) photo shoot. I must have uploaded twelve photos of her in the dress from all angles to Facebook. Then we were off to the park. I had to show her dress off to the world!

5 P.M.

I hate crafts. I was walking on air over the amazing dress I'd handcrafted for Aubrey for about ten minutes. That's when, with Aubrey sitting innocently on my lap—maybe I was showing her off a little—a mom in shorts and a pink tank top pushed her jogging stroller next to me and sat down. I thought she was going to ask me where I got Aubrey's fabulous dress, and had already prepared the look of surprise and gesture I'd make (my hand to my neck) as I said, "Oh, this is just something I made this morning!" But the words out of her mouth were, "I want to bless you today."

At first I was confused. Bless me?

"Bless me?"

She put a hand on my hand and leaned in. "Yes, honey. We all go through hard times. You know, my youngest daughter just turned two and I have a bag of clothes at home that I think will fit your little one just right until you get back on your feet."

I was speechless. I literally could not speak. I tried, but all that escaped my mouth was a weird honking cough. She kept talking.

"No, no, it's fine. You just give me a call and tell me where to drop it off and I'll come to you. I'd love to bring you and your daughter dinner, as well."

She then put a piece of folded paper with her number on it in my hand and walked away, to spare me some dignity, perhaps.

Apparently, my pillowcase dress is so terrible people think I'm struggling to clothe my child. I wonder if this happed to Maria in *The Sound of Music* when she made the children play-clothes out of the curtains.

I could barely move for ten minutes I was so embarrassed. Aubrey did not look that bad. I mean, okay maybe the stitching was a little crooked, but that gave the dress character. I suppose I did make the armholes a little big. And the ribbon was slightly frayed.

And then I finally came to my senses. Who was I kidding? She looked like a cross between *The Real Housewives of New Jersey* and *Oliver Twist*.

Then I remembered. FACEBOOK. I had shared photos.

I pulled out my phone and saw that I had twenty-five notifications. Twenty. Five.

The comments.

Joy: Ashley, is this a Halloween costume? Baby calf? I don't get it.

Mom: Very cute…this is an indoor outfit I'm assuming?

David: LOVE IT! (He types in all caps when he's lying.)

Amelia Davis (high school frenemy): Wow.

I didn't read the rest. I just deleted the photos and hoped that I'd somehow erased them from everyone's minds at the same time.

I've learned my lesson. Level II crafts are not for me. I need to stay in the shallow end of this pool. I aimed too high. Wish I had more of those truffles.

Dear Pinterest,

When we first started dating, you lured me in with Skittles-flavored vodka and Oreo-filled chocolate chip cookies. You wooed me with cheesy casseroles adjacent to motivational fitness sayings. I loved your inventiveness: Who knew cookies needed a sugary butter dip?

You did. You knew, Pinterest. You inspired me, not to make stuff, but to think about one day possibly making stuff if I have time. You took the cake batter, rainbow and bacon trends to levels nobody thought were possible. You made me hungry. The nights I spent pinning and eating nachos were some of the best nights of my life.

Pinterest, we can't see each other anymore. You see, it's recently come to my attention that some people aren't just pinning, they are making. This makes me want to make, too. Unfortunately, I'm not good at making, and deep down I like buying way more. Do you see where I'm going with this? I'm starting to feel bad, Pinterest. I don't enjoy you the way I once did.

We need to take a break. I'm going to miss your crazy ideas (rolls made with 7Up? Shut your mouth). This isn't going to be easy. You've been responsible for nearly every 2 a.m. grilled cheese binge I've had for the past couple of years, and for that I'll be eternally grateful.

Stay cool, Pinterest.

PS. You hurt me.

PPS. I'm also poor now.

Xo

Me

10 P.M.

On the plus side, David made it back from work before dinner tonight. He came home with a bouquet of red roses for me. If I hadn't been so exhausted I would have made it worth his while.

Watching him walk through the door with flowers was like watching a unicorn jump over a leprechaun—the stuff of fantasies.

I made the Frito Casserole and he devoured two-thirds of it himself. There weren't even leftovers for him to take to work. I'm ashamed to admit that I felt jealous. He'd never eaten anything I'd made like that.

Then, of course, he tried to get frisky as soon as Aubrey fell asleep. I'm no prude, but it's hard to jump into bed with someone you've barely spoken a paragraph to over the past few weeks. He's just been so busy... I mean, okay, he bought some roses before he came home. But I need actual romance, I need ulterior motive–free seduction. I tried explaining to him that it was impossible for me to get in the mood after two seconds of kissing and while he said, "It's fine," before rolling over and going to sleep, I felt bad. Maybe I should have tried harder.

Note to self: Craft yourself a libido.

Motherhood Better Bootcamp Message Board Entry
Hello ladies and Emily: I took a good stab at crafting this week and I definitely feel different. My family and friends couldn't believe that I was behind some of my creations! The mugs I made were en fuego. The pillowcase dress I sewed for my daughter turned so many heads. And the truffles I made were to die for. Some of you have asked for the recipe and I'll get it to you ASAP (do any of you have pets?). I hope everyone is doing well! Can't wait for our call tomorrow. Xo, Ashley

Thursday, February 7, 9 A.M.

Working from home is the best of both worlds: you get to spend time with your precious children, flex your creative muscles and bring in an income. My first year blogging at Motherhood Better by Emily Walker, I made six figures and that was while my babies slept.

—Emily Walker, *Motherhood Better*

Aubrey woke up at 4 a.m. this morning which gave me time to think about what's missing in my life: purpose. Of course Aubrey and David will always be my #1, but I need something outside of them to fulfill me. I've decided that since crafts aren't for me, I'm going to get a work-at-home job. Emily started her empire when she was a stay-at-home mom to three kids, and if she can do it, why can't I? The only difference between us is that she's organized, driven, resourceful and…never mind.

It only took two hours searching online, but I found something. It was like magic and just goes to show you that when you want something enough, it will happen. I replied to an ad on an online job board with my résumé and they called me within half an hour. Something about my work experience must have really impressed them. So this is what the Law of Attraction is all about!

My official job title is Customer Satisfaction Specialist for a company called Dreamstar Direct. They didn't have a website, but when I worked for Weber & Associates we held focus groups to understand consumer trends all the time. I figured this was the same thing—just over the phone. It's a step down from what I used to do, but I have to start somewhere. The plan is to dazzle them with my skills and work my way up. Six months from now, who knows, maybe I'll be a team leader with a squad of super work-at-home moms under me. We'll have conference calls, I'll convert the garage into my office, and all with Aubrey steps away from me. I'll have it all.

I may have fibbed a little during the interview. When the raspy-voiced regional manager, Wanda, asked me if I'd ever done work like this before, I said yes. I mean, I have talked on the phone. What could be so hard about doing it from the comfort of my own home? She asked me when I wanted to start and I said "yesterday" to which she replied that I must really need the money.

I would have explained that while the money is appreciated, it's really just about feeling useful in a capacity that doesn't have to do with wiping dried yogurt off a high chair, but that seemed unprofessional.

The stars must have been aligned in my favor, because my very first shift starts tomorrow at noon! It's a short one, just four hours. Wanda didn't give me much instruction other than that the customers would call me with their needs. These marketing types are so secretive. She was probably worried about my feeding info to a competitor. I've made it my mission to earn their trust.

I found a little notebook in the hall closet for writing down customer feedback. I'll keep impeccable notes and ask open-ended questions like, "How do Dreamstar Direct products make you feel?" and "Do you think Dreamstar Direct values you as a human being?" My shift would fit in perfectly with Aubrey's schedule. I'd feed her an early lunch, get her down for her nap by noon, and go back and forth between playing with her and taking calls for the last hour or so of my shift.

I'm making $20 an hour. If I work five days a week, that's $1,600 a month.

I can't wait to tell David.

It just goes to show you that with positive thinking and a proactive mindset, you really can do anything you want. I'm officially a work-at-home mom! It sounds like the best of both worlds and I'm so excited.

Friday, February 8, 11 A.M.

Working from home is simple. If you don't have a spare room for an office, create a space for yourself at the kitchen table or in the corner of your children's play-room.

—Emily Walker, *Motherhood Better*

Thirty minutes before my first call, I was still working through the paperwork Wanda sent me the night before. The plan was to wake up before Aubrey and learn all about the company, but she woke up no less than four times last night and I was beat. So there we were, at the kitchen table, me with my open computer on one side and a screaming, tired baby waiting for her next spoonful of mashed rigatoni on the other. I could feel the stress rising.

I pushed the spoon into Aubrey's mouth, and she hungrily chewed while banging her hands on her high chair.

I turned my attention toward my worksheet. Wanda said

filling out the New Hire questionnaire would help me learn what made Dreamstar Direct so special.

Some of the questions were a little odd.

"What's your favorite fantasy?"

If I were being completely honest, I would have written down "Free nanny and a bedroom with a built-in hot tub," but instead I said "Being part of a fantastic team and making the world a better place." It was a little Miss Universe, but I supposed they'd heard worse.

"What's your secret passion?"

Secret passion? I supposed the truthful answer would be "Making s'mores on the stove at midnight while my husband and daughter sleep." I wrote "Success."

An email notification popped up on my screen. It was Wanda.

To: Ashley Keller
Ready? We've routed your phone with your own 900 number. First call is in 20 minutes. I'll be listening in. Remember to write down customer requests so we can log the changes in the market. Don't forget to use a fake name.

Log customer requests. Check. Fake name! I'd completely forgotten. Wanda said that in customer service, pseudonyms are often used. Probably so that if a client starts yelling, they can't actually insult you accurately.

I didn't remember her telling me that she'd be listening in. I turned to Aubrey who wasn't even halfway through her lunch. If I cut her off now, she'd turn into an angry baboon baby and I'd be fired on the spot.

I knew what I had to do. I picked up my cell phone and punched in the number.

"Joy? I need you. Right now."

Seven minutes later, Joy rang my doorbell. I met her at the door with Aubrey.

"Take her, now. My call is in five minutes!"

Joy juggled Aubrey and Ella, who was dressed in a pale pink crocheted ensemble with white tights and a matching white beret. On her feet were delicate cream-colored plush booties. I kissed my niece on the head.

Joy sputtered, "Ashley! Okay, okay! Since when do you even have a job? I can't do this every day, you know. I'm busy." Joy headed toward the kitchen to finish feeding Aubrey.

"Busy doing what? Dressing Ella in perfect outfits?" I would have said if I hadn't needed my sister so much.

"Thank you, thank you, thank you!" I said instead, leaping upstairs with my phone and notebook in hand.

When I was finally sitting down, cross-legged on my bed-spread, my home phone, notebook and pencil in front of me, I took a deep breath. I'd done it. Joy was probably in my kitchen judging the number of dirty dishes in the sink, but I'd done it.

I waited.

And waited.

And waited.

I could hear the dishwasher whirl downstairs. Typical Joy.

The phone rang. I answered it immediately.

"Dreamstar Direct, how can I help you?"

A hoarse male voice answered. "You're supposed to tell me your name."

I flushed. He was right. And Wanda was on the line.

"Thank you for calling Dreamstar Direct. My name is Tiffany."

"Hi, Tiffany. I'm Greg. What are you wearing?"

My mind went blank. What am I wearing? Is Dreamstar Direct some kind of fashion hotline?

I looked down at my red and gray checked pajama pants and oversized black T-shirt.

"Sir, I'm wearing a designer black dress and Gucci slingbacks."

"Take it all off," said Greg, his voice thickening.

"EXCUSE ME?" I yelled into the receiver. I heard a click and Wanda's gravelly voice interrupted.

"Greg, we're going to redirect this call to Cinnamon, your regular girl."

Another click.

Wanda came back on the line.

"Ashley. You're fired."

The line went dead. I sat with the phone to my ear in disbelief. What just happened?

Standing up, I made my way downstairs and into the kitchen in a fog.

Joy was standing at the counter chopping pears and dropping the pieces into a mini blender with FirstFoods written across the side. Neat little jars filled with pale green puree sat on the counter beside her. She was wearing a sleeping Aubrey in the baby wrap. She must have found it balled up in my laundry basket in the living room.

Ella sat in Aubrey's bouncy seat, jumping up and down. In her formal day outfit, she looked like some kind of little duchess.

Joy takes care of two kids better than I can take care of one.

"Already done, Ashley? This wrap is divine. Do you ever use it?" Joy gushed without looking up.

I sat down at the kitchen table behind her and put my face in my hands as hot tears slid down my cheeks. Within moments, they turned into sobs.

Joy rushed over and put her hand on my shoulder. "Ash, what happened? What's going on?"

I sniffled and raised my head. "I got fired."

"Fired? On your first day? Did you sign a contract? They can't just fire you without notice!" She pulled out her cell phone. "I'm calling Grover. He plays racquetball with an employment lawyer. What's the name of the company?"

I wiped my face with my arm. "Dreamstar Direct... Joy, don't, it's f—"

Joy's face went red and she plopped down in the seat next to me. "Did you say Dreamstar Direct?"

My face flushed with embarrassment.

"Ashley. Why were you working for a phone-sex hotline?" she said and I felt like a fifteen-year-old being scolded by her mother after being caught smoking.

I blew my nose into a paper towel. Ella laughed at the sound. I'm glad someone was finding this funny.

"Because I didn't know it was a phone-sex hotline! I thought it was a customer service agency!"

Joy looked at me incredulously. "How could you not know? Their ads run nonstop all night! When I'm up nursing Ella, it's the only commercial on!"

I blew my nose again. "Yeah, if only I were breastfeeding, I wouldn't have accidentally become a phone-sex operator," I said sarcastically. I knew I sounded immature, but did she have to mention breastfeeding in every conversation?

Joy sat up straight. "That's not what I said."

I stood up. "I know. Sorry. Well, I'll take it from here, I guess. Thanks for coming over."

Normally I wouldn't have rushed Joy out so quickly, especially not before bumming a jar or two of organic baby food off her, but I needed to wallow alone.

Before heading out the door with Ella, she touched my arm. "Don't let it get you down, Ashley."

I smiled and kissed my niece again before closing the door.

8 P.M.

I personally have never needed a nanny, but when you
need help, don't be ashamed to get it.
                              —Emily Walker, *Motherhood Better*

I had a realization this evening as I was standing in the
kitchen trying to do dishes while holding a screaming Aubrey because David was working late for the 300th week in
a row: Mary Poppins isn't a child's fantasy, she's a mother's.
Isn't it your dream to have some maternal figure float in out
of nowhere, no background check needed, and take your kids
away for an indefinite amount of time? All of this and your
children come back better people with no money exchanged.

I've decided to hire a part-time babysitter so that I can...
wait for it...start freelancing again! I miss the marketing world
so much. The whole phone sex debacle was a wake-up call
(no pun intended). I need to do something in the field I love.
I know I can do this. Maybe David and I will end up doing
business together! Just the thought of us brainstorming client
product launches over hazelnut-flavored coffees got me excited. Finally, I'd be in my element again!

We don't really have extra money, but if I cut back on
spending we should be able to swing five hours a week. Now
I just have to find someone with the right qualifications.

I know I want someone younger than me. Not too much
younger. I want them to have common sense, experience and
a good head on their shoulders.

No one under twenty-six. I know someone in their early
twenties can be responsible, but I want the person to have seen
enough terrible things in life that they know to be alert with
a baby around. In your early twenties you still think life is all
good and that nothing terrible can happen. By twenty-six a
person starts to get a sense that bad things don't just happen

to other people, they happen to babysitters who leave babies in high chairs unattended. By one's mid-twenties, some of the glitter has worn off of life, leaving behind a matte finish.

Also, I don't want some hot young thing running around my house. Not while my stomach looks like some kind of front butt hanging out of my tank top. My fragile ego can't handle it.

Yes, there are lots of hot women in their late twenties, but they're less willing to lose their jobs for making a pass at their bosses' husbands, I think.

And the butt-stomach thing.

In summary, I need someone who is capable and not too hot.

David's working through the weekend so it's just me and Aubrey. I'm never going to get any work done if I can't find someone to watch her.

Saturday, February 9, 9 A.M.

Don't feel bad about needing domestic help. Not every woman can do it all, and until you can, the services of others bridge the gap.

—Emily Walker, *Motherhood Better*

What's so hard about finding a babysitter? When I was a kid the babysitter was the girl on the street old enough to stay home by herself but too young to date. And since when do babysitters make $12-plus per hour? When I was seventeen I made $2 and all the snacks I could eat.

So far I've email interviewed:

- a Russian au pair who was very interested in why Aubrey wasn't sleeping through the night and suggested I incorporate more ground beef into her diet
- a twenty-two-year-old very lovely young woman with a degree in early childhood education who suggested

that I not let Aubrey have any screen time until she's twelve and even then only twenty minutes a day and preferably Claymation

- a seventy(?)-year-old grandmother who asked if I offered a retirement package

After this, I'm considering hiring a dog to watch Aubrey, like in Peter Pan. I'm sure Nana wouldn't charge more than $10 an hour and the occasional Milk Bone. Maybe she'd work for stomach rubs.

Wish me luck.

10 P.M.

I found her. She floated in from a nanny website. Joy couldn't have been happier when I told her I was getting a babysitter. She was proud of me for getting "the help I needed." I made sure to tell her it's only part-time.

"Oh, it starts like that," was her response.

What does that mean? A month from now I'll be parenting Aubrey via Skype? I don't think so. And I can only afford three weeks' worth of babysitting without having any money coming in.

Chelsea, my twenty-eight-year-old angel sitter nanny starts tomorrow at 9 a.m. I interviewed her, will check her references tonight, and Aubrey seemed to take nicely to her. I can't wait!

Sunday, February 10, 9:20 A.M.

People ask me all the time how I run a successful company with five children. The answer is: naps! My littles are all on a regular sleep schedule, and while they doze, I take conference calls, fulfill orders for the Motherhood Better line of maternity wear and sign contracts. Where there's a will, there's a way.

—Emily Walker, *Motherhood Better*

I was sitting in the bushes at the park.

Okay, let me explain.

Chelsea arrived at 9 a.m. on the dot, and Aubrey was a bit fussy so I suggested she take her on a walk. Six seconds after they left I realized that while I interviewed this woman and checked her references, she could be anyone. What if she's an international child smuggler? What if those references were just her accomplices?

Bottom line: I realized I don't really know her and had just sent my child off with a potential criminal. I don't know if it's all of the episodes of *Crime Files* and *Gone Without a Trace*, but I pictured Aubrey's car seat in a van somewhere, off to her new family—or worse.

I threw a black sweatshirt over my black sweats and put a black beanie on my head so that I could follow them without being noticed. In hindsight, dressing up like a bank robber in broad daylight may not have been the smartest move but nobody could see me. This bush was thick. And there were three different toddler shoes behind it. So this is where they lose them.

Okay, back to Chelsea, aka Potential Baby Thief.

She was sitting on the bench near the swings with Aubrey in the stroller next to her. No sign of a van anywhere. She was looking around suspiciously—wait, that might just have been boredom. Wasn't she going to play with Aubrey or something? I know a baby can't do much, but she could at least sing to her. I mean, she was on the clock.

OMG.

No. Freaking. Way.

She was pulling out her phone. SHE WAS CHECKING HER PHONE. Instead of engaging my infant in age-appropriate play she was on her phone and…taking a park selfie? Was she serious? What was the caption? "Just neglecting my charge on this beautiful day at the park! Isn't being a half-assed babysitter awesome! Look at my youthful skin and hair that isn't falling out by the handful!"

Her phone rang. She answered it. This was insane. Aubrey was sitting in her stroller rotting away and Chelsea was laughing on the phone? What if someone grabbed Aubrey while she was distracted? Sure, she had one hand on the stroller, but this wasn't what she was getting paid to do. I was paying her to participate in the development of my daughter, not throw her social life in my face.

I was just about to jump out from behind this bush…

8 P.M.

The craziest thing happened today.

No, not the part where I was tailing my nanny and child through the park.

No, not the part where I was staking them out.

I'm talking about the part where I almost got arrested by a police officer for behaving suspiciously around small children.

Yeah, THAT PART.

Just as I was about to bust Chelsea for neglecting my child, a six-foot-tall officer yelled, "HEY, YOU! WHAT ARE YOU DOING OVER THERE IN THAT BUSH?" causing the whole park, Chelsea included, to turn their heads while I tried unsuccessfully to shush him. Hasn't he ever been on a stake-out? First rule: inside voices.

Apparently police officers don't like to be shushed because he pulled me up by my arm. I know. Crazy. Aubrey immediately recognized me and started crying. I was horrified, but a little touched that she recognized Mommy in her all-black cat-burglar ensemble.

Chelsea rushed over. She looked a bit confused, then angry when I explained to the officer that I was supervising my babysitter from afar. I thought it was completely inappropriate for the officer to agree with Chelsea that "spying" was a better word.

Chelsea quit and called me a crazy b-word in front of Aubrey, which pretty much proves she's not cut out for this job. The police officer laughed at me.

I now have no babysitter and no dignity.

I give up. I'd try another nanny, but I'm obviously not ready to let anyone else watch Aubrey yet. It doesn't make any sense. All I could think about for the past few months was getting a break from her, but the second I did, the moment freedom peeked over the horizon, I sabotaged it. Is this what motherhood is going to be like? Spending all day dreaming about getting a break and then, when it comes, wanting nothing more than to be with Aubrey?

I felt dread wash over me. I'd never be content again, would I? I love Aubrey more than I've ever loved anything or anyone, but when I'm with her, I feel smothered. And when I'm not with her, I feel incomplete, like a piece of me is missing.

How do other moms do it? Maybe it'll be easier once she gets older.

Maybe I need to stop resisting motherhood and just dive in headfirst and learn to "live in the beauty of the moment" like Emily says. I'm going to turn around and Aubrey will be eighteen, moving out, and I'll have spent her entire childhood wishing I was somewhere else.

The thought of Aubrey living somewhere else made my chest seize up. So this is motherhood. You pour your entire life into someone and then they just leave? It's insane. I'm insane. I keep watching those crime dramas and eating my weight in peanut butter. Since becoming a mom, I simultaneously have no stomach for these shows, but feel as if I need to watch every episode to know exactly how terrible the world is that I brought my child into.

Confession: Last night Aubrey barely slept and I cursed motherhood at 1 a.m. I cursed motherhood as in, "I hate this so much."

Now, watching these detectives break the news of a son's death to his elderly father, I felt so guilty. I love you, Aubrey. I'll try to protect you in every way that I can. I want you to have a happy, full life. I get tired sometimes, but I love you.

What kind of mother curses motherhood?

I'm awful.

PS. I think the elderly father is the perp.

Monday, February 11, 11 A.M.

Your lover should be your #1 priority. Every Friday night, my husband and I go out on a date to keep our fires burning brightly. We also go on a no-kids vacation three times a year and, after five kids, we're closer than ever!

—Emily Walker, *Motherhood Better*

Today's call was even better than the last one. When Emily popped up on the screen everyone gasped—she was wearing a sparkly gold-sequined gown and her hair was swept into a fancy updo. Her makeup was done with dramatic smoky eyes and deep red matte rouge on her lips. She looked straight off a Hollywood red carpet.

"Hi, everyone! I'm coming to you live from my photo shoot with *SHE* magazine! They've chosen me as one of the twenty women in their Sexy Entrepreneur Women edition!" she said, her sparkly white teeth gleaming through the monitor.

Looking down at the faded pink Gap sweatshirt that I was wearing, I felt a dull twinge of embarrassment. I'd fed Aubrey raspberry yogurt that morning and half of it was smashed into my chest. I did my best to wipe it off before the call, but it just looked like a giant bird had made me its poop target. I leaned in to conceal my dishrag of an outfit. That, coupled with my hair being days from its last washing, made me look especially homely next to dazzling Emily. I tried to focus on her words and not the fact that I looked like I'd been put away wet.

"If you follow me on Instagram, you already know that my incredible husband, Thomas, is with me on the set, taking care of the children while I work. He and I are not only a team, but we're best friends and—" she leaned into her webcam and lowered her voice "—passionate lovers."

I felt my face get hot. Passionate lovers? With five kids? David and I have one baby and our sex life is in the crapper.

"It's so important to keep the fire in your marriage burning with hot, sizzling embers of desire. Having children is no excuse for letting the spark that brought you together smoke and fizzle out."

Yeah, I'm pretty sure that, in my marriage, the "fire" is actually a pile of damp, charred sticks.

Emily went on. "I want all of you to read through Chapter Four, entitled 'Keeping Your Marriage Red Hot,' and then put into action some of my tips. Does anyone have any specific goals for their marriage?"

A shy-looking mom with short blond hair raised her hand.

"Yes, Lillian?" asked Emily.

Lillian look petrified to be the center of attention, "Hello everyone. I'm mom to three-year-old twin girls. I've been married to my husband for ten years. I'm just trying to figure out how to jump-start our sex life. He works so much and I'm exhausted after a full day staying home with the girls. They run me ragged."

Emily nodded sympathetically. "I totally get it. What's your main objective?"

"Ideally, we'd have more...you know...relations. Right now our encounters are dwindling. On a good week we only have sex three or four times."

"WHAT?" I screamed aloud unintentionally. Three or four times a week? David would be in heaven!

Emily held up a hand. "Now remember, this is a safe space for Lillian. Lillian, I totally understand. My husband and I used to have sex multiple times a day and we're down to just once per day. Read the chapter and let me know if it helps."

I couldn't believe what I was hearing. Compared to Emily and Lillian, I was living on a passion iceberg.

Something caught Emily's attention off camera and she made a thumbs-up sign before continuing. "Okay, they're ready for me so I have to go, but this week is the Marriage Challenge. Find that spark you and your partner in childrearing used to have and let it burn!"

All of those "burning" and "fire" metaphors were simultaneously making me think of yeast infections and BBQ. I was grossed out, hungry and completely overwhelmed at the task of turning my laundry-strewn bedroom into a lover's den. Sure, I wanted my marriage to have fireworks, but after spending an entire day wiping down counters and shuffling around braless, it was easier said than done. Not to mention, I was always tired. Where was I supposed to find the energy to stoke the embers of this "love furnace"?

I stood up and studied myself in the full-length mirror behind my bedroom door, trying desperately to find any signs of a vixen lurking beneath, but all I saw were dark circles, a dingy outfit and a mom who would give her left butt cheek for an afternoon nap.

"I'm more of a spaghetti squash than a seductress," I said

to no one. Aubrey laughed and jumped up and down excitedly in her zoo animal-themed exersaucer, causing it to sing
a catchy but annoying song about bears.

I picked her up and grabbed my keys off the counter.

I needed coffee.

11 P.M.

It is always so hard to fall asleep after Aubrey screams me
awake. Somehow she always knows when I've just entered the
most delicious REM sleep. Thanks, honey.

I didn't want to wake David with my tossing and turning,
so I sat on the couch in the living room with my laptop and
a cup of tea. While I'd rather be sleeping, it was nice to sit
down for a minute knowing the phone wouldn't ring, a meal
didn't have to be made and Aubrey (hopefully) wouldn't need
me for a few hours. I looked around the darkened room and
sank deeper into the buttery leather.

Yes, I thought. This is the life. Motherhood may be the
hardest thing I've ever done, but it sure makes a few moments
of silence feel like the most luxurious of vacations.

Then the thought hit me: the Marriage Challenge. Maybe
I should check into the portal and see how the other moms
are doing.

I opened my computer and after my eyes adjusted to the
glare, clicked my way into the website.

What on earth...?

We hadn't had this challenge for twenty-four hours and
some of the moms had already posted updates.

Tonight after our son went to bed I surprised my husband
with chocolate-dipped strawberries that I'd made that afternoon during naptime. He was absolutely delighted and, after

the evening we just had, so am I.—Samantha Davidson, mom of 2-year-old Henry

Girls! My hubby and I are about to hit the town and have a date night! I picked up a strappy red number and he made reservations at my favorite Italian restaurant. We're definitely making this a weekly thing. Can't wait!—Kimmie Reardon, mom of four

Strappy red number? The closest thing to a strappy red number I'd worn since Aubrey was born was when I wore a pair of black tennis shoes with red laces.

I thought these women were supposed to be underachievers, like me.

"These moms are frauds!" I whispered angrily, shutting my laptop with more force than necessary.

I needed to think of something and fast. Tapping out on the second challenge was not an option, especially when this program meant everything to my whole family.

I opened my computer again and began to type.

Hi ladies! I'm thrilled to see all of you doing so well. #Sexy-Mamas. I had a busy day of yogurt-making, but I can't wait to start this challenge tomorrow! Get ready, hubby!—Ashley Keller, mom of one

So maybe I stretched the truth a little on the whole "yogurt-making" part, but it's not all false. The yogurt cultures on my sweatshirt must have multiplied throughout the day due to my body heat, so technically I did make yogurt.

I looked at the clock—11:25. Time for bed. Tomorrow was a new day and I was determined to make it a sexy one.

Tuesday, February 12, 8 A.M.

My husband and I met at a fundraiser supporting the preservation of antique teacups. It was early in my modeling career and I'd been escorted to the event by a rising designer watch model, but as soon as our eyes met, I knew I wanted him to be the father of my children. His face was so symmetrical. I wanted that for my babies.

—Emily Walker, *Motherhood Better*

I love my husband, but sometimes I want to scream in his face. These days all it takes is one of his insensitive remarks, and I start picturing my life as a single mother, the two of us passing Aubrey between us at mutually agreed upon locations like a highway truck stop. Naturally, I'd be thin by then, due to all of the stress.

Let me tell you what happened.

Aubrey has been waking up at 2 a.m. on the dot for the past few days. Teething, growth spurt, I don't know. But last night I woke up my doting husband and asked him to go get her. Just this once. For the first time EVER in the eight months since OUR baby was born. Did I mention how this is OUR baby? The one we made together? Do you know what the man who promised to be there "for better or for worse" said to me?

"I have to work in the morning."

I have to work in the morning.

I know there is no salary for stay-at-home moms, but is this not a job of some kind? Isn't what I do work? I know I'm not getting paid, but it's not like I can just pop a squat and have a nap whenever I want.

"I have to be up in the morning, too," was my seething response in the dark.

"Yeah, Ashley, but you can sleep when the baby sleeps," he said through a yawn.

Sleep when the baby sleeps? And am I supposed to wash dishes when the baby washes dishes, fold laundry when the baby folds laundry, and sweep the floor when the baby sweeps the floor?

If it weren't for the marriage passion fire challenge, or whatever it's called, I would have flipped on the lights and told him exactly what I thought of his "sleep when the baby sleeps" idea.

All I asked was that he get up with her, just this once, and he threw his important job in my face.

I feel like I've gotten a glimpse into his subconscious. I'm the nonworking stay-at-home mom who should get up nights because he's an oh-so-important contributing member of society because obviously I don't need a good night's rest every now and then. Motherhood can be run on fumes alone. Good to know.

So far the only thing burning in our love furnace is any chance that he'll be getting any of this spaghetti squash before Aubrey's eighteenth birthday.

8:45 P.M.

My husband is my best friend. He understands exactly what I'm going through as a mom. Sometimes it's like we're twins!

—Emily Walker, *Motherhood Better*

I was prepared to be in a huff when David got back from work. The plan was to barely speak and close the fridge too hard until he asked me what was wrong five billion times. Five billion times I'd say "nothing" until he let his guard down. Only then would I unleash a heartfelt torrent of emotional diarrhea. That's how we do things. But I never had the chance.

He missed dinner entirely without even calling. This has never happened. Ever. Not in our entire marriage.

I texted my standard What time today? at 4 p.m. when I was at my brink. Aubrey had been screaming every time her favorite episode of *VeggieFriends* ended, meaning I'd been watching it on a loop for forty-five minutes.

His reply? Late.

One word.

I typed, Okay, what time?

He replied, Not sure busy.

He knows Estimated Times of Arrival are the only things that get me through afternoons. Could it be possible that he's angry about last night? That would be rich. But coming home late isn't his anger style at all. Usually he just gets quiet until I gently coax him with rapid-fire questioning.

When he hadn't come home by 7:30, I called him. Aubrey was fresh out of the bath and squirming in my arms as I balanced the phone between my shoulder and ear.

"Where are you?"

His voice was curt, "Work. Where else would I be?"

Excuse me? I let it slide because Aubrey was thirty seconds

away from wiggling out of my arms and onto the floor. What is it about being naked that makes babies so athletic?

"What's going on?"

I heard a muffled side conversation. He wasn't listening.

"David? I said what's going on?"

He finished talking to whoever needed his attention more than I did. "Pepperoni and olives," he said.

"Are you ordering pizza?" My voice was shriller than I meant it to be. Aubrey glanced up at me, probably wondering if I was yelling at her.

"Ashley, I really need to go. We're swamped. I worked through lunch and, yes, we're finally getting some dinner."

"Who's we?"

"Barry, the partners and myself," he said slowly, as if speaking to a three-year-old.

I felt stupid for having asked. What, did I think he was having a romantic candlelight pizza with a woman in his office? Some hot twenty-one-year-old intern who has nothing else to do but burn the midnight oil with my husband? An intern who showers daily and whose healthy, fragrant hair isn't in a greasy half bun? An intern who isn't on day three of the same pajama pants? Of course I didn't.

"Oh, sure. I know. When are you getting home? I made lasagna but since you're eating…" I hadn't meant that to come off like a guilt trip but as soon as the words came out of my mouth I knew they sounded like one.

Silence.

"Probably around nine. We're swamped with the Denta-Fresh proposal."

Duh. His firm has been trying to land the toothpaste conglomerate since they launched a year ago. This deal, if they get it, would be huge for them.

"Of course! I totally understand! Work as late as you need

to. I'll be here. Aubrey just got out of the bath. Do you want to say hi?"

He sighed into the phone. "Ashley, I'd love to but I really have to—"

"Go—no problem, honey. Good luck. See you later."

"Good night." Click.

Good night? I guess they'd be later than I thought. An hour ago I thought he'd be apologizing to me, and now I felt horrible for wanting him to get up with Aubrey the night before such a big day at work. How was I supposed to know? He doesn't tell me anything. I tell him everything. Twice. Three times if I'm feeling particularly chatty.

I placed the phone in my pocket and stared at Aubrey. Her still-damp hair framed her cheery face, making her look like a drenched cherub. She giggled, her eyes squinting and cheeks forming small apples. Something in her mouth caught my eye. Using my finger to examine her gums I could see two bumpy white nubs smack dab in the middle of her bottom molars.

First teeth! I squealed, which made her smile even bigger and then laugh. I couldn't stop staring at them as if they were ruby-encrusted gold nuggets rather than a couple of barely-there baby chompers.

Just as quickly as it came, the wave of excitement turned bittersweet. It was all happening so fast. My baby was growing up. First teeth, then braces, then I'll turn around and she'll be filling out college applications. I can almost see her driving away in a car packed to the brim with boxes, off to start her life…away from me. Only to come home on the odd weekend. Tears sprang into my eyes and I hugged her tightly. The moment was interrupted when a strange warmth flooded my midsection.

"Aubrey, did you—" Pee. I pinched the soaked edge of my T-shirt with my free hand and looked down at Aubrey. She glanced back at me innocently, as if to say, "Are you sure that was me?"

It's only pee, I said to myself as I made my way to her bedroom to get her ready for bed. I read somewhere that it's sterile, anyway.

As I walked down the hallway, I couldn't help but wish David were with me. He'd love to know that she'd gotten her first tooth. I could imagine him laughing as I told him that she'd marked her territory on me yet again. But I didn't want to disturb him—again.

"Sorry, business partners, I need to take this call. My eight-month-old just grew two teeth and pissed on my wife." Yeah, that screams professionalism.

Wednesday, February 13, 11 A.M.

David didn't make it back home until after 1 a.m. Right after he pecked me on the cheek and collapsed into bed, Aubrey started fussing.

My hopes that the arrival of new teeth finally popping through would settle her sleep nonschedule were in vain. It took me half an hour to get her back down. I've spent the morning researching the "cry it out" method.

Here's what I've learned so far.

Half of the internet thinks crying it out is hard to carry out but a perfectly healthy way to get babies on track to becoming fantastic sleepers for their entire lives, which in turn will lead to happy, successful adults who excel both at work and in their personal lives.

The other half of the internet believes that if you let your baby cry it out you will permanently damage their spirit and their brain, and they'll end up selling their bodies down by the train tracks for illicit drugs and dying of an overdose before they hit thirty.

What. Am. I. Supposed. To. Do?

I was desperate for sleep at this point. This morning I wore two different shoes to the café. I didn't even realize it until a five-year-old loudly asked her mommy if it was "crazy feet day" while pointing at them. I replied, "Why, yes it is, darling," in the sweetest voice I could muster, in case you're wondering where I'm operating, maturity-wise.

I bought a book called *Love Sleep Repeat*, which sounds like the insomniac's guide to the *Kama Sutra*, but it is really the go-to manual for learning how to do the whole crying-it-out thing. The book was written by a medical professional, Dr. Faber, who, according to the internet again, is both the best and most evil man to ever walk the planet.

Aubrey was hell-bent on eating the prologue, so I only managed to read the first few pages, but I get the idea. Instead of rocking your night screamer to sleep, you simply give them what are called "verbal assurances" until their dependence on you to soothe their night wakefulness vanishes. I hope Dr. Faber is right, because these double vanilla lattes are getting expensive.

Speaking of beds, I have four more days to get Operation Love Furnace up and roaring hot, but between Aubrey keeping me a zombie mom and David working around the clock, what's a mother to do?

Then I remembered. Emily said that if we need extra help to just ask. I mean, what could an international TV host, businesswoman, mother of five and jet-setting author have going on that would prevent her having the time to help me with my love shack problems?

It's better than flunking out.

Private Message
Hi Emily! I know you're busy with the book and your kids and

your life (that, by the way, is the stuff dreams are made of, you inspire me every single day, thank you so much for having me in this incredible program, I'm learning tons), but I was wondering if you could give me some advice. I'm having a bit of a time lighting my passion fire. Any easy tricks to share? Thank you so much! Xo Ashley

A month ago if you'd told me I'd be asking Emily Walker, my momspiration, for relationship advice, I'd have said you were crazy. And yet here we are.

I pressed Send. Looking over at Aubrey, I saw that she was doing her telltale squished-up, breath-holding poop face. How a baby on a mostly liquid diet can create such horrifyingly large emissions, I'll never understand.

Five minutes later I was done changing her and heard a little *ping* from my laptop, which was still open on the couch. One new message.

Private Message
Dearest Ashley,
I feel so honored that you trusted me with such an intimate inquiry. Progress in the Motherhood Better Bootcamp depends on the openness and earnestness you've shown. When Thomas and I were new parents to our sweet twins, we had a little ritual. Every night after they drifted off to sleep, we would take a bath together. Essential oils and sustainable beeswax candles transformed our bathroom into a Sharing Lair. We'd pour our hearts out to each other, cradled in the warm waters of life, a womb keeping our love aglow.
Never hesitate to reach out to me.
Love, Emily

I'm doomed.

9 P.M.

David is working late again. He let me know via a very personal text message: Late night. No dinner.

He sent the text at 5 p.m., which meant I'd already started cooking. I wish he'd let me know earlier. Does he think I'm cooking for myself? I'd be perfectly happy eating a couple of frozen waffles slathered with chocolate-peanut butter spread. They pair beautifully with cheap red wine. I'm certainly not cooking for an eight-month-old who takes ten minutes to polish off a single cracker.

I dutifully finished up the spaghetti and meatballs I'd been working on for the last hour and dined alone with Aubrey. I know technically that if Aubrey is there I'm not alone, but infants aren't known for their dinner conversation.

I may not have been alone, but I was lonely. Very lonely. He had to have been planning a little something for Valentine's Day, I hoped. Though, at this point, I'd be thrilled to receive a box of drugstore chocolates.

Maybe if I'd tended to our love furnace earlier, the nights David works late wouldn't be so hard. The furnace would be hot enough to keep me warm or something. The metaphors were starting to irritate me.

All I kept hearing from everyone—Joy, my mom and strangers at the grocery store—is how lucky I was to be a stay-at-home mom, but I wondered, if people knew how much time I spent by myself, whether they'd still say that.

I missed David. I looked forward to him getting home, not just to throw Aubrey at him the second he walked through the door, but to have him here with me. I really, really missed him.

An unexpected tear slid down my cheek just as Aubrey glanced up at me from her pile of shredded noodles. She cocked her head to the side like a puppy trying to understand, and then returned to pounding the pasta into her high chair tray with her bare hands. At least someone was having a blast.

Thursday, February 14,
2 P.M.

Date nights are a must for all couples with children. You don't have to make them elaborate: dinner, a movie followed by drinks, can make for a very special night out. I like to buy a new outfit to really get myself excited. If you don't have time to shop, many boutiques will send over a concierge with samples.

—Emily Walker, *Motherhood Better*

Happy Valentine's Day! I couldn't be happier than I was at this moment. David had just called me from work. Not only was he coming home early, but Gloria was babysitting tonight because he was taking me out to dinner!

"I've been working late and I know you're exhausted with Aubrey. Things haven't been easy. I appreciate everything you do." Those words came out of my husband's mouth.

I felt like the high school quarterback had just asked me to go to prom.

He'd be home at 6, which left me four hours to tidy up

(hide everything I didn't want Gloria to see), shower, do my hair and makeup, and pick out something that fit.

The timing couldn't be better, I was all out of ideas for this week's challenge and had two days to write my journal entry.

Can I just say that I have the sweetest, most intuitive husband ever?

5:55 P.M.

The house was clean (enough), and Gloria should be here any second. But none of my prebaby dresses would zip up completely, so I'd ended up running out just before dinner with Aubrey and finding a simple yet elegant three-quarter-sleeve black wrap dress. It was on sale for $49, marked down from $220. Score. The saleslady was quick to tell me that the gathered fabric over the midsection was "very forgiving" and "great for postpartum mommies."

Ugh. Thanks, size zero college student. I'm sure she was just parroting sales copy, but maybe a little less emphasis on my stomach? I'm surprised she didn't ask me how far along I was. Postpartum? I don't think I qualify for that exemption anymore, although I have heard it takes a full year for internal organs to reposition themselves correctly and for bloating to subside 100 percent. See? My thirty-two-week post-pregnancy pooch isn't my fault. My stomach doesn't know where to be. And my fluids haven't gone down. But you wouldn't know about that would you, body-shaming saleswoman?

Or so I thought.

Before I walked out of the store, the associate ran over to me with another coworker in hand.

"Doesn't she look just like Melissa?" she said, gesturing at Aubrey.

I smiled. "Is Melissa your sister?"

She grinned. "No, she's my daughter! She's six months old."

I coughed to prevent myself from cursing at the stranger. *How dare you look so good and have a baby younger than mine?* is what I wanted to say.

"Oh, how nice! You look fantastic…and rested."

"Thanks," my new lifelong enemy said, running her hands down her sides. "I still have a few more pounds to go. And Melissa's been sleeping through the night since she was two weeks old, bless her."

With that, I walked away for her own safety.

I wasn't letting anything get me down, though. Tonight was my night!

6:30 P.M.

David still wasn't home and hadn't returned any of my five texts or two voice mails.

"Leave him be, darling. He's hard at work. He'll get here when he gets here," Gloria said from the living room couch, bouncing Aubrey on her lap.

I tried the office line. No answer.

I couldn't stop pacing. What if he'd gotten into a car accident? What if something happened? My calls were going straight to voice mail. What if he was robbed going to the ATM machine and the thief forced him to chuck his phone into an ocean or something? Aubrey's never going to see her daddy again. I could feel the tears start to rise again.

7 P.M.

Did you know that 911 doesn't consider anyone a missing person until they've been gone for twenty-four hours? Insanity.

10 P.M.

David walked through the door at 9:30, fifteen minutes after I had insisted Gloria go home.

"He just got caught up with work. I'm sure of it. A mother can sense these things," she said, lingering at the front door.

"Normally he'd call. I'm worried."

"In my day, you know, during the war, we wouldn't hear back from our men for months at a time," she said, waving a finger at me.

I didn't say "These aren't war times," because all I really wanted was for her to leave so that I could try David's phone again.

"Okay. I'll call you as soon as I hear anything."

Fifteen minutes later the door opened and I felt my heart jump into my throat.

I practically ran toward him.

"Where were you? What happened? Are you alright?"

"I'm fine. My phone died."

It was like someone punched me in the chest. "Your phone died? Your phone died?" I couldn't stop repeating it over and over.

He walked over to the kitchen and put his briefcase on a chair, then took off his coat.

"Yes," he said, rubbing his eyes with his palms. "Didn't you get my email?"

"Email? I haven't been on my computer all day. Why didn't you call me from the office?"

"I've been in back-to-back meetings all day. I left as soon as I could."

I stood in the kitchen, unable to process what he was saying.

"I'd love to talk, but I'm exhausted," he said, kissing me on the cheek before walking past me.

I followed him into the bedroom and watched him undress and lie down. His eyes were just about to close when I blew a fuse.

"David." My voice was so calm it scared me. It was scary calm. The kind of tone only serial killers use. "David, do you see what I'm wearing?"

His eyes fluttered. "Yeah. A dress. You look good."

I was dumbfounded.

"Do you know why I'm wearing a dress?" I felt like a kindergarten teacher quizzing her students on their ABCs.

He raised his hands, exasperated. "Ashley, I'm tired, okay? I don't have energy for whatever it is you're getting at. Can you just spit it out?"

I felt a searing heat creep up my spine like a volcano about to explode lava, destroying everything in its path.

"Date night. Valentine's Day. Need I go on?"

His face went blank and then...recognition. He jumped out of bed and walked over to me cautiously. "That was tonight. Oh, my—I completely forgot. I completely—it's work. It's been so stressful, Ashley. I will make this up to you."

I took a step back. "Stress? Do you think you're the only one stressed out right now? I haven't had eight hours of continuous sleep for over a year. I'm overwhelmed every single day. Yet somehow I don't forget to show up for the first date we've had since Aubrey was born."

I tried my best not to raise my voice and my words came out like hissed accusations.

David cupped my face with his hands. "I'm so, so sorry. You have no idea how sorry I am. It's this DentaFresh proposal, at the last minute they let us know their marketing initiatives for the calendar year were changing and—"

"Is this how it's going to be?" I interrupted.

He froze, confused. "How what is going to be?"

"Am I, are we, going to come last after your job? Will I always be waiting at home for you to toss me whatever crumbs are left over from your important life in the outside world?"

David's face fell. "No. It won't be…it's not like… I'm not tossing anything—"

I narrowed my eyes at him. "I plan my entire day around you and Aubrey. I cleaned all afternoon today. I bought a dress."

His eyes flickered. "You bought a dress? For dinner? You have a closet full of dresses."

"Yeah, and none of them fit me," I retorted painfully, each word feeling like it burned on its way out.

David crossed his arms. "Then work out!" he erupted.

As soon as he said it, he looked shocked by his own words.

The air felt like it was sucked clean out of the room with one of those infomercial vacuum sealers, but instead of raw cuts of rib eye, two people were suspended in time.

He started to speak. "I didn't mean… I'm tired…you look…"

I held up a hand. "Just stop."

I turned around and walked toward the door. Before leaving, I turned back and said, "Happy Valentine's Day." His shoulders dropped. I headed for Aubrey's room. Once the door was closed behind me, I switched off the baby monitor on the dresser and peeked at her. She lay still and I didn't move until I saw her take a deep breath.

I closed the door gently and made my way downstairs. I felt like a zombie curled up on the couch. The fight with David and his words sat in my chest, heavy and hollow. A few tears slid down my cheeks and I pulled my phone out of my pocket.

Motherhood Better Bootcamp Journal Entry

Hi everyone. This week has been really busy but I did my best with the challenge. My husband planned a date night and I won't get into the details, but I got to see a new side of him. ☺ Xo Ashley

Friday, February 15, 6:30 A.M.

I woke up at 6:30 on the couch with a blanket over me. David must have put it there. I just didn't feel like sharing a bed with him, not after how we'd ended things last night.

His words still stung.

I sat up. Something felt strange. Something was off. Then it hit me. Aubrey. She hadn't woken up all night. My heart started pounding. Was she okay? As I stood up and flew upstairs I prepared myself for the absolute worst. Pure terror pounded in my chest.

I pushed her door open and it hit the back of the wall with a bang as I lurched toward her crib. "AUBREY!" She was still there. I put my hand on her chest and felt it rise while I tried to control my still-shaky breathing.

She was fine. Just sleeping. I stared down at her face in disbelief. Did she sleep through the night?

"I got up with her," whispered David's voice behind me. I jumped, startled, and turned around to see him standing in the dark doorway. "She woke up at one and then again at 3:30. I don't know how you do it."

I turned once more to Aubrey. A peaceful half smile played on her serene face. She sniffled in her sleep. To think I almost woke her up. I crept toward the door and shut it, being careful to catch the latch with the doorknob before it clicked.

I turned to face David. He stood there, looking down at me with his *I feel so bad but I don't know what to say* face. I can't resist that face. He opened his arms.

Without speaking, I fell into his hug and he wrapped it around me. I closed my eyes and let the side of my face soak up the warmth of his cotton T-shirt against his hard chest.

"I'm sorry," he murmured into my hair. "I'm a jerk. I didn't mean that you need to exercise, I was just trying to think of something to say... I'm an idiot."

"I know," I breathed out.

He took my hand and led me to the top step, where we sat, side by side. "You're perfect. You've been doing everything around here while I've been trying to keep the business going."

The gravity of his tone startled me. "Keep it going?"

His brow furrowed, "Work has been hard lately, Ashley." His face was serious. I studied his face and saw...was that fear?

"Companies aren't hiring new marketing firms the way they used to and our start-up cushion is almost gone." His voice shook.

I took his hand. "David, it's going to be okay..."

He drew his hand back. "It's not. Not unless I can land this DentaFresh deal. If we don't get this business..." His voice trailed off, and from the way he looked around the house, I understood.

I felt helpless. Maybe I should have looked harder for a job. No wonder he blew up about the dress. "I'll spend less money. I can take the dress back."

He rubbed his forehead. I'd never seen him this stressed. "I'll figure something out. In the meantime…if I have to work late—"

"It's no problem. Work as much as you need to. I'm here." I rubbed his back. Everything was going to be okay. It had to be okay.

I took his hand and looked him dead in the eye, "David. I believe in you."

He stared at me for a moment before putting his hand gently on my cheek.

"I love you. And your body," he whispered into my ear.

He kissed me. I leaned into his kiss and felt my heart flutter the way it used to. I heard him sigh and we both giggled.

He rested his temple on mine and drew me close. "Why, Mrs. Keller… I don't think we've kissed like that for a while."

I lifted my arms over his shoulders and locked them around his neck. "I guess you should stand me up more often."

He laughed his deep quiet laugh and wrapped his arms around my waist. "May I interest you in a date right now? Party of two."

"Maybe," I said, teasing.

"Fair enough. But first, I have something for you." He reached into his pocket and pulled out a rectangular black jewelry box. My eyes grew to the size of dinner plates. I thought he'd forgotten.

"Happy Valentine's Day, Ash."

I blinked back a few tears as I opened the box. Inside was a gold locket attached to a gorgeous braided-gold necklace.

"David," I said, holding the necklace up. "It's beautiful."

I opened the locket. Inside, the date was engraved and three sparkling stones gleamed in the dim light of the hallway.

"Those are our birthstones. You, me and Aubrey. So that we're always together and right next to your heart."

That did it. A waterfall of feelings poured out of my face. I blubbered while he helped me put the necklace on.

He spun me toward him and kissed me again. I felt a tingle run up my spine.

"So," I began coyly, "how about we have that date right now, but skip straight to dessert."

Saturday, February 16, 11 A.M.

Marriage is a partnership. My husband has supported me on my journey to creating a worldwide brand from day one. He even helps me pick out Instagram filters.

—Emily Walker, *Motherhood Better*

Aubrey clapped her hands and jumped up and down in her exersaucer as I played peekaboo with her. Every time my eyes closed behind my hands I fought the urge to fall asleep right there on the floor. She woke up four times last night and the day was creeping by. I was on my third cup of coffee, but my mind was still a thick fog.

All I could think about, other than how utterly exhausted I felt, was David. How could I be so blind? And selfish? Here David was trying to get his company up and going, and I was angry because he wasn't home for dinner. I couldn't imagine the amount of pressure he was under every day to make this work. He was so brave—he could have stayed at Paulson International and eventually become CEO, but instead he chose to build something for himself…for all of us.

Aubrey squealed as I popped out from behind my hands and made a silly face. I pulled her out of the exersaucer and put her in her Pack 'n Play surrounded by toys. Maybe she'd entertain herself for a few minutes while I sprawled across the living room floor.

No dice. As soon as I put her down she started wailing, her arms outstretched. I picked her up and fought back tired tears. It wasn't even noon.

My thoughts returned to David as I sat on the couch, Aubrey squirming in my lap, trying to pull my hair out of its messy bun. I hoped he got the DentaFresh account.

I feel so useless at home, just frittering the day away with Aubrey when I could be helping him succeed. There has to be something I can do; after all, this business is the family business and it's not like I don't have experience in marketing.

"Think, Ashley, think," I said to myself. After a night of almost no sleep, my mind felt like a muddy pond, but I was determined.

And then, an idea.

When I was with Weber & Associates, one of the ways I used to encourage potential clients to sign with us was by hinting that a competitor was interested in our services.

Maybe that's what DentaFresh needed: a little healthy encouragement. I grabbed my laptop.

It took me all of two minutes to find their press contact and make up a bogus email account.

To: Cynthia Burton, cburton@dentafreshco.com
From: Rebecca Squash, mssquash123@mail.com
Subject: Upcoming Dental Seminar
Hello Cynthia,

My name is Rebecca Squash.

I'm a reporter with a small regional newspaper looking for a quote from DentaFresh regarding marketing trends in the oral hygiene industry. Do you have any news you'd like to share? We're reaching out to the All White toothpaste brand, as well. According to reports, they're collaborating with new firms such as Keller & Associates to come up with innovative campaigns next quarter. We would love to hear your thoughts on the matter.

Best,

Rebecca

I smiled at the screen. So, is this what spies feel like? I felt both satisfied and utterly pleased with myself. It was just like old times in the office, except this time I'd completed a task with a baby batting at my face. Back in the day, my superiors used to praise me for my resourcefulness when it came to making things happen. It's just like Emily always says, "Opportunity waits for no mom."

The day felt like it couldn't get any better. The only thing left to do was stop by the grocery store.

8 P.M.

Grocery stores should have signs in front of them for new moms that read like this:

Dear valued shopper, if you are entering this store with a young child, please know that you will lose your mind. If you should find yourself in an aisle having a complete nervous breakdown, find a customer service agent who will promptly hand you a square of our finest chocolate and small glass of pinot grigio. You will then be led to one of our several massage rooms while your child is

taken to our state-of-the-art nursery. We will happily
finish your shopping for you and deliver your groceries
to your home.

I made the mistake of taking Aubrey on a post-nap errand
today. Aren't naps supposed to relax babies? Aubrey woke up
the Chucky-doll version of herself.

I should have known things were going to be bad when
Aubrey screamed the whole fifteen-minute ride to the store.
By the time we arrived my nerves were already fried. After
parking the car I did my best to do what Emily Walker calls
"be present for your child's needs." She didn't want her pac-
ifier. She didn't want her blanket. Her diaper was dry. She
didn't want a teething cracker. I even waved my phone in
front of her face and she took it alright, then threw it out of
the open car window. The screen now has a tiny crack up
the side. Fantastic.

"Do you want to stretch your legs, honey?" I cooed to her
as she let out another feral holler. Yes, that's it. Once we're
inside, she'll calm down.

For my baby shower I received one of those huge shopping
cart covers that are supposed to prevent your child from getting cholera from other people's kids. I've been using it reli-
giously, but even that had to go horribly wrong.

Aubrey was still screaming like her hair was on fire for the
few seconds it took me to grab an abandoned shopping cart. As
I opened the trunk to pull out the cholera-prevention cover,
I must have been frazzled, because it slipped out of my hands
and onto the cement.

That wouldn't have been such a terrible thing, but of course
I had to have parked in the only spot that was directly over
a huge puddle of brown, murky water with a thin gasoline-
film rainbow over the top and what looked like a plastic bag

full of vomit. I picked up the cover as quickly as I could, but it was already half sopping wet with putrid muck. No way was I putting my kid in that thing. Who knew what was in that water? Flesh-eating bacteria? I couldn't leave it in my car. I stuffed it into a nearby garbage can.

By that time, Aubrey's wails had settled down to desperate little hiccups, so I quickly cleaned the cart handle with a baby wipe before placing her inside. By "placing" her, I mean practically forcing her squirming, defiant little body to sit down and then doing my best to strap her in.

My luck continued when I noticed that not only was one side of the strap hard, caked with some sort of film, the other one was broken.

It took three more tries before I found a cart with functioning straps. Who are all of these kids breaking shopping cart straps with their Hulk muscles and bare werewolf teeth? And what are you spilling on them? Glue?

Aubrey's hiccups started to gear back into an angry cry as I sprinted through the store, haphazardly throwing things into the cart. Between speeding down aisles and yelling "No" every time she tried to peel off her shoes, I had no idea what I was buying. I'd made a grocery list, but it was in the car and there was no way I was starting all over.

Twenty-five minutes and two family-sized bags of tortilla chips, produce I'll probably never eat, overpriced chicken breasts, two frozen lasagnas and who knew what else later, we were done.

Standing in the line, Aubrey began looking at me strangely. Her eyes went blank and her head fell back a little before... she barfed. Projectile vomited, all the way down my shirt. Everyone in my immediate vicinity gasped and leapt away.

Ten to fifteen seconds passed before I could fully absorb

what just happened. Aubrey just stared at me, looking some-what relieved.

"Ma'am? Can I…get you a paper towel?" said the checker who couldn't have been a day over seventeen. He can thank me later for the free birth control.

"Yes," I stammered, fully aware that I had an audience of close to twenty people who seemed unable to look away. "A few would be great."

I did my best to clean myself up. All Aubrey needed was a dab on the chin; she'd managed to keep herself completely barf free. After the paper towels were all in a plastic garbage bag, a friendly mom shopping with her two toddlers handed me a container of disinfectant wipes.

"Keep them," she said, smiling sympathetically at me.

When we finally got home, I peeled off my shirt and called the nurses' hotline.

"If she doesn't have a fever, you don't have anything to worry about," the nurse told me matter-of-factly. "These things just happen."

"How often, do 'these things just happen,' exactly?" I asked dryly, sipping a cold glass of white wine as Aubrey splashed her bathwater with her palms. "I'd like to be prepared next time."

She laughed, not realizing I was serious.

When David arrived home a few minutes after I put Aubrey down, I was sitting on the couch with another glass, dazed out in front of a reality show featuring moms as rich as they were childish.

"Hi, babe, how was your day?" He leaned down and kissed me on the cheek, then scrunched up his nose. "What's that smell?"

"Motherhood."

Sunday, February 17, 1 P.M.

Positive Affirmation of the Day: Mama-hood fills me with joy! I am a goddess who radiates hope, wisdom, and maternal beauty!

—Emily Walker, *Motherhood Better*

Almost a full month into the Motherhood Better Bootcamp I have lost no weight, my hair is still falling out like it's offended by my scalp, and Aubrey knows zero sign language while Ella is up to forty-five words and has her own YouTube channel. Joy says she has 300 subscribers and is being scouted by baby modeling agencies.

I am a complete loser.

Off to drown my sorrows in a bag of chips. Chips always understand.

Monday, February 18, 10 A.M.

I don't know what I'd do without my group of mommy friends. There are ten of us in our village and we aren't just best buddies, we're sisters. We spend so much time together that even our housekeepers are friends now.
—Emily Walker, *Motherhood Better*

The fourth Motherhood Better Bootcamp video conference is this morning. Aubrey woke up at 4 a.m., so by 8 a.m. she was in a deep sleep. I placed her in her crib and by some miracle she didn't wake up. If it were any other day I'd immediately lie down on the couch and pass out until her cries woke me up, but I rushed to put on a bit of foundation and lip gloss.

Over the past few calls, I'd noticed something: each time, the other moms looked more and more put together. For the first one, everyone was in raggedy ponytails and had the same dark circles under their eyes I know so well. For the second one, hair was brushed and clean, lips were tinted. And then, suddenly, the moms looked like they'd been airbrushed:

straightened or expertly curled hair, full makeup, no clutter in the background. We looked better, but I couldn't help but wonder if we felt better. We were in full-blown silent competition with each other.

I looked in the mirror and decided that a moderately clean black tank top, sweatpants that nobody would see, powder and plum gloss were going to have to do it today. I pulled back my hair into a bun. Not bad.

I opened my computer and logged in. It was only a few seconds before I heard Emily Walker's voice sing over my speakers.

"Aloha everyone!" The camera zoomed into focus and there was Emily, lying out on a beach chair in a gold bikini. She was holding some kind of selfie-stick-type camera that allowed her to pan right and left. Beside her were three other women in blue, red and white barely-there swimsuits, looking perfect.

I glanced down at my sweats.

"I'm coming to you live from the island of Kaio! My three best friends and I are here for the next few days enjoying a little break from my whirlwind book tour! The dads are officially on duty—am I right, ladies?"

They hooted and giggled. Hot jealousy pumped vigorously through my veins.

Emily took off her sunglasses and looked deep into the camera. *How are her eyelashes so long?* I wondered.

"My family is everything to me, but I wouldn't be able to survive without my mama village. These three women mean the world to me. That's why, whenever we can, we hop on a jet and go somewhere where we can connect."

A mystery gloved hand holding a platter of champagne flutes, appeared from the side.

The women cheered. Emily took a glass.

"This week, the challenge is to find your village of moms! Join a playgroup. Make a best friend. You can do it!"

She clinked glasses with her friends and took a long sip.

"I believe in you! Oh, and before I let you go, remember that you only have three more weeks before our trip to Napa together! I can't wait to make all of you my besties for life! Who knows, maybe next year we'll be on vacation together. Make today a great one!"

With that, the connection switched off.

Now that's the life. I tried to imagine jetting off to spend a few days with Emily Walker and her cast of mom models to drink sparkling wine on a secluded beach. I can already see the conversation.

"Gloria, can you take Aubrey for a little while? My best friend and television host, Emily Walker, and I are going resort hopping in Jamaica."

Could that really be my life? A shiver of excitement ran up my spine.

2 P.M.

Breastfeeding is the first and best gift you can give your child. It's not just perfect milk that's flowing through you into your child, it's perfect love. Some of my best memories are of being a young toddler and breastfeeding from my own mother.

—Emily Walker, *Motherhood Better*

Aubrey woke up soon after Laundrygate, so I popped her into the stroller for a coffee run. I've learned that staying home in the afternoon makes the day go by even slower than it usually does, so we often run errands (i.e., buy things we don't need or ice cream) to pass the time. If I'd known what was going to happen at the café, I probably would have stayed home.

It was quiet, the early afternoons just after lunch and before the later afternoon slump rush always were. There were plenty of tables to choose from, but I made a beeline toward the one with a stroller. It was empty—the owner must be in the bathroom, I theorized. Being a mom means being on the constant lookout for friendship, a listening ear, or just someone to complain to who gets it. I've found grocery checkers aren't the best listeners.

I quickly purchased my vanilla latte and gingerbread loaf with a madeleine for Aubrey and sat down, practically trembling with anticipation. Who was the mom? Or dad? Was I about to make my lifelong best friend?

Then she emerged from the bathroom, juggling her diaper bag and a baby wearing a blue romper who looked no older than six months. I cleared my throat in anticipation. The café was almost empty but I'd chosen a seat one table over so as not to come off as too desperate.

She crouched down and grabbed a lightweight blanket before sitting down, cradling her baby in her lap.

I stood halfway up, preparing to introduce myself, before I saw her slip one strap of her tank top down and flop the blanket over her shoulder. She was nursing. Oh. I'd been down this road before. When Aubrey was three months old I joined a mom group for about five minutes. That's how long it took me to figure out that I was the only one not breastfeeding. It's not that the moms were judgmental—the pitying, sympathetic smiles every time I pulled a bottle out were too much. Maybe it'd all been in my head, but watching them cradle their babies on their giant nursing pillows while I measured formula was more than I could take on a regular basis.

I didn't realize I was staring until I snapped to and saw the nursing mom looking at me. I smiled and she returned it.

I busied myself opening Aubrey's package of madeleines and

handed her one. "Here you go, honey," I whispered, trying not to notice the stark difference in what we were feeding our babies. Aubrey snipped off a tiny bit of the soft cookie with her gums and grinned.

I couldn't resist peeking at the mom again. She and her baby were lost in each other the way breastfeeding moms always are. She gazed down at him with a serene smile on her face. *What does that feel like?* I wondered to myself. *The feeling of knowing you're doing the absolute perfect thing for your child without a doubt.* She looked so calm and serene. The baby reached up from behind the blanket and touched her face. They were like a commercial. I gathered our belongings and headed for the door. When the daylight hit my face, I was grateful for the distraction.

One hand on the stroller, the other clutching my sweet coffee, I took Aubrey for the longest walk we'd been on so far.

4 P.M.

I was sitting in my living room watching Aubrey, who was currently fascinated by the twirling monkey mirror on her exersaucer. She was adorable. I was obsessed with her. But I was bored.

I really did need friends, but when you're a mom, that's easier said than done.

Yesterday at the park I tried to chat up a couple of moms who were having what looked like a really interesting conversation. They were whispering and everything. You should have seen how slick I was as I complimented one of the moms on her stroller and tried to use that as a segue to introduce myself. They looked at me like I had six boobs and an infant breastfeeding on each one.

They were polite enough, but it obvious that they wanted me to keep moving.

You know what really surprised me about motherhood? The slow realization that mothers aren't anything I thought they were to each other. I thought once you entered the mommy club they brought you into the fold with open arms. Look guys, my vagina/stomach/overall body got torn up just like yours and I'm pushing a stroller here, we're all going to be best friends, right? No. Maybe it was naive of me to think that just because we shared the experience of never feeling rested that we'd be blood sisters for life, but I wanted that. I needed that.

It killed me that one of the hardest parts of being a mom was sometimes dealing with other moms. The judgments, the looks, the advice that feels like a slow plunging of a knife into an already sore spot. They were supposed to understand better than anyone. They were supposed to be the only people I didn't have to pretend for. They should have been my safe space, but they weren't.

Anyway. If someone needs me, I'll be talking to the nine-month-old in my care.

9 P.M.

I met my best friend, Alexsis, at the Rainbow Orchid Spa in Napa Valley, California. We were both taking a little R & R. The minute our eyes connected over the steam in the sauna, I knew we'd be best friends for life.

—Emily Walker, *Motherhood Better*

I took some decisive action to find my "mama tribe" today, and even by my standards it helped me achieve a new low.

Okay, so I was at the café, like always. It took me almost a full three minutes to cram my T. rex of a stroller through the door. The Mitax Marathon is trendy, but why, oh why, are the wheels so far apart? I felt like the business people on their phones and students tapping away on their computers enjoyed watching me almost dump Aubrey out onto the floor as I tipped the stroller to an angle to finally get myself in.

"No, no, don't get up," is what I hope my eyes said at the 20-plus people who remained glued to their seats staring at me while I struggled. I don't expect help just because I'm a mom, but what happened to the whole "it takes a village" thing?

Back to the story.

Ten minutes later I was sitting down, vanilla latte in hand, when Aubrey started to fuss the way she always does when I've reached a pre-baby state of relaxation. A few twenty-year-olds turned to look at me and I could tell they were irritated. Obviously they were never babies and were born fully grown, so the sound of a human infant is completely foreign to them.

Or maybe they think a good mother would sedate her baby with tranquilizers before taking it out in public so no one would be subjected to the torture of hearing a baby get upset.

Either that, or my child's cries were distracting them from their oh-so-important Facebook posts.

After one of them sighed loudly for the third time, I took the hint and started preparing to leave. But then I thought, *Why should I have to vacate the premises every time Aubrey makes a sound? It's not like she's screaming her head off.* No. I decided to handle it right there.

I picked Aubrey up out of her stroller and could tell right away that she was exhausted. It's hard for me to get her to nap at home much less in a loud coffee shop full of judgy twenty-year-olds probably live tweeting my every move, but I was determined.

I cradled her firmly in my arms and draped a blanket across my shoulder and over her head to block out some of the light and started bouncing her. The Motherhood Gods must have smiled upon me because she fell asleep in ten seconds flat. I couldn't believe it! I was finally becoming the kind of mom I'd always wanted to be: capable. My arm fell asleep and started to burn, and I was pretty sure it was going to fall off, but my kid was asleep and I had coffee. All was right in the world.

Then they walked in. The moms I'd seen at the park a few days earlier. My dream mommy group. My dream village. There were five of them. They all wore their babies and toddlers in a rainbow of amazing carriers: long strips of tie-dyed cloth, gorgeous prints. One of them pushed a double stroller. They held the door for her. See? Mom friends are a must. They walked in and sat at the table directly behind mine. I could barely breathe.

I knew it was my chance. I needed to say something. But what? Introduce myself? I took a few very nervous sips of my latte and tried to think of something to say. I took a deep breath and, right as I was about to turn around, a woman standing in front of me cleared her throat loudly.

I assumed my stroller was blocking her way.

"Sorry, do you need me to move my—" I began.

"Do you mind not doing THAT in here?" She twisted her lips and pointed at sleeping Aubrey.

I was legitimately confused. Let my baby sleep? Drink lattes while looking like a Dumpster? What was she talking about? And it dawned on me. She thought I was breastfeeding. My boobs have been drier than a raisin for months but she thought I was breastfeeding.

My mind raced as I tried to find just the right words, but before I could speak a voice behind me boomed, "SHE'S NOT GOING ANYWHERE."

The moms. They came in like a wrecking ball and swarmed me before I could utter a single word.

A redhead in a maxi dress stood between me and the woman. "She has every right to feed her baby here. Breastfeeding in public is protected by law, or didn't you know that?"

A mom in a blue sweatsuit chimed in, her arm protectively around a curly haired toddler in a yellow-and-green checkered wrap. "She's not going anywhere and you have no right to ask her!"

People were turning around in their seats now. The whole café was watching and I think I saw one teenager filming with his phone.

Business lady clicked her tongue and shook her head disapprovingly. "It would really be more appropriate if you did that kind of thing in the bathroom."

I still hadn't said anything. I knew that this was the moment to say that I wasn't even actually breastfeeding but two things popped into my head.

If I WERE breastfeeding, this woman was way out of line for asking me to leave.

THE MOMS NOTICED ME. THEY NOTICED ME AND MIGHT WANT TO BE MY FRIENDS.

I'm not sure where the voice came from but the words, "I'm not going anywhere. Breastfeeding is natural," came out of my mouth before I could stop them. I may have hugged sleeping Aubrey closer to my chest area, also. I also may have said, "It's my right."

Business lady whipped around in a huff and stomped away. Of course I immediately thanked the other moms. Maxi Dress (whose name is actually Lola) put her hand on my shoulder and asked me what I was doing tomorrow. I said "Nothing," and they invited me to their playgroup. The only problem is…it's a La Lait meeting. For breastfeeding moms. And I'm not breastfeeding.

I said yes.

The good news is that I now have friends. The bad news is that it's based on a small (HUGE) lie.

Tuesday, February 19, 9 A.M.

I breastfed my first children, Eleanor and Gregory, until they were 4.5 years old. They're rarely sick and read two grades above their age. Breast milk can cure many common ailments including sore throats, the flu, eczema, burns and even hangnails."

—Emily Walker, *Motherhood Better*

What am I going to do? I'm a formula mom in a breastfeeding world. Just my luck that the first serious mom-group prospect I get since the pyramid scheme playdate is based on a huge lie. Maybe once they get to know me they can overlook the whole "I lied about breastfeeding and my baby is really living on the stuff you think is pure evil" thing.

Today was my first La Lait meeting. Operation Pretend to Breastfeed to Make Friends was in full effect. I wore jeans and a button-down shirt because I read on the MilkMums.net message board that they're the easiest to nurse in. I wasn't proud of myself, but I knew blending in was going to be important until I worked up the nerve to tell them the truth.

There was a small possibility that I also wore a nursing bra, but only because I had one lying around from before Aubrey was born. I'd given all but one of them to Joy after it was cemented that I wouldn't be breastfeeding. To be honest, I was still a little raw that she'd had the nerve to ask me for them.

"I mean, it's not like you need them," she told me while I was holding six-week-old Aubrey and still crying every time I made a bottle.

Aubrey was quiet as we drove to the meeting. She was ridiculously cute in her lavender overalls and white shirt. As we made our way out of the suburbs and toward the La Lait meeting in the hip part of town that was inhabited by college students, organic grocery stores and independently owned coffee shops, I reflected on how I found myself in this utterly ridiculous predicament. Technically, I never lied. My exact words at the café were "I'm not going anywhere. Breastfeeding is natural. It's my right." All of those statements are true. I wasn't going anywhere. Breastfeeding is totally natural. And it was my right. I just wasn't doing it.

They're the ones who assumed I was breastfeeding. If I'd corrected them in the café in front of that wretched woman I would have hurt the movement.

My heart began to race as I pulled into the community co-op parking lot. It was adjacent to a public garden with a hand-painted sign that read, "Come one, plant all." A few people, a young woman in a long patchwork skirt with a toddler strapped to her back, a man with an elaborate beard and wearing denim shorts, and an older woman wearing a mechanic-style jumpsuit, were harvesting the land.

I sat in the car for a few moments with my hands on the steering wheel. "I can't pretend to breastfeed Aubrey," I said aloud. "That's insane. It's deranged. Who does that?" I peeked at Aubrey in the rearview mirror. She gummed on a silicone teether in the shape of a giraffe. I'd received three of them at my baby shower. Apparently they were the hot must-have for moms. As I stared into her sweet brown eyes, I knew what I had to do.

Opening the door gingerly, I walked to her side of the car. I grabbed the diaper bag and undid her straps. With Aubrey on my hip and the diaper bag (with a bottle hidden in a tangled mess of pacifiers, toys and changes of clothes), we made our way toward the door.

"I'm not going to pretend to do anything," I decided. "I'm just going to show up to the meeting I was invited to." Anyway, I thought, who says it's for breastfeeders only?

A sign on the door in swirly script read: Welcome to La Lait—A Safe Haven for Breastfeeding Mothers.

Oh.

11 A.M.

> Breast milk isn't just wonderful for children. I pump and feed for premature shelter puppies once a month.
> —Emily Walker, *Motherhood Better*

Lola, the outspoken redhead from the café, was waiting for me in the lobby of the co-op when I walked in.

She wore her two-year-old son, Donovan, in one of those woven wraps that are way more expensive than they look. Maybe she'd be able to teach me how to wrap Aubrey. That is, if she can't tell just by looking at me that my girls are as dry as a bone.

"Ashley!" she squealed as she glided over to me. "You made it!"

She reached out and grabbed me into her arms, squishing Donovan against my chest. She held my arms.

"The ladies are so excited to meet you."

I forced myself to smile and hoped that I wasn't visibly shaking. "I'm...so excited to meet them, too!" Inside, I could hear a voice saying, "What are you doing, Ashley? Run! Run now!"

Lola tickled Ashley's cheek. She giggled. "We've got to get you a wrap, little missy! Mommy's arms are probably so tired!" She put a hand on my shoulder. "I have a spare in my car, if you want I can..."

I waved my hands wildly. I couldn't let her see that I have no idea how to use those contraptions. Not even seventeen YouTube videos and a ten-pound bag of flour as a baby stand-in could teach me.

Lola grinned. "Ah, you're one of those 'baby in arms' mommies. Old school. I love it."

I shrugged my shoulders and smiled as if I had any idea what she was talking about.

Lola led me down the hall, past a Tai Chi class for elders and a pottery class for the recently divorced, to a door with a poster of a woman tandem nursing (that means two babies—I learned that last night) her twins. The caption above her head read, I make milk. What's your superpower?

"Apparently, it's lying my way into mom groups," I said under my breath.

"What's that?" asked Lola.

"Oh, nothing! I just can't wait to say hello," I lied.

Lola put one hand on the door handle. "Ready to meet your fans?"

"Fans?" Before I could answer or sprint to my car, she opened the door and pushed me in front of her.

I'd decided to keep a low profile at the meeting. I wouldn't tell anyone what had happened; I'd just make a fresh start based on truth. That plan went out the window the minute Lola spoke.

"Our hero was arrived!" Lola practically yelled and the fifteen-plus women sitting in a semicircle on a large red rug with blankets and pillows broke out into applause. The ones without babies on their breasts even stood up to give me a standing ovation.

I died.

"It's so great to meet you! You are so brave. Can I interview you for my blog about normalizing breastfeeding?" said a bubbly brunette with thick glasses who turned out to be Nina, mom to six-month-old twins, Finch and Aiden.

"I'm, um, thank you, maybe," was my eloquent response.

I sat down with Aubrey, who was practically buzzing at the excitement. Everyone was staring at me, beaming as if I were some kind of lactating Joan of Arc.

Lola took her place among the moms and sat on her knees. "Hi, everyone! I want to formally introduce Ashley Keller, mom to Aubrey! She's the amazing milk warrior I met at the café yesterday. She stood up to ignorance and we're so happy to have her as part of our group."

Everyone clapped again and I did my best to conjure invisibility. *This was a mistake*, boomed in my head, over and over.

"Ashley, would you like to say a few words?"

I froze. Maybe now was the time for me to speak up and just tell everyone what had happened. Surely they'd understand, I thought. It's such a simple misunderstanding. If I told them now, maybe we could all laugh about it and I could be the Le Lait version of a football waterboy and make sure everyone stays hydrated while they nurse.

But as I looked around the room of smiling faces, hair as disheveled as mine, shirts with mysterious white, filmy, damp stains, eyes with dark bags under them, babies squirming around, I knew that these were my people. I know it sounds crazy, but besides the tiny fact that my diaper bag contains a bottle and powder that I'm pretty sure would leave them re-coiling in disgust, we're pretty much the same.

"Thank you so much for having me today," I heard come out of my mouth. "It's time people accepted breastfeeding as normal and natural."

They clapped.

What have I done?

Thursday, February 21, 1 P.M.

Today was everything I dreamed motherhood would be. The La Lait moms and I met up at the park for a lunch potluck. I brought my Lemon Poppyseed Cake (it turned out perfectly and everyone wanted the recipe).

I was finally *that* mom. The one I always saw laughing and giggling with a group of mommy friends all seated together on a huge blanket surrounded by their babies. Somewhere between eating cubes of cheddar cheese and sipping on Nina's homemade lavender lemonade (which was amazing, by the way), I realized that this is what was missing in my life. I looked down at Aubrey and felt like I was not just a mom; I felt like a whole person. I hadn't felt like that in ages. And for the first time in a long time, I didn't feel completely and utterly alone.

Nina, a seasoned mom of four, and I hit it off especially well. At the first La Lait meeting we spent some time chatting, while she bounced her six-month-old twins, Aiden and Finch, one in each arm.

I almost said, "Wow, you have your hands full," but remembered how much I hate when people say that to me. It's basically code for "Your life looks unmanageable." She dresses just like me: black stretch pants that she woke up in and long-sleeved shirts or hoodies. But our bonding wasn't just over clothing preferences—I love how relaxed she is. Nothing seems to faze her. When Aiden and Finch both started projectile spitting in a stream of white milk, one over each shoulder like some sort of marble water fountain, she just looked at the three-foot-long splat mark on the linoleum and said, "I think that's a new record, boys. Well done." Then she set them down on a mat and wiped the whole thing up with a burp cloth. I would have wanted to sink into the floor. Nina just rolls with the punches. I'd love to be like that one day.

The craziest part about her is that she has FOUR kids, including the twins. Besides Finch and Aiden, there's Everdeen, four, and Lillyanne, six. I have no idea how she does it. She's so cheerful and sarcastic. She told me that the trick to making it through the day is to "always have a glass of wine or piece of chocolate waiting for you at the end of the day…or with lunch, whatever." I love her.

Lola's toddler, Donovan, is her first, but she's hoping for another. When I told her that I'm probably one and done, she said "Just wait," and winked. I got the feeling she's been trying for a second for a while now but didn't want to pry.

I also chitchatted with a mom named Kristen. Her little girl is Alice, who's just three months old. She reminds me of myself when Aubrey was a newborn: quiet, insecure, and trying so hard to find her groove. She was learning how to use a beautiful purple-and-black striped baby carrier on my first day with the group. Three moms were helping: one held the baby while the other two wrapped her up. As I watched her stand there, surrounded by friendship and encouragement, I felt a little pang of sadness. Maybe I wouldn't have had such a hard time getting used to this whole motherhood thing if I'd had a group like this.

Sitting on the grass on overlapping blankets, babies, moms, and containers full of fragrant salads and sandwiches, I felt like I'd finally come home.

Today was an absolute success.

Except for one small incident.

After lunch Aubrey started fussing and I knew she wanted a bottle right away.

Lola knew, too. "Looks like someone wants lunch!"

I froze. Letting Aubrey just starve was out of the question but was I supposed to whip out my plastic container of devil's dust and say, "April fool"?

Aubrey started fussing louder, and within moments was in a full-blown cry. I saw Nina glance at me questioningly and did the only thing I could think of.

I sniffed her bum. "Phew! She's ripe! I'm going to change her in the car before I feed her. Don't want to ruin anyone's appetite." And then I dashed off, diaper bag in hand.

As I sat in the back of my car, feeding Aubrey, I stared down at her face and tried not to cry. What am I doing? I felt like a fugitive. A fake. But I can't lose my friends, I just can't.

I checked into the Motherhood Better Bootcamp portal and nearly everyone has found their way into a playgroup or book club and seems to be having a blast with their new clique. It's too late for me to find a new playgroup and I really, really like these moms.

I know the truth will have to come out eventually, but until then, is it wrong to just enjoy finally having people to talk to?

9 P.M.

Honesty is the foundation for all friendships and it's no different for mommies. Always tell your village what's on your heart. I've found that the soothing, warm water of a sea-salt hot tub makes for a comforting place to get vulnerable.

—Emily Walker, *Motherhood Better*

I had the best day with Nina today. After the picnic lunch we took the kids to the zoo. Well, I took Aubrey. Nina brought—or should I say "corralled"—her four. I have no idea how she does it. She wore one twin (Finch, I think), used a double stroller for Aiden and Everdeen, and Lilly-anne walked.

She makes having one kid look like a walk in the park. It felt almost criminal complaining to her about Aubrey's sleep problems, but she was sympathetic. It was so good to have someone to talk to. Someone who gets it. With David it's like talking to a brick wall. I love him, but trying to get him to understand what motherhood is doing to my brain and body is an exercise in futility.

Nina told me that she remembers what it was like to be a first-time mom and that everything I'm feeling is completely normal. When I'm around her I feel less like a screwup and more like a mom who is just trying to make it through the day, just like them.

Aubrey is starting to really love our outings, too. I don't know if it's because I'm more relaxed, but she was giggling and pointing at all of the animals. She just looked happier. Lilly-anne's only six but she was a huge help. When I was changing Aubrey, she reached under the stroller and handed me wipes just when I needed them. Maybe there's something to this whole have-more-than-one-kid thing.

I know I need to come clean about not exactly being a breastfeeding mom sooner than later, but…we're having so much fun together.

★ ★ ★

When we got back home, Aubrey was wiped out and slept for two hours. While she dozed, I chopped tomatoes and diced onions for Kristen's homemade pasta sauce. Turns out she's a chef. I told her about my kitchen fiascos and she assured me this one is foolproof. By the time Aubrey woke up it was done, and my house smelled like a basil wonderland. For the first time since I can remember, David went back for seconds at dinner. He's even taking the leftovers to work for lunch.

I wish I could have enjoyed the meal as much as he did. Sure, the sauce was great, but each bite just reminded me how much I need my new friends and that it's all going to end, probably terribly, any day now.

While Aubrey splashed around in the bath, I realized that for the first time in a long time, I actually felt good about myself. I didn't feel like a failure. I felt like a normal mom and was actually enjoying the days, not just getting through them.

As I watched Aubrey's chubby hands slap the water, I made a decision. I had to fight for my friends. I was not going to let them slip away from me. Whatever it took, I was willing to do it. Maybe, just maybe, I could prove that, even though I'm not exactly who they thought I was, I was still a really good person and fun to be around.

David put Aubrey to bed so I had a few minutes to write my wrap-up for the Mama Village Challenge.

Hi everyone. This week was incredible. I'm proud to say that I made a group of great friends! I'm loving getting to know each of them personally and feel like they're really starting to get to know me.
Xo, Ashley

Friday, February 22, 1:30 P.M.

Aubrey just went down for her nap. I had the most incredible morning with the La Lait moms.

I arrived at the meeting at 9:45 a.m., fifteen minutes before it officially began, and helped Lola set up. Aubrey was snug as a bug in a rug in a baby carrier Nina lent me the day before.

"You're really quiet today," Lola said.

"Oh, I'm just thinking," I responded, setting up the coffee and cookies.

"Thinking about what?" Lola had stopped working to breastfeed Donovan on the carpet. She patted the area on the carpet next to her. I took a seat.

"I'm just really happy. I never thought I'd have friends like this again after having Aubrey," I said, stroking the top of Aubrey's head as she lay contentedly against me.

Lola smiled warmly. "You've got a tribe now. No mom should be alone in raising children." I looked at Donovan, who was nursing quietly. His face was hidden in the folds of

Lola's multicolored wrap, but his fist was wrapped around one of her long strands of crimson hair.

As we sat there together, in the silence of the community center, I felt something I hadn't felt for a long time. Peace. I realized that it wasn't a lack of crafts, my terrible cooking skills, my crushing sleep deprivation, or even David being gone so much that had made motherhood so hard for me. It was not having this. Real friendship.

Aubrey began fussing.

Lola peered over at her. "Someone wants a snack," she said, eyeing me from the side.

"Oh, yeah," I said, fumbling. I pulled out my phone. "My husband just called me. I'll be right back."

As I ran out of the room to feed Aubrey in my car, I knew I'd have to find a way to make this work.

Sunday, February 24, 3 P.M.

When I was a mom of only one, I designed my home after the Montague residence in Romeo and Juliet. Since then, my design taste has changed, but my commitment to making my home a place of beauty, organization and relaxation has not wavered. You'll never see piles of laundry in my family room or toys strewn about, not because I have live-in help, but because I believe your home should be a place you are proud to call yours.

—Emily Walker, *Motherhood Better*

Only eighteen hours until the next bootcamp video chat. And I could barely contain my excitement, as it was going to tackle something I have tried, and failed, to get under control: my home.

Before Aubrey was born, David and I lived in a tiny one-bedroom condo that could be cleaned from top to bottom in under an hour, probably because we didn't own that much stuff. We had a set of dishes for four people. There were no baby spoons, baby forks, bottles, baby plates, baby bowls, or sippy cups with lids and weird plastic tubey parts I didn't understand practically bursting out of the kitchen cupboards.

Everything was minimalist, which I loved. There was no item that didn't have a place. Magazines went on the rack beside the couch. Shoes were all lined up in the entryway closet. My bags hung neatly in the bedroom wardrobe.

Now? Aubrey's five pairs of shoes are strewn in a messy pile in front of the door. My diaper bag is lying on its side like a drunken college student in the entryway with a trail of individual infant socks, an empty package of travel wipes and two canisters of sweet-potato-flavored puffs falling out of it. We traded our gorgeous small circular throw rug and slate coffee table for a huge, interlocking, brightly colored foam mat—the kind I said I would NEVER have in my home. All it took was imagining Aubrey hitting her head on a hard edge or the hard floor for all of our beautiful things to go on Craigslist.

When we got married, I said everything in our home would be charcoal and cream. That was our official color scheme. I rubbed a bare foot along the hard plastic of the foam mat. Green, blue, yellow, and red. Primary colors. That's my color scheme now.

Plopping myself on the floor beside Aubrey, I had to admit that our flooring was pretty comfortable. It was like living inside of a children's play center, except with less stomach flu. Aubrey noticed me beside her and took the opportunity to attack my head. In three seconds my hair was damp with drool.

I pried her baby orangutan arms off my head and rolled her onto her tummy. She giggled gleefully as I blew raspberries into her back.

Within a few seconds, Aubrey's laughter dissolved into fussy yelps as she tried to flip onto her back.

"You need tummy time, Aubrey! How are you going to learn to crawl?" I crooned while placing her back on her front.

She screamed at me and waved her arms pathetically, like a beached baby sea lion, before pushing herself onto her back again.

"How can a baby have such a strong will?" I asked her, hoping the self-satisfied glint in her eye was just a figment of my imagination and not a glimpse into her future stubbornness.

Joy posts videos of crawling Ella almost every day now. I'm sure her friends must love the five-minute-long montages of my niece set to classical music.

"Has Aubrey started crawling yet?" she asked me the last time we spoke.

"Not yet, but she sits up and is rocking. She will any day now." I tried to sound confident.

"Don't worry. Some kids are just late bloomers. Maybe if you cleaned up your living room a little you'd have more space for her to move around," was my sister's response.

Double whammy. Note to self: Mail Joy an envelope full of glitter.

She's not all wrong, though. Currently, there are four full baskets of clean(ish) laundry, an exersaucer, a bouncy chair, four throw pillows and a ton of other miscellaneous goods on my living room floor.

I checked my phone's clock.

Only 17.5 more hours until I learn how to finally be someone who is proud of her home.

Monday, February 25, 10:30 A.M.

My interior designer and I worked together to give each room in my home a personality of its own. You spend 85 percent of your life within the walls of your house; you should love every square inch of it.

—Emily Walker, *Motherhood Better*

The Motherhood Better Bootcamp call had been at 9 a.m., a full hour earlier than normal. Emily wanted us to catch her at home before she left for the studio to film her show.

"Good morning, mommies!" she chirped from the screen. Even in pink sweats and a hat with her pink EW logo on it, she looked fabulous. "I hope you guys had fun with your mama village last week. Now are you ready to tackle the Home Challenge?"

The other moms smiled politely. I wondered if any of them were doubting that they could whip their cluttered, overridden-with-toys houses into shape in just one week.

Emily adjusted her hat and continued, "Your home isn't

just a structure, it's your family's safe and sacred space. It's your temple. This week you're going to learn how to treat it as such."

Temple? I looked around my living room where I was sitting barefoot and cross-legged because the laundry baskets left little space to stretch out.

"I've left some instructional guides for you in the portal, but right now, I want to show you around my house! Ready for a tour?"

Emily's camera rose as she stood. She shifted her computer to face out, and a sparkling white room filled the screen. Luxurious eggshell suede couches, a cream rug, glittering chandelier lamps, blue and gold porcelain accent vases…did children really live in this house?

"This is the formal family room. It's where I receive guests. My children love to play in here."

Play what? Sit Still and Try Not to Break Anything?

"Let's move on to the kitchen!"

The camera panned down a long hallway with smooth oak hardwood floors and family photos hanging on the walls, and then opened into a rustic, high-ceilinged kitchen. Pots and pans hung from the beams over the chef's kitchen. Stainless steel appliances with not a trace of fingerprints twinkled as they caught the sunlight.

"The kitchen is where my family gathers several times a day not just to feed their bodies, but their souls."

Over the next half hour, we saw every immaculate room in Emily's house, including her children's themed bedrooms (Unicorn Wonderland, Horses Galore, Nighttime Whimsy, Forest Magic and Beyond Space and Time), her bedroom— it looked straight out of *Arabian Nights*—the den, her many bathrooms, her meditation room, her dining room, her craft room, her office, her garage and the backyard.

At the end of the tour, there was just jealous silence.

"I hope you got inspired to create a truly beautiful living space of your own. As always, if you need any direction, consult your copy of *Motherhood Better*, chitchat in the portal, or send me a message. Love you guys!"

Consult the portal? Are there a few hundred thousand dollars in there for me to make my home look like a magazine spread?

Ugh. I clicked through to the message boards and opened the Home Challenge Guide Emily had written for us.

"Ready to start? First I'm going to teach you how to clean up your space, naturally. Check out these recipes for homemade cleaning products!"

I snapped my computer shut. As I looked at Aubrey, who had fallen asleep in a pile of mismatched socks, I knew it: this challenge was going to end me.

5 P.M.

> Keeping your home clutter-free should be a priority for all mothers. When a home is tidy and organized children are far more relaxed and better behaved. If you don't have live-in help, spend 40 minutes a day picking up and keep all toys out of sight.
>
> —Emily Walker, *Motherhood Better*

David should have already come home. Balancing a still-pajamaed Aubrey on my hip, I stood in front of the stove and stirred the rice, soy sauce, cubed chicken and broccoli concoction I'd thrown together half an hour earlier. If only the recipe website I'd used had been more specific about cooking the rice before mixing it with the other ingredients. I hoped David didn't mind it a little al dente.

Other than my blasphemous attempt at stir fry, I felt more

put together than normal. Aubrey'd had a great nap and I'd already done the obligatory pre-husband-coming-home speed clean. David and I had an unspoken rule that he wasn't allowed to see the state of our home before I could take it from Dumpster Rat Wedding to Somewhat Livable. It wasn't about my feeling like I had to show off for him, it was about my dignity as a person. I couldn't let him see how I lived during the day.

My phone buzzed on the counter. It was David. Be home in 20 min.

Put all the toys back in their bins.

Clear the dining room table of breakfast plates, milk splotches, dirty bibs, baby socks, empty bowls with dried-up baby-food goo and junk mail.

Sweep the Funny O's off the floor.

Wipe my hair off the bathroom floor (seriously, it looked like an infestation of seaweed on a dried up beach).

Pick up the clothes that I'd left all over the house during the day.

Hastily make our bed.

Wipe down the kitchen counters.

Spray some all-purpose cleaner into the air to give the impression that someone who lives here cares.

This is the type of cleaning that affects the top layer of the house only. If you were to open a closet door, an avalanche of random goods would come bursting out, revealing me as the fraud I am. To move any appliance half an inch to the left or right would expose a grime outline like some sort of waiting-to-be-filled-in coloring sheet. Peek into a linen closet and you'd find bunched up fitted sheets, towels strewn about and random panties.

A quick once-over of the interior of my home would fool you into thinking that someone conscientious and domestically proficient resides within these walls, but no. Anyone with an eye for detail, i.e., my mother-in-law, would know better in a matter of moments.

I've gotten really good at the speed clean over the past few months but the Motherhood Better Home Challenge is all about making real change. I don't want Aubrey to grow up in a pigsty, embarrassed to bring her friends over to the house.

Flash-forward to ten years from now...
Me: Aubrey, why don't you have a sleepover this weekend?
Aubrey: (taking my hand) I'd love to, Mom, but the other parents won't let their children spend the night here on account of the... (She gestures around the room at the laundry pile that is now to the ceiling.)

No. I needed to get this under control now. Tomorrow I tackle the clothing situation that is haunting me like some kind of 100-percent-cotton phantom of the opera.

I shifted Aubrey onto my other hip and mixed our sorry dinner some more.

"All it needs is a little love," I sang to Aubrey as I brought a mouthful of the now-congealing goo to my lips, blowing before tasting it. The gummy rice was somehow still hard in the middle. I felt the grains crack under my molars.

Aubrey winced, "Yucky."

She wasn't wrong.

Tuesday, February 26, 10:30 A.M.

"What have I gotten myself into?" I whispered. There I sat, smack dab in the middle of my bedroom, surrounded by no less than eighteen loads of laundry that represented every item of clothing my family owned. The oppressive cotton and poly-spandex blends formed valleys and peaks, they mingled, socks with ties, panty hose with infant tutus, conspiring against my sanity like rebel forces. The dark wood was completely hidden under the sea of multicolored, wrinkled fabric.

At 9:30 that morning I decided to jump into the Home Challenge headfirst and tackle the first of three of Emily's sub-challenges.

Motherhood Better Mail
From: Emily Walker
To: My Mommies
Good morning from Manhattan! I'm meeting with buyers from Neiman Marcus (hush-hush!) this morning and will have a big surprise for you in a couple of days. But first, as you know,

I've divided the Home Challenge into three bite-sized goals that I just know you ladies are going to rock.
Declutter
Deep Clean
Design
Today we're tackling a hot topic: laundry. Are you REALLY wearing all of those clothes? Lay everything out in front of you and get rid of what you haven't worn in the past ten days. Only store pieces that 1) you truly cherish, such as your wedding dress or a piece from the Emily Walker MAMA collection coming out this fall, or 2) you can say with 99% certainty you'll wear again one day—like how the MAMA collection can follow you through all of the stages of motherhood. Do the same for your kids. This challenge is all about making your life and homes LIGHTER! Can you feel it? You're a cloud. Love you!
Xox Emily

I'd tried earlier that morning to organize Aubrey's closet and was doing pretty well until the crushing nervous breakdown complete with heaving sobs. It didn't happen all at once. In fact, everything was going fine up until I found her newborn socks. Newborn socks that she'll never wear again, to be more specific.

I'd been sorting her clothes into two storage containers: one massive gray one for donating and one medium-sized blue one for keepsake items to reminisce over when I'm seventy or to give to my grandchildren. After twenty minutes, the donation container was next to empty, other than an over-the-top stark white, frilly newborn dress, complete with a scratchy tulle liner and headband that Gloria tried to insist I bring Aubrey home in.

I declined, of course. It seemed cruel to make an infant go

from floating within the soft, warm walls of the embryonic sac to scratchy tulle in a matter of hours. The only solution had been to misplace the hideous dress until Aubrey grew out of it.

I'd just thrown the garment into the donation container and was scraping around the back of her closet when I found the socks. Two little yellow fuzzy socks that never seemed to stay on her plucky newborn feet. They were like chicken legs; I remembered how her toes would fray when she cried.

And, oh, how she cried. I'd heard babies cry before and it had never affected me, but her screechy wails sent pangs to my heart in a way that was so unexpected and all-consuming. Sitting on Aubrey's pale pink carpet, I thought about how it seemed like yesterday that I would swaddle her in a white muslin blanket (my wrapping style was rather sloppy and she often looked like a messy burrito) and tug those socks onto her feet. Three seconds later they were off again.

I know they say newborns can't smile and it's just gas, but I swear, every time I, exasperated, put those socks back on her, the edges of her mouth would turn up as if to say, "I don't think so, lady."

As I held the socks, sitting on the floor of her bedroom, watching my now nine-month-old play with her toes that were so much bigger and less chicken-like and more toddler-like, I started to cry. Almost a year had gone by. It was all happening too fast. I can't even remember what it felt like to hold Aubrey as a newborn. All I had left were her socks, and I was supposed to just give them away?

I began to pull out all of her newborn sleepers, blankets and bitty hats. These were not just clothes, they were memories from my first few months of being a mom. I couldn't throw them in a black garbage bag and leave them outside of a donation center on the sidewalk like trash. It's easier for Emily, she has five kids and gets to see the same socks worn over and over. I only have Aubrey and frankly, my plate feels full, overflowing, really.

I added the socks to the Keep pile. And then the sleepers. Then the hats. Then the burp rags, so soft from multiple washings. In half an hour, I'd gone through every item Aubrey had ever owned and not only had I failed to part with anything, I also had a headache from crying.

#Success.

Then I remembered a DIY quilt tutorial I'd seen on Pinterest. Who knew—maybe one day I'd turn all of this into a fabulous, handmade blanket. The chances of that are about as high as me taking up competitive deep-sea diving, but it was the only excuse I needed to put all of Aubrey's outgrown clothes right back in the closet where I found them. At least they were folded now. That had to count for something.

Things went a little better with my own clothes. As I already knew, I owned a separate wardrobe for each of the different versions of myself.

Pre-Pregnancy Me

This person was always trying to improve her body despite being quite hot. She owned pantsuits, fitted sports jackets (that I can no longer button over a wobbly muffin top), skinny jeans for spending the day shopping or reading in a bookstore, matching exercise outfits, bras that wouldn't come close to containing the gals today and cute, teeny-tiny panties that would maybe cover one of my butt cheeks.

Pregnant Me

This person started off cute enough: fashionable, boot-cut maternity jeans and silky tops that were professional but showed off my teeny-tiny bump. Dressing for the beginning of my second trimester was a blast. I had a perfectly round bump that was downright adorable under baby-doll dresses and clingy tops.

Somewhere between the end of the twenty-eighth week and the beginning of the thirtieth, I exploded into a sea creature and grew so large that strangers winced as I waddled past them. Bye-bye stretchy denim, hello yoga pants. Dressing for comfort meant breathable fabrics, dark colors (to hide the food stains) and whatever shirts would cover my rapidly expanding bump.

Postpartum Me

Even if I could fit back into my pre-pregnancy clothes, I wouldn't wear them. My days are spent collapsing strollers, rolling around the living room floor, running errands and foraging for coffee. Pantsuits? Yeah, right. I wear absorbent fabrics because they double as a paper towel. If it looks and feels like pajamas, sign me up. A fashion designer might call my look Sleepwear Chic or Bedroom Casual.

All I could do was stare at my entire adult life represented in skirts, bras and tops. Where to even begin?

Aubrey let out a muffled squeal from under a maternity shirt. I pulled it off her and she beamed. Silly girl. I rubbed the pale blue stretchy cotton between my fingers. This was the shirt I was wearing when I first felt her kick.

"That's enough, little missy," I said, plopping her into her jumparoo hanging in the doorway. She began pushing off the floor with her footie-pajamaed legs, launching herself into the air and then bouncing back again. They really should make those for adults.

I dragged four large storage containers into the room from the hallway. Time to organize.

An hour later, Aubrey was asleep in her playpen and I snapped the last storage container shut. On my bed were six pairs of black stretch pants, eight tank tops, two dresses and four sweatshirts. That's it. That's all I wear. I basically had the wardrobe (but not the body!) of a yoga instructor.

Now the big question: What to do with the two humongous storage containers of clothes that either a) not even a 10-day juice cleanse would get me into or b) are impractical for my life as a stay-at-home mom? Giving them away seems hasty. What if I go back to work?

And my maternity wardrobe cost a small fortune. I bought it before I knew how much formula cost. Even if I didn't intend to get pregnant again, I should at least try to sell it. Yes, that's what I'd do, I decided. Not today, obviously. I'd already overextended myself. If anyone had earned a break, it was me.

I quietly pushed the storage containers into the hall, knowing that David would move them to the garage as soon as he got tired of tripping over them.

All in all, I felt like I'd aced the day. Maybe I didn't get rid of anything, but I did move it all around, which counts for something.

8 P.M.

David was working late again, so with Aubrey sleeping soundly, tuckered out from another splashy bath, I took the opportunity to learn a little more about my Motherhood Better Bootcamp competitors. While we're buddy-buddy on the conference calls, at the end of the day, we all want to take home the $100,000 grand prize.

Based on their Motherhood Better community posts and profiles, I think I know who'll be the biggest competition.

Fiona Martin: mom of three. Despite probably being up to her armpits in diapers, during the craft challenge she learned how to jar fresh tomatoes from her garden and crocheted hats for an entire neonatal intensive care unit.

Janice Paulsen: mom of three girls ages three months, four, and six. She took the body challenge and ran with it. Literally. She completed her first marathon last week and is launching her own line of weightlifting DVDs for postpartum moms.

And last, but not least, Samantha Davidson: mom of two-year-old Henry. I knew her face looked familiar. Samantha's a hugely popular mom blogger. Her website, Homestead Mama, is full of gorgeous photos of her ranch and horses, and her down-home country recipes.

I can't even look at her dishes after 9 p.m. They say her macaroni and cheese changes lives. What is she doing in this competition? Every other pic on her blog is of her beautiful son running through wheat fields in overalls with a red bandana around his neck and a cowboy hat sitting atop his golden ringlets. I read all of her Motherhood Better journal entries and she's completing them perfectly. For the marriage challenge she took it a step further by organizing a massive in-hospital date night for pregnant moms on bed rest. It was catered by a Mexican restaurant and she even hired a mariachi band.

I know I said I wasn't only in it for the grand prize, but I've been thinking of what I could do with $100,000…anyway, it's out of the question for me unless I can figure out a way to make myself stand out—and fast.

Wednesday, February 27, Middle of the Night Sometime/Too Tired to Care

Establishing a sleep schedule is vital, not only for your child, but for your own well-being. Thanks to the Family Bed, all five of my children slept through the night by three days old.

—Emily Walker, *Motherhood Better*

Aubrey woke up again. That's four times in one night, not that I'm counting. I refuse to look at the clock right now. I don't even want to know what time it is.

I've tried everything to help her teething: an amber tree sap necklace that the woman with henna tattoos on her arms at the health store promised would work like a miracle, aspirin and mouth-numbing cream. I even tried homeopathic remedies, although David said they're practically water. At this point I'll give anything a shot.

Nothing is working. I'm starting to wonder if something more serious is wrong with her. I'm researching online now. Maybe something terrible is wrong in her body. Like a tumor. Here I am, worried about my sleep, when my baby's kidneys are being squished by tumors.

To: Dr. Ross
From: Ashley Keller
Subject: Emergency Appointment
Dear Dr. Ross,
I know it's late, but I couldn't find your home or cell phone online anywhere. I'd like to set up an emergency full-body scan for Aubrey first thing in the morning. She's been screaming all night and something is seriously wrong. Attached are 47 pages of my findings.
Thank you.
Ashley

To: Ashley Keller
From. Dr. Cynthia Ross, Pediatrics
Subject: Re: Emergency Appointment
Hello Ashley,
I'm sorry to hear that Aubrey isn't feeling well. She seemed fine at her last appointment. It sounds like she's teething and possibly going through a growth spurt. I went over your "findings" (which seemed to be links to various blogs and obscure pseudo-scientific medical websites) and would like you to stop Googling her symptoms.

Full body scans are not done on children Aubrey's age, nor does she need one.

I suggest Tylenol and something cold to chew on, like a frozen washcloth.

As for my home and cell phone numbers, I don't give those

out to patients. You are free to leave a message at the office or email me anytime. As always, in a (true) emergency, don't hesitate to call 911.

Take care,
Dr. Cynthia Ross

To: Dr. Ross
From: Ashley Keller
Subject: Re: Re: Emergency Appointment
Thank you so much for the advice. Did you happen to check out any of those links? I'm wondering if the connection between dust mites and molar pain have any substance to them? I already purchased the dust mite elimination ray advertised and plan to sweep the whole house with it. They're on sale for $399 if you're interested in one for the office.

If I had your cell phone number it would much easier to just text you the direct link. I would only use it in emergencies like this, and wouldn't give your number to anyone else.

Aubrey's settled down a bit. Most of her crying is done at night. Do you make night appointments? House calls? Like in old movies?
Ashley

To: Ashley Keller
From: Dr. Cynthia Ross
Subject: Re: Re: Re: Emergency Appointment
I don't make house calls or book "night appointments." The article about dust mites was complete lunacy and I hope the dust mite ray comes gold-plated at that price.

Feel free to call the office and make an appointment anytime. I only ask that you not bring your binder of printouts from the internet as they tend to make our visits last much longer than they need to.

Take care,
Dr. Ross

10 A.M.

> I credit fresh air, good food and exercise for my chil
> dren never having so much as a sniffle. Mother Nature
> is their pediatrician.
>
> —Emily Walker, *Motherhood Better*

There must be a way to let someone know that their baby doesn't have a dust mite-induced infection without laughing in their face, right? If there is, Dr. Ross hasn't heard of it.

If I wasn't so tired I would have said something like, *Excuse me if I don't have more experience with teething, but if you'd heard my child crying you would have thought her internal organs were being disintegrated by the toxic feces of microscopic pests, too.*

But I didn't.

We were in the driveway. Aubrey was sleeping in her stroller. There was no way I was moving her. Maybe I could catch some Z's, too. So tired.

11:45 P.M.

> For teething pain I highly recommend using aromather-
> apy. My babies love the smell of lavender and jasmine dif-
> fused through Baltic sea water. Who needs big pharma
> when we have precious oils?
>
> —Emily Walker, *Motherhood Better*

Aubrey woke up again. I brought her into our room even though Joy's #1 rule of parenting is "Never let them into your bed." Aubrey was sleeping at my side now, and I had about six inches of space so I figured I'd just stay awake until morning.

I couldn't go back to sleep if I tried. The type of shrill yell she woke me up with sent about fourteen gallons of adrenaline into my bloodstream. David, of course, slept peacefully through the whole thing. Would it be wrong to heat a fork and poke him with it? Kidding.

Thursday, February 28, 5 A.M.

I was beyond exhausted. Over the last few days I'd probably gotten eight hours of sleep total. Aubrey would only doze when I was holding her. I'd tried every over-the-counter remedy, every hippie remedy and everything in between. I even burned sage in the corners of her bedroom to ward off bad energy. That was Joy's idea.

"Have you considered taking her to a channel to see if there's something in a past life upsetting her?" was another bit of Joy's brilliant advice.

"No, but thanks for the tip."

"It's all so strange. Ella sleeps soundly. So does George."

The worst thing a mom can do is brag when you're complaining.

"Oh, you're struggling to lose ten pounds? I can't seem to gain weight!"

"Oh, you're having financial problems? We can't figure out whether to buy a yacht or another summer home!"

So there we were, at 5 a.m., once again standing in the

kitchen, Aubrey in her pink-and-white footie pajamas and me in one of David's old college T-shirts and sweatpants. The sad fact was that I was dressed for the day. One great thing about being exhausted is that you don't care what anyone thinks of your outfit choices.

Aubrey leaned into my chest and I pushed the black start button on the coffeemaker while I hugged her to my body with my free arm. She nuzzled. She was obviously tired—why wouldn't she sleep? Was this normal?

Facebook Status: I remember when I thought eight o'clock classes were too early. Zzzzzzz.

The coffee machine sizzled as it finished pouring the steaming black liquid into my Best Mommy Ever mug. David had surprised me with it in the birthing center. Wishful thinking, I suppose.

I dumped in all the vanilla creamer that would fit into the cup without splashing out and stirred it quickly with my finger.

Toting my coffee and daughter, I shuffled over to the couch and flipped the TV on to some home makeover show. It was always entertaining, seeing a dilapidated basement go from unfinished baseboards and exposed wires to an impressive, impeccably designed playroom.

I took a greedy sip of my coffee. Sweet and delicious. What would I do without this comforting blend of caffeine and sugar? Motherhood would be absolutely impossible without it. Suddenly, I realized that with all of Aubrey's sleep issues I hadn't checked in to the portal for over forty-eight hours. I wonder what I'd missed. Probably Samantha Davidson sharing photos of a baby calf she delivered with her own hands or Serena Hossfield posting a recipe for homemade toothpaste.

There was a message from two days ago, but it was from Emily herself! What did I miss? I shifted Aubrey, who was now sleeping, in my arms, and moved as close as I could to the screen. What had she said?

Motherhood Better Message:
From: Emily Walker
To: <<Entire Group>>
Hello ladies! I'm loving your posts about the Home Challenge. Samantha, your hand-reupholstered dining room set looks fantastic! Bravo! And Heather, the canary yellow paint is just what your kitchen needed. It looks full of sunlight!

I have a surprise for all of you. As I hinted during our last web call, I'm launching a new line called Emily at Home that will feature beautiful and practical items from furniture to hand towels. To make this challenge a little more exciting, I'm sending my right-hand man and chief designer, François De La Rose, to each of your homes for a one-on-one consultation! He'll help you use what you have, along with a few complimentary pieces from my line, to finish out this challenge with a bang!

I've posted appointment assignments below. If you need to reschedule, let me know ASAP, otherwise I'll assume we're good to go.
Happy designing!
Love and Hugs,
Emily

I scanned the bottom of the email with all of the ladies' names, cities and dates until I found mine.

Ashley Keller....what? That date can't be right. I opened my computer's calendar and sure enough...today. François De La Rose was coming to my house today. In three hours, to be exact.

I looked down at Aubrey, who was snoring contentedly in

my arms, and then up at the pile of underwear and socks in the middle of my living room, three days' worth of mail, one day's worth of breakfast and a week's worth of snack remnants on the dining room table. A trail of granola bar littered the entire floor. The kitchen sink was overflowing with dishes. My bedroom was a mess. Aubrey's bedroom had toys everywhere and this famous French interior designer, who reports directly to Emily and influences who wins the Motherhood Better Bootcamp, would be here in three, no, two hours and forty-five minutes.

Well, shoot.

I crept up the stairs and gently laid Aubrey down in her crib. She gave me two seconds before she stirred awake and began to cry softly. I picked her back up knowing that she'd be in a full-blown howl in minutes. The only thing left to do was to speed clean. With one hand, naturally.

With Aubrey in one arm and a garbage bag in the other, I began throwing things into the bag. It made no difference whether it was clothing, a paper plate, socks or a checkbook, it went in the bag. I could sort it out later. For now, I had to convince François De La Rose that I was not the maternal version of Oscar the Grouch.

An hour and six bags hidden in my closet under a comforter later, the house looked deceivingly put together. Aubrey still lay comfortably in my arms, even though I'd had to switch her from side to side numerous times as my cut-off circulation turned all sensation in my arms to pins and needles. I rushed over to the sink. The dishes. The dishwasher was full so I rinsed the cups and plates before stacking them in the oven.

The house looked cleaner than it had in months and I still had a full hour to get dressed.

I was halfway up the stairs when the doorbell rang.

"Please be the mail, please be the mail," I murmured to myself, running toward the door.

I swung it open and standing before me was not the mailman, unless the mailman was a four-foot-three, tanned and Botoxed Frenchman wearing an all-white satin suit and crimson crocodile shoes with a matching red bow tie, who traveled with a full camera crew.

"*Allo*, mama!" the man said, waving his hands with flourish. A camera flashed and the light blinded me and caused Aubrey to stir. "*Je m'appelle* François De La Rose!" he said, entering the house while looking madly around.

The crew of three burly men dressed in black work pants and black short-sleeved shirts, and one mousy-looking intern in a wool skirt and collared T-shirt covered with a dark vest, followed.

I followed François as he made his way into the living room. He looked around with a troubled expression on his face, as if the place were on fire or crawling with poisonous snakes.

He remembered I was there and turned to face me.

"*Chérie*. You must be Ashley," he said sweetly before kissing me on either cheek. He inhaled sharply, "And this precious *bébé, elle s'appelle comment?*"

He gently tapped Aubrey, who was fully awake now and staring at the men with lights and cameras, on the head.

"She's Aubrey. It is so nice to meet you! Thank you for coming! Can I get you anything? Coffee? Tea? Wine? I would have had something prepared but…" I rambled on.

The camera crew stayed close, focusing the lights and microphones on us. Their lights felt like a laser beam. I had no idea this would be videotaped. Could I be any less prepared? I smoothed the front of my T-shirt and sucked in while trying to remember the last time I had washed my hair.

"I'm so sorry, I was just about to get in the shower—" I

blubbered, wishing they would turn the damn cameras off for a minute.

François held one hand up. "No, sorry. You are a busy mama of..." He looked around the room as if something was missing. "How many kids zoo you have?"

I felt my face get hot and coughed self-consciously into my hand. "Just the one. I have one child."

François's eyes grew large and he laughed loudly. "One? *Mais non*, surely there are three or four children who live in zee home. Whose things are zese?" he asked, gesturing at the overflowing toy bin, walker, bouncy chair, exersaucer, sippy cups and piles of baby clothes. "Zoo you run a daycare?"

I shifted from foot to foot. "No daycare, just the one."

François gestured around the room, unable to comprehend what I was saying. "*Mais* surely, you are hiding some extra children somewhere?" He lifted a couch cushion, perhaps hoping to find triplet three-year-olds, but all he discovered were three stale French fries and a heavy dusting of crumbs.

He jumped as if the furniture food had startled him. "OH, MY!"

Forcing a smile, I lowered the couch cushion and gestured for him to sit directly on top of it.

François sat next to me, shifting as if he could feel every hard morsel under the cushion a la Princess and the Pea, and took my hand, "I see now why you have joined zee challenge. But do not worry, *chérie*. François is here to clean up your space."

One hour and frantic half-French, half-English phone calls to an interior designer, professional organizer and commercial cleaner (François thought a domestic cleaner might get overwhelmed by my home) later, everything was in motion for my home to go from raccoon Dumpster party to gorgeous family home. The cleaner was coming tomorrow morning, followed by the designer, then the organizer. They weren't doing anything drastic, but "optimizing my space."

I was overwhelmed with excitement.

"Thank you so much, François," I gushed.

Without answering he bent down and pulled a black binder out of his satchel. "Wait, mademoiselle, zere is more." He smiled devilishly.

Tickets to Jamaica? Free babysitting for life? A sister wife?

He opened the binder. The first page was a glossy insert with Emily Walker Home printed in white calligraphy.

"Emily Walker has arranged for all of zee women to preview the Emily Walker Home line," he said in a hushed tone as if the CIA were listening in.

My heart skipped a beat. I'd get to have the Emily Walker line before anyone else? Imagine the Facebook posts. Joy would perish from jealousy.

He handed me the binder and I began to flip through page after page of stunningly beautiful furniture.

François leaned over and turned to a spread. "Allow me. Zis one would look beautiful in your family room."

Before me was a beige leather couch, loveseat and recliner, a coffee table and an entertainment center with loads of hidden storage called the Verdanza Package. It was amazing. I felt tears spring into my eyes. So this is how celebrities feel.

"Yes. I love it. I'll take it," I whispered.

François clapped his hands. "Perfect! How would you like to pay?"

I blinked. "Pay?"

"Ah, *chérie, oui.* Your designers and organizers, and a few pieces are free, but zee entire Emily Walker Home line is being offered to you before the general public at wholesale price because you are in zee...bootcamp."

"Which pieces are free?"

François flipped through the catalog and pointed to a set of three throw pillows. "Zere."

I held my breath. There was no way, even at wholesale prices, I could afford a new living room set.

"How much is it?"

François flipped to the next page.

Verdanza Package: $1,025

That's it? I thought. You can't even buy a couch in some stores for that. This is brand-new designer furniture at prices that will be gone in three months. The pieces themselves will probably sell out. Yes, David is worried about money, but he's always worried about money. That's never going to change. Anyway, he's probably securing the DentaFresh account right now. If I don't buy this set I'll be wasting money, throwing it down the drain.

Furniture is also a great investment. It's so well-made it will last forever. The holidays are coming up. I'd love to host everyone and see the looks on their faces when they see such a chic collection in our home.

François cleared his throat. "Would you like to call your husband?"

I exhaled sharply. A year ago I was managing million-dollar client accounts and now I'm some stay-at-home mom who has to call her husband before making a purchase? Absolutely not. I'm a modern woman. Just because I'm not making the money doesn't mean it doesn't belong to both of us. We're both contributing. If I didn't take care of Aubrey, he wouldn't be able to work. I don't need his permission to spend our money. I'll just use the credit card he doesn't know about.

"Is Visa okay?" I heard myself ask.

"Absolutely."

François copied my card information and promised to send

me a receipt by email. The furniture is set to be delivered a week from tomorrow.

Before leaving he looked around again, perhaps expecting a busload of children to come running down the stairs. I really do need to pick up more. The new living room set is really going to inspire me.

11 P.M.

I just checked my email for the receipt from François.

6-piece Verdanza Package: Emily Walker Home
Ashley Keller
Visa 4875-****-****-****
Total: $8,025

My entire body morphed into an ice cube. Eight thousand and twenty-five dollars. There had to be some mistake. This was someone else's order. I scanned the itemized bill.

3-section couch: $2,500
Loveseat: $1,025
Recliner: $1,025

As I kept reading, *no, no, no, no*, echoed in my head. The price François had shown me was for just one piece, not for the set. How could I have been so dense? I didn't even know if I had that much credit available. I immediately hit Reply to tell François to cancel the order, but something stopped me. If I did, Emily would find out, which would mean not only would I be humiliated in front of my idol, I'd lose any chance of winning the grand prize. I closed the email window.

What was I going to tell David?

Nothing. I was going to tell him absolutely nothing. He

was already worried about money; this would send him over the edge and he'd demand everything go back immediately, which would make all the hard work I'd done in the Motherhood Better Bootcamp a complete waste.

I had to deal with this myself. Either I'd win the prize money or I'd pay it off without him knowing. All I needed was a little side money. How much was $8,025 anyway?

A lot. It was a lot.

Oh, crap.

Friday, March 1,
4:45 P.M.

I spent the entire day trying not to think about the fact that I spent almost $10,000 on furniture behind my husband's back. That's the price of a car. Not a brand-new car, but a good one. That money could have gone toward our mortgage. I remembered David's reaction to the dress I bought for our date that never was and tried to picture his face if he found out about the furniture. He'd blow a fuse. What if he walked out of the house and just drove away? He'd never do that to us…to Aubrey. As I popped a frozen lasagna in the oven, I tried to snap myself out of the fear cycle. "It's only money," I said over and over.

"Ma-nee. Ma-nee," Aubrey repeated from her high chair. She was starting to talk a lot more lately. Note to self: Be careful what I say around her.

I heard my phone vibrate against the countertop.

David. Going to be late. Also, I'm taking my car to the shop tomorrow. Transmission. Oil change. I'll need yours for work.

Well thanks for the notice, I thought. Just because I'm a

stay-at-home mom doesn't mean I actually stay at home all day. Use of a vehicle would be nice. Also, François and his team are coming over to give the house the grand makeover I can't afford. I'd planned to be out all day. Without a car what was I supposed to do? Hang out in the backyard with Aubrey? Set up a tent at the mall?

I quickly fired off a text to David explaining my predicament (minus the furniture we couldn't afford part).

He responded five minutes later with a simple, Problem solved! My mom will pick you up at 9 o'clock and take you to her house.

WHAT? Yes, she may have come through for me with dinner before, and I may have said a few times that I wanted to get to know Gloria better outside of the context where she tells me things like "Your house sure is full of stuff," and "Any thought on when you'll be getting the baby some proper shoes instead of those overpriced granny slippers?" But an entire day?

I was just about to call David when he texted he was going into the DentaFresh pitch. I wished him luck. Now wasn't the time to stress him out. I slammed my phone down on the counter.

"Crap." An entire day with Gloria.

"Cwap. Cwap. Cwap!" Aubrey yelled, hitting her high chair tray to punctuate each word.

I really needed to watch my language.

What was I going to do? There was only one thing I could do. Eat my feelings; tuck them safely into my stomach and thighs. I popped a corn chip into my mouth and washed it down with a generous splash of pinot noir out of a lidless sippy cup.

Aubrey giggled at me from her high chair.

"Tomorrow, we're going to grandma's house." She clapped her hands gleefully.

Saturday, March 2,
8:30 A.M.

I'd spent the last three hours cleaning the house from top to bottom. No more French fries in the couch. I even cleaned out the high chair and discovered that Aubrey has never eaten anything, ever. She's been tucking food away like a rodent under the plastic cushion of her chair. I swear I found enough food to feed a small nation for weeks. But that's all gone now.

Joy called me while I was a tornado of all-purpose cleaner and rags.

"You actually cleaned?" she asked in an irritated tone. As I predicted, she was teeming with jealousy once she found out (via my dramatic Facebook post—the one I'd made before knowing what I'd actually spent) that I'd ordered the Emily Walker Home line and was getting my home redone. Since I'd been accepted into the Motherhood Better Bootcamp, Joy had been downplaying it as my "little support group." It felt good to finally have something over her.

"Yes, I cleaned. I do it all the time," I answered, out of

breath from trying to remove a month's worth of grime from inside the microwave.

"So, what time is Gloria picking you up?" Joy knew how to take the buzz out of any situation.

Gloria. I'd been trying not to think about the fact that I'd be spending the entire day with my mother-in-law.

"Hopefully never o'clock. Are you sure you can't come get me?" I really must have been desperate if I was begging my sister to let me spend the day in her Stepford-land.

"Like I said, I'm making the drive up to see Mom with Ella. We're going to see Veggie Friends on Ice."

I already knew that. I'd tried, and failed, to get tickets to the show even though the televised version makes my ears bleed and the three-hour drive to the arena and back with Ella sounded like pure hell. Anything to avoid the awkward afternoon that lay ahead of me. But they were all sold out.

"Fine. Abandon your sister in her time of need."

Joy huffed. "Oh, stop being so dramatic. Maybe you'll learn something."

I started to say, "What's that supposed to mean?" but Joy cut me off.

"Ella needs a change. Talk to you later!"

As I clicked off, the doorbell rang. Of course Gloria would be early.

I picked up Aubrey from her playpen and held her in front of me like a bulletproof vest. I swung open the door and was surprised to see a team of five women in crisp pink cotton dress uniforms with white aprons holding buckets full of cleaning supplies.

"Happy Maids to the rescue!" one sang.

Another chimed in, "We're happy maids, we love to dust. Get a sparkling house without the fuss!" she belted out.

Aubrey shrieked with happiness at the impromptu musical.

"Wow! That's...something," I said. "Come in, come in." I invited the barbershop quintet inside and they immediately spread out in all directions with mops, buckets and spray bottles filled with a rainbow of colors. I heard water running in the bathroom.

"Okay then, let me know if you need anything..." I'm not sure if any of them heard me as the only two in sight were already sweeping underneath the couches and vacuuming the drapes in the living room.

Suddenly I felt a tap on my shoulder. I turned around and a cheery-looking Happy Maid was standing there, holding a business card.

"I'm Mary! I love being a Happy Maid! We'll be in and out in an hour, Mrs. Keller," she practically sang before running off into the kitchen.

The doorbell rang again. This time when I opened it, standing in front of me was an impossibly tall, slender woman in brown slacks and a T-shirt from the concert of a band I'm probably not cool enough to know. Over the T-shirt she wore an expensive-looking caramel leather jacket with brass buttons. Her hair was in tiny black braids all the way down her back. She looked oddly familiar.

"Hi, I'm Ashley Keller." I stretched out my hand. Aubrey babbled on my hip.

"Hi, Ashley, I'm Shelly Harbor," she said, studying my porch.

Shelly Harbor! The interior designer to the stars! The brains behind every celebrity baby nursery was about to enter the aesthetic disaster I call my home. I gulped.

"Oh, my goodness, Shelly! I'm a big fan. I love your work!" I couldn't believe she was here. In the flesh. A TV person who rubs elbows with famous actors every day. I bet she just came from a mansion with twenty-foot ceilings. My home was going to look like a campground compared to what she normally deals with.

"It's nice to meet you," she said sweetly, entering the house. She carried a white suede clutch with gold accents that somehow paired perfectly with her slacks and T-shirt. Even in white ballet flats she was so glamorous.

"Can I get you anything to drink or eat? Breakfast?" I asked. *Yeah, Ashley, she wants some eggs and orange juice. Get it together. Pretend like you interact with people on a daily basis*, I thought.

She smiled. "I'm fine. It's so great to meet you. Emily sent me the photos from your home and I think there's a lot we can do here."

It was only then that I remembered that I'd sent in photos of every room as part of the bootcamp contest entry form. There was a slight possibility that I'd edited out a little bit of the clutter. If Joy can Photoshop her kid's lashes, is it so wrong to make a little laundry disappear?

Shelly sat down at the kitchen table and opened up a sketchbook with all kinds of collages from magazines. Two feet away from us a Happy Maid was spraying and wiping down the cabinets. We're supposed to clean the cabinets?

Shelly barely seemed to notice, but I found it tough to stay focused with all of the excitement.

"Your home is already beautiful, and the paint looks recent. All that's missing are livable storage spaces for things. I'm thinking a modern country look updated to suit a growing family. How many kids do you have?"

Not again. I shifted Aubrey from one knee to the other. "Just the one."

Shelly touched her face. "Oh… I thought from the photos…"

Apparently I hadn't edited ALL of the clutter out.

"She has a lot of toys."

Shelly smiled kindly. "I'm sure it's normal. You should have seen Emily's house before I redesigned it." She laughed.

Before she redesigned it? I thought Emily did all of her own interior design.

I cleared my throat. "Doesn't Emily—" But I was interrupted by the beeping of a truck backing up.

Shelly stood up. "We have a surprise for you, Ashley! Your Emily Walker Home furniture is coming in today and we threw in a few extras. You're going to love it."

I felt a bubble of excitement begin to rise into my throat. It was followed by a bubble of dread. Who knows, maybe I'll win the lottery...

The doorbell rang again.

Shelly stood up. "It's showtime!"

I swung the door open again and there was François. I was relieved to see that there was no camera crew this time.

"François!"

"*Allo*! I just wanted to pop by and help out any way zat I can!" He pushed past me and hugged Shelly. Of course they'd know each other.

"Did she tell you zee good news?" François said while pulling a little black-and-white striped handkerchief out of his lapel to dab at his brow.

"Yes, the furniture is here! I'm so excited!"

It was then that I noticed François had brought a guest who was still in the doorway. He was tall, in his fifties and was wearing a gray suit and tie. His formal appearance was in stark contrast to Shelly's rockstar glam and François's French chic looks.

"Hello, I'm Ashley." I reached out my hand and he shook it curtly.

François cut in. "Ah, yes. Ashley, I want you to meet Dr. Simpson."

Dr. Simpson stared at me as if he was trying to figure something out. He noted the flurry of cleaning ladies running around in dresses and nodded.

"How brave of you to let them into your space," Dr. Simpson said, nodding toward the Happy Maids. "How are you feeling about this?" He removed a notepad and pen from his jacket pocket.

"Excuse me?" I asked, puzzled.

François touched my elbow. "Is zere somewhere we can sit down?"

"Sure."

Shelly coughed nervously and then excused herself. "I'm going to help the delivery men...good luck."

I led Dr. Simpson and François to the couch where a Happy Maid was using a broom to hit toys out from under the recliner. A sippy cup filled with what had probably been milk at some point came shooting out and hit the wall, causing the top to fall off and a cottage-cheese-like substance to come spraying out. I was mortified.

I stood to help. "I'll get that." But the Happy Maid just waved me away and began cleaning it up with gloved hands.

At the sight of her forgotten cup, Aubrey tried to leap out of my lap and slurp down its rotten contents.

"No, Aubrey, yucky." I distracted her with a stuffed octopus with mirrors on each tentacle.

I looked up to see Dr. Simpson and François staring at me. François had a look of abject horror on his face. It's probably not every day he sees homemade cheese spray all over a wall.

Dr. Simpson and François sat on either side of me.

François shifted nervously. "Ashley. I brought zee doctor here after seeing your condition yesterday," he spoke calmly, as if talking down a toddler holding a Sharpie.

"What condition?" I asked, while Aubrey pulled my hair.

I looked at Dr. Simpson whose presence was starting to feel more and more looming, especially with him studying my face as if I were a specimen under a microscope.

The doctor cleared his throat. "Ashley, being a hoarder is nothing to be ashamed of. I'm here to see if we can make some breakthroughs today."

I choked on the air and burst out laughing. "A hoarder? I'm not a hoarder! Would a hoarder's house look like this?" I gestured around the room and quickly figured out that while it looked clean to me, three laundry baskets of clothes, an entire wall of toys, and the recent cup o'curds weren't helping my argument.

"No one eez judging you. We only want you to not live in your own filth." François nodded patronizingly.

I sputtered, feeling insulted. "Okay, look. I buy my daughter a lot of toys but I'm not a hoarder. Dr. Simpson, feel free to tour my home and see for yourself."

Dr. Simpson nodded without saying a word as if he were witnessing massive denial.

Suddenly a Happy Maid holding a large garbage bag was standing in front of us.

"Mrs. Keller, what would you like to do with this?" Oh, no. It was one of the "hurry up people are coming" bags from my bedroom. To my absolute shock she emptied the bag right there on the living room floor. Dr. Simpson, François and I stared at the foot-high pile of underwear, solo socks, candy wrappers, a wine bottle or two, stuffed animals and other random goods.

I set Aubrey on the floor and began hurriedly tossing items back into the bag.

I looked up at Dr. Simpson. "I was in a rush to clean." I swiveled my head to the Happy Maid whose ever-present smile had slightly faded. "I'll take care of this."

It took half an hour and a tour of my home, but I finally convinced Dr. Simpson and François that I wasn't a hoarder, just very bad at home management.

"Ah, so you are just very messy, zen!" François declared happily.

"Exactly!" I agreed.

François took my hand "I'm so, so sorry, Ashley. I was simply worried," he explained.

"It's quite alright," I said, feeling both embarrassed and relieved. At least now when David complains about the house I can say that a psychiatrist signed off on it.

"If you ever want to get to the root of your issues, feel free to get in touch," Dr. Simpson said before handing me his card.

François and I bid Dr. Simpson adieu. When we closed the door I gave him a look.

"I am so sorry, Ashley. I just had to be sure," he sputtered.

"It's alright," I assured him. He probably just hadn't seen many homes cared for by first-time moms with an Amazon Prime account. Which led me to wonder. What did the other moms' houses look like?

"Am I the first bootcamp mom you're visiting?" I inquired.

"*Mais* no, I have already completed five home transformations!" I gulped. That means he had seen other houses and mine was the worst.

"And my house was the messiest so far?" I squeaked.

François tapped my shoulder the way someone would try to comfort a potentially volatile person.

"Zere, zere, Ashley. It's not a competition."

Actually, it was. And $100,000 plus my pride was on the line.

François puttered off to consult with Shelly about the placement of the new furniture. I couldn't bring myself to look at it quite yet. Not when it symbolized the potential destruction of my husband's trust in me. As I walked upstairs to change Aubrey, I passed a Happy Maid pushing my bed away from the wall to vacuum. We're supposed to do that? Move furniture to clean?

Once Aubrey was changed, I packed her diaper bag and sat on the front porch with her while she devoured a bag of crackers. It felt so weird to have people in my home. François assured me that he would stay until the last person left and lock up. "You are going to be dazzled when you return." I had to admit that I was excited.

Aubrey shoved another cracker into her mouth and greedily gummed it until it dissolved.

"She might eat more at meals if she didn't snack so much," a voice said. I didn't have to look up to know who it was.

"Hello, Gloria." I picked up Aubrey and handed her to Grandma.

Gloria was dressed resort casual in white capris and a brightly colored, flowing button-up top decorated with a tropical jungle print complete with several toucans. Her large white sun hat was tied under her chin.

Aubrey screamed happily as Gloria nuzzled her.

"My sweet girl! What are you eating? Oh, you're so hungry! Did you have breakfast? You feel lighter. Does she feel lighter to you?"

She bounced Aubrey up and down like a melon.

"She is a little bit lighter but only because I'm starving her," I joked dryly.

Gloria pursed her lips. She never did appreciate my sarcasm. "Are we ready to go? I can't wait to spend the day with you!" she squealed, looking at Aubrey.

"It's going to be fun!" I tried to convince myself, grabbing my diaper bag.

Gloria began walking Aubrey to the car. Thankfully David

had installed the car seat the night before. She turned back to me. "Did you remember the diapers? I'd hate for my grand-baby to have to suffer through another panty debacle."

My face went hot. "Diapers are all here."

Five minutes later we were rushing down the highway, Gloria in the driver's seat, me in my own personal Hades.

To Grandmother's house we go.

When we arrived at Gloria's house I was prepared to hear Terry yapping away as we walked up to the door, but it was quiet.

She guessed what I was thinking, "He's at the vet today. Gall bladder surgery. A doggy mommy's work is never done."

Gloria opened the front door and Aubrey and I followed her inside David's childhood home.

The décor was tropical island chic, her favorite. Crystal palm trees from every vacation spot she'd ever been to, paint-ings of beaches with white sand and little dancing figurines that shook their hips when touched could be seen in every cor-ner. It looked more like a hotel gift shop than a home. It had been many years since Mr. Keller had passed away, but Gloria had kept the massive three-story house rather than moving into a condo like David begged her to, and no wonder—half of her things would have to go into storage.

I set the diaper bag on the floor near the stairs. Aubrey put her hands in the air toward her grandmother, begging her to come get her.

"I have a treat for my little princess!" Gloria sang, as she whisked Aubrey into her arms and took her into the family room.

I followed them and heard Aubrey scream in delight. When I rounded the corner, before me was a three-foot by three-foot by three-foot plastic multicolored cube of flashing lights, whirring parts and spinning tops.

"It's the BabyBox!" declared Gloria. "Have you heard of it?"

My mouth hung agape. Yes, I'd heard of it. It was listed on VillageofMommies as the most obnoxious toy of the year. It was twenty-seven cubic feet of migraine-inducing noise and seizure-inspiring lights, had only one volume level and was known to turn on spontaneously in the dead of night. It was designed as an interactive toy for toddlers—there were buttons to push and levers to pull all around the cube—but I'd made a mental note to never own one because it broke my number-one toy rule: never own a toy louder than your child. It was also HUGE.

"Wow, Gloria..." I struggled to find the words. "This is so neat!"

I bent down to sit on the floor next to Aubrey. She poked a bright blue button and a song erupted like an outbreak of herpes. "WE LOVE SHAPES! SHAPES LOVE US! SHAPES ARE FUN SO FUN SO FUN!"

This was the kind of music that, when played backward, said things like, "Get a knife. Kill kill kill." There was no way this was coming home with us.

Gloria clapped her hands, "This one is for my house."

I breathed a sigh of relief. "I bought one for yours, too. You still have to put it together, though."

She pointed to an enormous box in the corner that looked like it contained several thousand individual parts.

Why me? Why?

"Thanks, Gloria. Aubrey seems to really love it."

"I'll go check on lunch. I have minestrone soup in the slow cooker. Slow-cooker meals are really easy, Ashley. Even for people with not a lot of experience in the kitchen. I'll give you the recipe," she said, walking into the kitchen.

I gritted my teeth. Aubrey pushed another button. "SQUARE! RED SQUARE! YOU DID IT! HOORAY!"

At home Aubrey's attention span lasts ten seconds and she floats from toy to me to another toy to me so quickly I get dizzy. But when it came to the Hell Cube, she played with it for a solid hour and a half until it was time for lunch. Maybe it wouldn't be so bad. I'd just have to figure out a way to disable the sound. I could already feel a headache coming on from the incessant noise.

I rooted around my purse for an aspirin. I'd never been so happy to hear someone say, "Lunchtime!"

Gloria insisted that we eat in the formal dining room and had set three places.

"Are you expecting someone?" I said, looking at the third plate and flatware.

Gloria picked up Aubrey and placed her on the chair in front of an adult bowl, plate, fork, knife and glass. An actual glass.

"If you train children to sit at the table, it encourages good eating habits," she said, in a kindergarten teacher tone.

I said nothing and sat down, placing the beige linen napkin on my lap. I decided to let the natural consequences play out. Of course, I'd make sure Aubrey didn't hurt herself with the table knife or the broken glass when she inevitably threw it against the wall like she does with her sippy cup for every meal, but I wasn't going to save the day.

Gloria fit a little white bib around Aubrey's neck. It was the size of a dollar bill. For meals at home, I've resorted to stripping Aubrey naked. For a while I used those full-frontal plastic bibs intended for toddlers when fingerpainting to keep her clean, but even that didn't stop her from mashing a handful of potatoes into her back.

"That's a very cute bib," I said pleasantly.

"Now say ahhh," Gloria instructed, bringing a spoonful of room-temperature soup to Aubrey's mouth. The spoon contained beans, pasta and green peas swimming in a red broth.

The last time I tried to put a mix of foods in Aubrey's mouth, she spat it directly in my face. This should be interesting. I looked down so that my smile would be concealed.

"Ahhh!" I heard my daughter's voice say.

My eyes darted upward just in time to see her eat the entire bite, chew it with her gums, then open her mouth for another.

What kind of witchcraft was this? I watched in disgust and amazement as the process was repeated until Aubrey finished the entire bowl of soup.

"You were a hungry girl, weren't you!" exclaimed Gloria, placing the bowl and spoon in the sink. "Ashley, you really must attempt this recipe."

Attempt?

When lunch was all cleaned up, I watched while the two played with the Torture Cube for a few minutes before Gloria announced that she was putting Aubrey down for a nap. I relaxed into the couch. Finally, I'd have some time to myself. Nap time meant twenty minutes of rocking Aubrey before she finally settled down. If Gloria wanted to take that on, she was more than welcome.

I kissed Aubrey on the cheek and handed her to Grandma. "Good luck!"

When I heard Gloria walking back down the steps after two minutes, I stood with a start.

"Do you need some help?" I offered, a smug smile playing across my lips.

"No." Gloria took a seat on the recliner. "She went right down. She always does when she's here. It's all about having a routine."

"We have a routine," I muttered, sitting back down.

Now what were we going to talk about? Being alone with Gloria isn't something I look forward to.

"So, Ashley. How is my David?" she asked innocently.

Why did she always call him "my David"? Of course, he'd always be her son, but the phrase sounded so unnecessarily possessive.

"Your David is fine. He's a little stressed about the business, but they've all but landed a huge account."

"The DentaFresh account?"

I sat up, startled. How did she know? "Yes, actually."

Gloria took a sip of her tea. "No, that client went to another company. David called me yesterday. He was really upset. He didn't tell you?"

My body stiffened. It took everything not to run out of the room and call David immediately. What did she mean he didn't get the account? And he told his mom, but not me?

"Oh, I must have confused them for another company. My mind is so jumbled these days." I slowly pulled my phone out of my pocket. "Excuse me. I'm just going to check on how the home makeover is going."

I ducked into the kitchen and fired off a quick text to David. Did you lose the DentaFresh pitch and not tell me but tell YOUR MOM?

I slid my phone back into my pocket. I walked calmly back into the living room and sat back down.

Gloria cleared her throat. "How is that…bootcamp going? Is it helping much?"

Why didn't she just say "Is it helping you be less of a screwup?" That's what she meant, I was sure.

"I'm actually learning a lot," I said flatly. I'd hoped not offering any other details would mean the end of the conversation. I was more than happy to sit in silence on my phone, like I do at home while Aubrey slept.

"You could have just come to me, of course. I can teach you everything you need to know about raising kids."

"Yes, you're very knowledgeable." I smiled tightly. In my pocket, my phone buzzed.

I discreetly pulled it out. On the screen was a text from David.

I was going to talk to you about it tonight. I didn't think she'd say anything. Sorry.

That's all he had to say for himself?

Is everything going to be ok? I texted.

"Tell David I say hi," sang Gloria.

I looked up and smiled.

We'll talk about it later, he texted back.

I tucked my phone away again.

"I think I heard Aubrey. I'd better check on her," I lied, standing up.

"Feel free to lie down in the guest bedroom if you'd like. You should always sleep when the baby sleeps."

I took her up on the offer and, after peeking in on a peacefully sleeping Aubrey, fell into an exhausted sleep in the Caribbean-themed guest bedroom.

I woke up to Gloria gently whispering my name. "Ashley. Ashley. David is here to pick you up."

My head swam. What day was it? What time? Where was I?

Gloria read my mind. "It's 4 o'clock in the afternoon. Aubrey woke up an hour ago and we've been playing. I didn't want to wake you."

Bless her for that. I must have been exhausted. I rubbed my eyes and reluctantly lifted my head from the soft palm-tree-printed pillow.

"Thanks, Gloria," I said, putting on my shoes. "I really appreciate it."

Gloria sat next to me on the bed. "Don't be mad at David for not telling you. He probably just didn't want you to worry."

This wasn't a conversation I felt comfortable having. "I know."

"Maybe he'd feel more comfortable talking to you if you didn't seem so angry all the time…"

I felt my heart skip a beat.

"Angry?"

"Yes, he says you're always upset and stressed."

I turned to face her. "He talks about me?" My blood began boiling.

"Just a little. I *am* his mother."

And he's still your baby boy, apparently.

I couldn't hold back my emotions, they were coming at me faster than I could screen them. "I appreciate you letting me sleep, but please stay out of my marriage."

Gloria sputtered. "I didn't get into your marriage. David brought me in when he couldn't talk to you…"

"Well," was all I managed to say. With that I stood up and began walking toward the door. I didn't want to be rude but angry tears had already sprung into my eyes and I wanted to hang on to the few shreds of dignity I had left.

My legs were still struggling to wake up as I made my way down the stairs, and I tripped a little on the bottom step. David's arm reached out to steady me.

"Hi, Ashley! Did you sleep well?" He was grinning and holding a contented Aubrey.

I shot daggers at him with my eyes. "So you think I'm always angry?"

David shot a pleading glance up the stairs to where his mom was standing.

"She can't save you now." I picked up Aubrey's bag and walked out the door to wait in the car.

When David finished buckling Aubrey into her seat, he turned to me. "Ashley, I just—"

I put up a hand. "Don't. I'm not talking to you with your mom watching from the window." I turned toward the house, and sure enough a drape fell where Gloria had been watching.

"Okay, fine." David turned over the ignition.

When we were a block away, I unleashed.

"How dare you discuss our marriage with your mom? And tell her about the DentaFresh account before me, knowing I was spending the day here? You made me look like an idiot. An angry idiot."

David kept his eyes on the road and struggled to find the words. "I was just stressed and needed someone to talk to, Ashley..."

"The person you talk to is me. Not your mom."

"I'd love to talk to you but you're either complaining, frustrated, angry at me or exhausted from Aubrey," he spit out.

"And you're not preoccupied at all? You're at work almost all the time and when you're home, you're relaxing from work. Do you see me ever relaxing? That nap I had was the best rest I've gotten in months."

David erupted. "Yes, I know! You hate your life. I'm failing at work and I'm failing to make you happy. I get it, Ashley! Okay?"

He was practically shaking. I sat, shocked, staring at him.

"I don't..." I put a hand on his on the steering wheel. "I don't hate my life... I'm just stressed. And you're not failing..."

David was quiet for a moment. "Yes, I am, Ashley. We lost the DentaFresh account. It's over. We're going to have to sell the house."

I felt the wind get knocked out of me. I knew things were hard but I didn't know they were that bad. Sell the house?

Where would we live? My blood ran cold. The furniture bill. I still hadn't told him about the $8,000.

I took a deep breath. "David, I have something to tell you."

He turned to glance at me. "What is it?"

"The home makeover… I thought I spent a grand on the furniture…"

David clenched his teeth. "Ashley, we don't have an extra thousand!"

I kept going, determined. "But I really spent $8,000. I put it on my credit card. It's nonrefundable." It was true. It was in the fine print.

David slammed the steering wheel with his hand. "Dammit, Ashley! That's our entire savings. It was going to help us find a rental if we move."

I felt a tear slide down my cheek. "I'm so sorry."

David's shoulders hunched over in utter defeat. "If I don't get another account, we won't be able to afford a rental. We'll probably have to stay with my mom for a while."

My stomach flip-flopped. "With your mom? For how long?"

"A few months. Hopefully."

We didn't speak for the rest of the ride home.

When we arrived at the house, everything was locked up, just as François had promised. The door swung open and all was dark. It wasn't until David flipped on the light that I saw it. I gasped. It was a whole new house. Everything sparkled and shone.

Even David said "Wow" under his breath. "I'm going to put Aubrey down," he said gently, before heading upstairs. I could barely reply as I looked around.

It was like walking into one of those home-and-garden magazines. The wooden floors were brighter than I'd ever seen them. I floated into the kitchen and, as the light flooded it, I was dazzled. Nothing was out of place and everything looked so fresh, like it was right off the assembly line. I couldn't find a speck of grime or a crumb anywhere. I opened a cabinet, and instead of almost being buried in plastic containers falling out, found everything stacked neatly.

I wandered into the living room. The furniture. It was even more beautiful than the catalog had promised. The living room set was perfectly placed and screamed "luxury." Aubrey's toys were nowhere to be seen—I lifted up the soft leather ottoman and found them tucked out of sight. They'd even thrown in a large chestnut area rug and several beautiful wooden spheres for the mantel. Was this really my house? I collapsed onto the couch and it supported and hugged my body at the same time. It all certainly looked like $8,000. Or more. I felt like I was in an episode of *Lifestyles of the Rich and Famous*, only in a parallel universe where I'd only get to enjoy these things for less than a month before we had to sell them online to afford utilities.

I wrung my hands together. I looked at the corner where Aubrey had rolled over for the first time on the colored mats that were nowhere to be found. I guess Shelly thought they didn't fit in with the décor. I stared at the middle of the floor, where I'd spent more afternoons than I could count folding laundry while Aubrey lay on her back and tried to bite her toes. The laundry was gone; finally put away. Everything was how I'd always wanted it, but not at all right. For the past ten months I'd felt trapped in this house, and now it was all going away.

I curled up on the oversized couch, tucked my knees into my chest and cried.

Sunday, March 3,
9:30 A.M.

David barely spoke this morning, other than to tell me that a Realtor was coming to look at the house sometime this week. I couldn't believe this was really happening. He said if we couldn't find a place to rent for the right price, he'd have to ask his mom if we could stay with her for a few months.

He'd already put in résumés with marketing firms, but in the meantime, he said we were in what he called "money-saving mode." I think that was code for "don't spend another $8K on furniture, please." What he didn't seem to understand was that I was the one who would be staying home with Aubrey and his mom all day. He asked me if I wanted to go back to work and have Gloria watch the baby, and suddenly all I wanted to be was a stay-at-home mom.

For the past ten months I'd been complaining about how hard life was and not realizing how hard it could get.

I looked over to where Aubrey was sleeping peacefully on her back in her playpen. The last Motherhood Better Boot-

CONFESSIONS OF A DOMESTIC FAILURE   255

camp call was tomorrow. I'd submitted my Home Challenge diary entry already.

Hi everyone,
I'd like to thank Emily for the amazing work her team did on my home. It's cleaner and more organized that I've ever seen it. It's how I always dreamed my house would look. The new Verdanza living room set is an absolute dream. My home looks incredible. The only thing I could ask for now is for great memories to be had in it.
Ashley Keller

I included Before and After photos, and everyone oohed and aahed in the comments. The difference really was striking, but it all felt so hollow. It was such a cruel twist of fate for me to finally have the house I wanted but to have to give it away in two weeks.

The one piece of good news was that I'd be flying out to Napa this week for the Motherhood Better Bootcamp Finale. Did I mention that I was going to be on TV? No? That's because I only just found out. Emily posted in the portal early this morning that we'd be spending Thursday relaxing in outdoor hot tubs, being treated to massages, and getting a personalized makeover. But on Friday we'd be broadcasting live on *The Emily Walker Show* to announce the winner.

At this point, I'm not holding my breath. While I was conning my way into mom groups and working for phone sex companies, Janice Paulsen from Minnesota lost twenty-five pounds and raised $20,000 for a charity that matches foster children up with available families. Heather Logan has pumped over 300 ounces of breast milk for preemies, and Naomi Price knitted 150 quilts for moms on bed rest in her local maternity ward.

Tomorrow is my last La Lait meeting before my trip and I've decided to come clean. Before the general announcements, I'm going to stand up and apologize to everyone for misleading them and beg them to let me stay. I owe them the truth.

Having to give up the house is putting everything into perspective. I can't live any more lies.

Monday, March 4, 10:30 A.M.

The last Motherhood Better Bootcamp video chat was this morning. Emily looked as chipper as ever wearing her new line of athletic gear: EW Move. She had on a white crushed-velvet tracksuit with her initials monogrammed over the chest.

"Is everyone ready for our Napa getaway tomorrow? I've been reading your wrap-up posts and can't think of a group of moms more deserving."

The wrap-up posts she was referring to were the 200-word personal reflection essays, due by tonight at midnight, that summarized what we'd learned from the bootcamp. I hadn't submitted mine yet.

"Don't forget to send yours in by tonight. No matter what happens on Friday, you're all winners in my book," Emily said, her hand dramatically placed over her heart.

Winners, right, I thought, bouncing a squirmy Aubrey on my lap. I tried to focus on the call but couldn't stop thinking about the La Lait meeting in an hour.

What were they going to say? I pictured myself standing in

the middle of the room being squirted aggressively with milk from all directions, straight from the nipples of the moms I'd offended. "Please, stop. I'm sorry!" I'd yell, trying to shield Aubrey from the sprays of milky anger.

Emily's voice cut through my nightmare. "This week, I want you to reflect on everything you've learned because you'll be sharing a few words live on my show. I can't wait to see all of you on Wednesday night. My personal chef will be preparing all of our meals, and for Thursday I've also booked you head-to-toe makeovers!"

Everyone oohed giddily and clapped their hands. I managed a halfhearted smile. A month ago, the thought of a few days away, a haircut and a soak in a hot tub would have left me dizzy with glee, but between our impending move and the inevitable loss of my only friends, I couldn't get excited.

"I'm just so proud of all of you. Hugs and kisses, ladies!" Emily said, blowing a kiss to her webcam.

When the chat screen closed, I shut my computer and carried Aubrey into her bedroom. I changed her diaper and put her into a pair of gray sweatpants and a matching hoodie. I looked down and realized we were wearing almost exactly the same outfit.

Half an hour later we were walking through the front doors of the community center. I held my breath as I pushed the La Lait meeting doors open. This was it. There was no turning back.

I inhaled deeply and walked through, trying to steady my nerves against the weight of the moment.

"Hi, every…" My voice trailed off as I froze against the sight in front of me.

All twenty moms, including Lola, Kristen and Nina, were standing under an enormous white construction-paper banner that read "Good luck, Ashley!"

Lola threw a handful of confetti in the air. "Surprise!"

Nina pulled a cord, sending a cascade of balloons from a net affixed to the ceiling. Aubrey squealed with delight.

Lola's booming voice filled the room. "Ashley, we just wanted to send you off to the Motherhood Better Bootcamp knowing that we're behind you one hundred percent. We love you!"

With that, all of the moms rushed forward and surrounded me, hugging me from all sides. I felt a warm bubble of emotion rise from the pit of my stomach and get lodged in my throat. My eyes filled with tears, and as they streamed down my face, I actually, genuinely, wholeheartedly laughed.

"I can't... I can't believe this!" I sputtered. Nina wrapped me in a bear hug, the twins strapped to her chest. "No matter what happens in Napa, remember that you're already a great mom." A fresh batch of tears ran down my cheeks.

I turned every which way, hugging the women around me. I'd never felt so supported in my entire life. Every mom had different words of encouragement for me, but they all were in the same thread: "You're amazing just the way you are." That's all I've ever wanted to hear.

After ten or so minutes everything settled down and we were sitting and lying on the giant rug surrounded by pillows and toddling, squirming babies. Every few minutes a different mom would pop up and hug me, wishing me well on my trip.

The meeting flew by. I looked at my phone. I'd almost forgotten that I hadn't done the only thing I'd intended to do. There were only ten minutes left. I wrung my hands together and watched Aubrey crawl her way over to Donovan and tap him gently on the head as if to say, "Hello friend!" They both dissolved into delicious baby giggles.

It wasn't the right time. I couldn't. My confession would have to wait until I returned from the bootcamp finale.

Wednesday, March 6, 6 A.M.

The morning hadn't been an easy one. Since Aubrey was born I'd dreamt of taking even just one night off, but putting her down last night was next to impossible, as I couldn't stop hugging her. I knew I'd only be gone two and a half days, but if you were to peek in on me, both arms tight around her pajamaed body, rocking her in the glider in the dark room, tears rolling down my cheeks, you would have thought I was leaving for war. Tonight was going to be my first night away from her, ever.

I'd hardly been able to sleep, either. Even though I'd set multiple alarms on my phone and David's phone, I woke up every half hour.

"You're going to be great," David said, cupping my face in his hands as the Town Car driver pushed my suitcase into the trunk. "And don't forget to relax. Have some fun."

He kissed my cheek and I turned toward the waiting car. Leave it to Emily Walker to arrange a fancy black car for a pickup. As I slipped inside and glided across the black leather interior, I felt like a movie star. I watched David disappear into the house.

People always complain about travel, but I found navigating through the bustling airport and a particularly grumpy TSA agent easier than grocery shopping with a tired baby. For the first time in forever, I only had myself to worry about. By the time I was seated in 4A, a window seat in first class, I felt like I'd spent the day at a spa.

I'd never flown first class before and was slightly embarrassed to board before everyone else. The main cabin was still empty as I, along with a few business people, made myself comfortable in a large, plush seat in the luxury section of the plane.

"Can I interest you in a beverage? Tea? Coffee? Wine?" the perky brunette flight attendant asked me.

"Coffee would be wonderful, thank you," I said, trying to sound as gracious and unspoiled as possible.

"How do you take it?"

It took everything inside me not to say "Cold, and with a baby on my hip."

"Sugar and cream would be fantastic. Thank you very much."

A few minutes later, a piping-hot mug of caramel-colored coffee was placed on my tray, alongside a glass plate with a warm blueberry muffin.

"They're freshly baked," the flight attendant said, winking at me.

I was speechless. Coffee and a muffin? And I didn't have to share it with anyone? I was on cloud nine.

The main cabin began filling up as passengers shuffled past first class and into the main section. Suddenly, I felt self-conscious of not only my priority seating but the continental breakfast in front of me. I noticed a few people struggling to make their way through the narrow aisle steal judge-y glances at me, and I wanted to say, "I'm not rich! I usually eat stale cereal off my daughter's high chair for breakfast in stained yoga pants and an oversized sweatshirt!"

The familiar sound of a fussing baby caught my ear and I saw a young woman juggling an infant car seat, diaper bag and carry-on bag, while wearing a baby who could be no more than six months old in a wrap.

A pang of sympathy shot through my chest. The look in her eyes was a familiar one: a mix of defeat, frustration and determination. Our eyes met and I smiled empathetically. I'd been there. The diaper bag strap slid down her arm into the crook of her elbow.

"Let me help you with that," I said, standing. I slid the strap back to its rightful location. "I have a baby, too. Hang in there."

She smiled appreciatively at me. "Thank you. It's been one of those mornings."

She continued making her way back, stopping in the first row of economy seats, just behind me. I watched in awe as she pushed her carry-on into the overhead compartment and placed her belongings in her seats, all while bouncing her increasingly upset baby in the wrap. As she took care of business, I noticed an older man behind her get fussy over the hold-up in the line. My blood began to boil. What happened to common courtesy? Instead of tapping his foot, he could be helping her!

I stood up in my seat again. "Can I help you with anything?"

She blew a strand of hair out of her face and tilted her head gratefully in my direction. "I'm okay. But thank you. Again. You're very kind," she said, shooting a glare at the gentleman who was now twitching with impatience.

Finally, she slid into her seat and unwrapped her baby from

her chest. The pajama-clad infant let out a shriek of discomfort over being removed from his cozy cocoon.

"Shhh, shhhh...you're okay," she cooed.

Ten minutes later, everyone was in their seats and the emergency landing routine had just wrapped up.

A voice over the intercom said, "Hello, everyone, I'm your captain, Jack Ross. Thank you for flying Air United today. Our flight time is approximately three hours and twenty minutes."

I'm not sure when I dozed off, but the next thing I heard were the sounds of a baby in full meltdown mode. I awoke with a start, and for a moment, I forgot I was on a plane and had the urge to run upstairs and collect Aubrey from her nap.

The sound was coming from behind me and was slightly muffled by the closed First Class curtain. I pulled it to the side and peeked through. The young mom was frantically trying to comfort her baby, who was strapped into his car seat in the seat beside her.

"Oh, great!" I heard a woman's voice from the middle of the plane exclaim.

The mother's face said it all. She was mortified.

"Can I help you with anything?" I whispered to her.

"No... I'm so sorry about the noise. He's just tired."

"No need to be sorry," I said softly. "Babies cry."

A female flight attendant with a tight bun crouched beside the mother. "Ma'am, we're getting some complaints from other passengers. Is there anything you can do to calm your little one down?"

It was like someone slapped me in the face. Was she serious?

"I'm doing my best..." I heard the mother's voice crack. "I'll feed him."

I slid back into my seat, feeling utterly devastated for her. The next thing I knew, the same older gentleman from before who was sitting in the aisle across from the young mother was roaring, "You've got to be kidding me! Now you're going to flash us?"

I heard the mom's feeble voice, "I'm feeding my baby…"

I peeked through the curtain again to see the baby happily nursing, the mother's tank top slightly lifted to make room for his head. Her eyes were full of tears.

It was like someone lit a match under me. I stood up and whipped the curtain open. I leaned over my seat.

"HEY, YOU!" I heard myself say. "SHUT UP! She's a mother trying to take care of her baby. News flash: they cry. They need to eat. Moms need to take them places. We can't stay home twenty-four hours a day to save your precious little ears and eyes from our HARD work raising the next generation. If you can't handle it, maybe you should be the one to stay home."

The man's face turned red and he fumbled the newspaper in his hand. "I'm just asking for common decency!"

I stood and walked right up to the man who was now almost trembling. I pointed in his face. Something inside me had snapped.

"Why don't you have the DECENCY to let this mother tend to her baby in peace! She's doing an excellent job and shouldn't have to put up with jackholes like you!"

I gestured to the rest of the plane. "Do any of you know how hard it is to be a mom? You're supposed to be perfect and invisible at the same time! This mom is just trying to do her best and you're making her feel like crap! Moms can't win!"

I felt a tap on my shoulder. It was the female flight attendant. "Ma'am, I'm going to have to ask you to take your seat."

"I'll sit down when I'm done!" I was on fire now. "Moms can't win with any of you. If we work, we're neglecting our children. If we stay home, we're wasting our lives. If we don't breastfeed, we're failures. If we do, we need to do it in the dark, under a blanket, on a different planet so we don't offend your fragile, weak sensitivities! Give a mother a freaking break!"

I felt a tap on my shoulder again. I turned around. "WHAT?" And was face to chest with what I had to assume was a human giant. He had to be seven feet tall. His voice was a deep baritone and he was cut, like, bodybuilder cut.

"Can I help you?" I said, indignantly.

"Yes, ma'am, I'm going to have to ask you to take your seat."

I flipped my hair. "And just who are you, exactly?"

He pulled a badge out of his jacket pocket. "I'm a flight marshal."

My body ran warm. "Oh. In that case, okay."

I started to make my way back to my seat, but turned around and faced the plane one more time. "And the next person that bothers this woman is going to have to deal with me!"

The flight marshal gave me a look.

"I'm sitting down, sir."

I took my seat and inhaled sharply, trying to steady my nerves. I looked at the mother whose mouth was hanging open. Tears were now streaming down her face. To my surprise, they were falling from mine, too.

"Thank you," she squeaked.

I was afraid that if I answered I'd start sobbing, so I mouthed, "You're welcome," before leaning back into my seat.

The rest of the flight was a quiet one. After we landed and people began collecting their things, I noticed that the older man sheepishly allowed the mom to collect her belongings without a hint of impatience. Our eyes met again before I exited the plane, and her beaming face said it all.

11 A.M.

There I stood, in the foyer of Emily Walker's beautiful wine-country home (yes, wine-country home). I closed my eyes and took a deep breath. Was this really happening? We were surrounded by row after row of gorgeous vineyards, heavy with the small purple grapes that made my evenings so delicious.

Was I really standing in one of Emily Walker's mansions? I could barely take it all in. The white and gray tiled floor sparkled in the California sunlight that poured in through the long vertical windows. Ahead of me were two staircases that met halfway from the top to become one—it looked like the kind of staircase a princess walks down to enter a ball. One of Emily's assistants, Anna, a short brunette with a classic bob and enormous glasses, had already had one of the many men and women I'd seen scurrying about in white sport jackets and black pants take my bags to my room. A room that I'd yet to see.

"Someone will escort you to your room in just a minute! First, you must be hungry from your long journey," Anna said, before disappearing down a long hallway. Ten minutes later she reappeared holding a clipboard and with a Bluetooth device in her ear, and led me down the same hallway and through three doors. I tried to remember which way we turned and what the rooms we passed through looked like, as if I were some kind of blindfolded hostage being taken away by car. I'd practically need GPS in this house!

Finally, she flung a set of double doors open to reveal a party in progress. I stared, gawking at round tables set with full flatware and centerpieces as if it were a wedding. Glittery lights twinkled in the multiple chandeliers. Women crowded the room—*the* women! I instantly recognized many of them from the bootcamp video conferences. Only one thing was wrong: they were all dressed to the nines. Every last woman had donned cute skirt and sweater combinations, pastel pumps, A-line dresses and dangly earrings. I stood, self-conscious, at the entrance next to Anna.

I leaned over, "Anna, is there any way I can change—" I gestured down at my black saggy leggings and university sweatshirt.

"Don't worry, this is just the reception brunch. It was on your itinerary. It's very casual."

I remembered the reception brunch, but I was thinking it'd be more scrambled eggs, croissants and mimosas over giggles in sweatpants, not what looked like Easter Sunday at the Vatican.

I took off my backpack and placed it by the door. David had insisted I take his hiking backpack as my carry-on "because of all the pockets."

Walking slowly toward the buffet, I redid my ponytail.

"Ashley? Ashley Keller, is that you?" A high-pitched voice cut through me right as I was reaching for what looked like a grapefruit champagne cocktail.

I turned around to see a six-foot leggy blonde in a pale pink, knee-length taffeta dress and matching heels running toward me. It was Heather Logan, mom of three-month-old twins from New Jersey. I recognized her from her posts featuring chalkboard paint tutorials, making door wreaths for every season and basically any craft you can think of. She was a star on the Motherhood Better Bootcamp portal.

She gathered me in a tight hug for several seconds before pushing me playfully away. I tried not to lose my balance.

"Hi, Heather! You look fantastic!" She really did. I wish I'd gotten the memo about dresses.

"Thank you, doll! And you look…no way, did you already find the gym? You are such an overachiever!" she practically yelled. She motioned toward several ladies who were gathered in a small circle near us.

"You guys, Ashley already worked out!" she boomed, pointing at me.

A woman in a black pencil skirt, red fitted blazer and red pumps turned toward us. "No way. I've been dying to get on the treadmill. Only two days until six million people are staring at us on TV." She flipped her hair and looked me up and down. "Where is it?"

I laughed nervously. "Where's what?"

A small crowd was forming now. They were eyeing me carefully, as if I were a threat, while simultaneously circling me like easy prey.

"There's a gym?" I heard someone mutter.

"Yeah, she already went," said someone else.

Heather waved her hands as if to clear the air. "Okay, calm down, ladies! You'll all have a chance to kill yourselves on the elliptical later!" The crowd dissipated.

I exhaled, relieved.

"So," Heather went on. "Have you met *Emily* yet?" She said Emily's name as if she were a third grader teasing her schoolyard friend about her crush.

I grabbed the fruity cocktail and took a big sip. "I just got here, no. Have—" Before I had a chance to finish the sentence, Heather was dragging me across the floor by my hand.

We stopped in front of a woman who was in conversation with one of the waitstaff, but even with her back turned to us, I could tell it was Emily. I felt myself get hot and then cold all over. No, no, no! I couldn't meet Emily Walker dressed like someone on laundry day!

But it was too late. Heather tapped Emily on the shoulder. As she turned toward me, I'm positive I saw a beam of light encircle her face. Her makeup was flawless, her hair perfectly done up in a stylish ponytail, not a raggedy slept-on one like mine. A short jade dress accentuated her lean, curvy figure.

I was speechless. For once I was grateful to have Heather's mouth do the talking for me. "Emily, have you met Ashley?"

Emily's eyes lit up. "Ashley Keller!" She took the sides of my arms gently and gave me a kiss on each cheek. I moved, stiffly, unsure of how this greeting was supposed to happen. I'd only ever seen it on a few travel shows.

"It's so wonderful to finally meet you! I feel like I've known you forever. This is Sage." She looked down and for the first time I noticed the toddler peeking through her legs. "He's a little shy." She bent down gracefully and scooped up the child whose curly brown hair framed his long black eyelashes. He looked like a child model in his white shorts and a white sweater with a little navy anchor on the chest.

"He's getting tired," Emily purred into Sage's ear and he laid his head against her chest.

I gawked, awestruck. If Aubrey were here, she'd be pulling at my earrings, screaming for a scone and generally raising hell, but here was Emily, being an amazing mom, hosting a party and looking fabulous while doing it. She was absolutely perfect.

"Ashley, I can't wait to talk to you more, but I'm going to give a little speech before everyone gets restless!"

"Okay," I sputtered, realizing that I hadn't said one word since meeting her.

I found my way back to the buffet, trying to choose between piles of freshly shaved, cured meats, mouthwatering platters of fresh fruit, pastries, cheese, and the crepe and omelet bar. I never wanted to go home.

I heard the telltale sound of a microphone being tapped and turned to face the front of the room.

Emily was holding a mic and grinning.

"Hello, everyone! I'm so glad that you've all arrived safe and sound! Welcome to the Motherhood Better Bootcamp Finale!"

Everyone cheered.

"I want you to take your time eating, drinking and mingling. Your only job here is to have a great time. You've earned it."

Heather "whooped" from inside the crowd.

"My number-one goal since I started the Emily Walker empire has been to inspire and support moms. I hope that the Motherhood Better Bootcamp has done that for you. No matter who is crowned as the winner in two days, I want you to know that, in my book, you're all queens."

Applause broke out. I could feel myself getting misty. If I hadn't had a plate full of ham and cheese omelets, mandarin-orange crepes topped with fresh cream and about six different kinds of meat, I would have clapped, too. I wished every mom could know what it felt like to be recognized like this.

I found an empty table in the back and proceeded to attack my plate.

Just when I'd stuffed a prosciutto-covered piece of cantaloupe into my face, a voice distracted me. "Ashley? Hi, I'm Kimmie Reardon."

Kimmie Reardon. How could I forget? I'd seen her name all over the Motherhood Better boards. Mom of four. Lives in Los Angeles. Loves to bake. Completed all of the challenges with ease and always has ten or twelve photos to prove it.

I stood up.

"No, no, don't get up," Kimmie said, taking a seat beside me. "You look…busy."

She looked just like the photos she'd taken: five foot five, long, wavy brown hair, pretty almond-shaped eyes. She was dressed more casually than the others: suede calf-high boots, black leather pants and a white denim cropped jacket over a black tank top. Where do all of these moms shop? And how can so many of them wear white?

I forced the appetizer down my throat. "It's nice to meet you," I said. She daintily shook my hand, as if human contact wasn't something she relished.

I took a bite of my crepe, eyeing Kimmie to see if she was going to stay.

"So," she said, watching me intently. "How do you feel about your chances?"

"My chances for what?" I asked, my mouth full.

"Winning," she said, staring me dead in the eye, expressionless.

I chewed. "Well. There are a lot of great women here." I trailed off, hoping that would be a sufficient answer.

Kimmie scanned the room, her eyes narrowing. "They're okay." She turned back to face me. "Don't let your guard down just yet. The competition's not over."

She gave a saccharine smile before standing up abruptly and walking away.

An almost-full plate of food sat in front of me, but suddenly I wasn't as ravenously hungry as I was before. Kimmie the Ice Queen was right. This wasn't a vacation. It was the final lap.

When I finished my meal, I opened the welcome packet Anna had given me.

Dear Ashley Keller,

It's our absolute pleasure to welcome you to the Napa home of Emily Walker for the Motherhood Better Bootcamp Finale! We hope this time will be one of rejuvenation and community. Below are your accommodation details and schedule, along with a map of the estate.

Wednesday

11:30AM Welcome brunch

Feel free to spend the rest of today relaxing! The spa, pools and kitchen are at your full disposal. If you need anything, please page Anna or James (the house butler), and our staff will provide it.

6:30PM Dinner in the Outdoor Garden Dining Room with Emily and her family

Thursday

6AM Yoga on the south lawn with Emily & Sven

7AM Breakfast in the Main Dining Room

8AM Basket and Dream Catcher Making in the Craft Room

9AM Organic Smoothie Workshop with Chef Evelyn

10AM Makeovers!

Noon Lunch & Sharing

1-5PM Free Time

6PM Dinner on the North Lawn

Friday

5AM Hair & Makeup

7AM We go live!

11AM Farewell brunch

"So much for a relaxing vacation," I thought. At least the makeover sounded fun. I scanned the sheet to find my room assignment.

Accommodations
Ashley Walker: The Pink Peony Room (locate on the map)
Roommate: Kimmie Reardon

Just when I thought things couldn't get worse.

When I finally made it to the room through the labyrinth of doors, I was taken aback. Pink Peony wasn't just the name of the room, it was the theme. Pale pink and white flowers with dainty green leaves filled every inch of the slate walls. A bedside table adorned with an antique desk lamp and a glass vase full of delicate peonies separated two double beds. The only other furniture was a white leather loveseat and a tall, wide oak dresser.

The bathroom door on the far right of the room opened.

"Hi, roomie," Kimmie said slyly, as she walked out and sat on a bed covered in garment bags.

I placed my suitcase, which had been left just inside the door by the staff, on the remaining bed.

"Hi again, Kimmie," I responded. "Did you know we were roommates earlier?"

Kimmie threw her head back and laughed. "Oh, yeah. I was just waiting for you to figure it out."

I smiled weakly. "It's going to be great."

Kimmie swung her legs over the bed to face me. "I'm so happy we're together. I can't imagine being with some of the other women."

I opened my suitcase and began slowly taking out my belongings, hoping Kimmie wasn't judging them. I didn't own anything nice enough to warrant a garment bag.

"Oh, really? Why not?" I asked, making my way over to the dresser. I opened drawer after drawer to find they were already filled with silk panties, tops, jeans and more jeans.

"Sorry. I'm an overpacker. I left you some space in the closet," she said flippantly.

I opened the modest closet to find it two-thirds full. Six hangers remained. "Thanks."

Kimberly pulled a black compact out of her purse and began puckering her lips. "Some of the moms here…wow. I mean, you can tell they needed the challenge, but there's no way they're going to win. I'm talking totally dumpy. Frump city. It's sad."

I silently stacked my clothes on the shelf at the top of the closet, next to four pairs of Kimmie's boots.

"Motherhood will do that to you," I responded.

Kimmie dug through her purse and retrieved a small glass vial and wrapped hypodermic needle.

"Oh, not me. Letting yourself go is a choice." She unwrapped the needle and poked it into the top of the vial. "Do you want some? It's better than Botox," she said, peering into the mirror and sliding the needle into her forehead.

I watched, shocked. "Um…no. But thank you."

"Suit yourself. We're going to be on TV in just under forty-eight hours. Your fine lines will be even more pronounced in high definition."

I slid my empty suitcase under my bed and sat on the chair. It was so odd not to have a baby to change, feed or put down for a nap while worrying she will wake up any second. I folded my hands and realized that I had absolutely no idea what to do with myself. Sleep was out of the question with Kimmie sitting three feet away, injecting God knew what into her brow line.

I coughed. *Make conversation, Ashley. It's not that hard*, my inner voice urged.

"So, Kimmie…how did you hear about the Motherhood Better Bootcamp?"

Kimmie put the needle in a black plastic box and snapped it shut.

"Actually, I've known about it for months. Emily Walker's husband works with mine. They're investors," she said, smiling rather smugly.

"Investors? What do they invest in?" I asked, leaning my head on my hand.

"Everything. Tech, retail… They went to the same Ivy

League and were even in the same frat. We were at each other's weddings."

"So, you know each other?" I asked, trying not to frown.

Kimmie stumbled over her words, "Well, yes, but no. We're in many of the same circles. Anyway, I'm going to take a shower before heading down for a swim. Let's sit together at dinner, okay? See ya," she said, standing up and tossing me a tight smile.

"Okay, bye."

Kimmie grabbed a plush robe from the closet before disappearing into the bathroom and closing the door behind her. I heard it lock, so it was clear she'd be in there for a while. I decided to go for a stroll.

This wasn't a house. It was its own village. Emily Walker's Napa estate had its own tennis court, two pools, a hot tub, a pool house with an area for manicures and massages, a room just for hot yoga, three kitchens—including one large enough for a full professional staff to prepare meals—four wings, four garages, a movie room and that's just what I'd seen so far. Did I mention there was an elevator? I wouldn't have been at all surprised to open a closet door to Narnia.

As I walked down a set of cement stairs from the main garden to the spa, I ran into a familiar face: Janice Paulsen, the do-gooder mom who matched foster kids to families. She wore a thoroughly bedazzled gray sweatsuit.

"Ashley! It is so wonderful to see your beautiful face! I'm Janice" she said in a Minnesota accent.

Ah, Janice. The needlepoint queen of the great Midwest. She'd found way to inject her love of craft needles into every single challenge. For the Marriage Challenge, she'd even knitted a set of yarn lingerie that I'd never be able to unsee.

"It's nice to meet you in person." I smiled, feeling like

for once I was nailing a social interaction with someone old enough to use the bathroom alone.

Janice took my hand as if she was trying to prevent me from leaving too quickly. "Lauren," she yelled, calling to a woman at the bottom of the stairs who was tying her shoe. "Lauren, Ashley's here. Remember? The tush girl?" she said, waving Lauren over furiously.

Tush girl? They couldn't mean the first video chat fiasco. There's no way they were talking about me.

Lauren, a woman with chestnut hair in a low ponytail, wearing bedazzled jeans and a T-shirt, hightailed it up the stairs. I recognized her from a particularly long post about how bedazzling saved her life.

"Tush girl!" Lauren exclaimed, loudly enough for everyone in the zip code to hear. She ran over to me and gave me a bear hug. "I tell your story to everyone I meet. You're practically famous in my book club. I love your little tattoo, by the way!"

I tried to will my body to melt into the ground.

"Thank you…for…it's nice to meet…" My words left my brain again.

"Hey." Lauren touched my shoulder and drew me close. "If you need anything bedazzled you let me know. I brought my Rhinestanator 2000 and have been hooking everyone up." I looked the women up and down, and by the no less than six trillion plastic gems on their outfits sparkling in the sunlight, I knew she wasn't kidding.

"I'll let you know!"

Somehow I managed to slink away from the conversation before they asked to take a photo of my tattoo for their scrapbooks.

Once safely back in my room, I opened the bathroom door to find Kimmie standing as naked as the day she was born in the shower with her arms and legs spread wide. She was wearing some kind of protective goggles and a woman wearing the same eyewear was spraying her with a large canister attached by a hose to an even larger tub.

I screamed.

Kimmie pulled up one side of her goggles. "Geez, Ash. You almost gave me a heart attack. What happened to knocking?"

I shielded my eyes with my hand. "I'm sorry, it was unlocked. I'm sorry."

I backed away into the door and bumped against it.

"No need to freak out," Kimmie said, folding down her goggles. "Amanda, meet Ashley. Ashley, meet Amanda. She's my personal tanner. She's staying at a nearby hotel. There's no way I was going on TV without a fresh one, am I right?"

"Yes, right, right," I said, finally finding the doorknob with my eyes closed. "Okay, enjoy yourself."

I sat down on my bed and opened my computer. One missed FaceCall request from David. I clicked on the notification and it started dialing.

He picked up after one ring. I could hear running water and the sound of someone gagging.

"David? Are you there?" The screen only showed the bathroom ceiling.

"ASHLEY!" I heard David yell before gagging again. "ASHLEY, HER DIAPER EXPLODED!"

"David?"

His face popped up over the monitor. His eyes were full of fear and there was a bandana tied around his nose.

"Ashley, I'm dealing with a Level Ten Poopsplosion right here and am two seconds away from—" He retched loudly.

"Oh, David..." I could hear Aubrey giggling hysterically in the bathtub.

"Ashley. If I pass out I'm going to need you to call 911."

I tried to hold back my laughter. "David, you're not going

to pass out. Are her clothes off yet? Let them soak a bit before you wash them—"

"Too late," he said, looking around wildly. "I had to cut them off. They were an unfortunate casualty."

It was then that I noticed he was wearing the yellow gloves I use to wash dishes.

"Feel free to burn those when you're done," I said.

David paused for a minute before I heard him say, "Oh, no, no, no, it's happening again. There's more coming out of her. Why is this happening? Is she possessed? Is she possessed by a demon? I need a young priest and an old priest. I gotta go, Ashley. I'll call you later."

"David, you're going to be okay." Before the camera clicked off, I'm almost positive I heard him chanting in Latin.

"Don't forget to get under my butt cheeks! They won't be on camera but I'll know!" I heard Kimmie scream from the bathroom.

I opened the bedside table drawer and found a pair of purple eye covers. They smelled lightly of lavender. I slipped them on over my head, lay back and, before I knew it, was in a deep sleep.

I woke up to Kimmie shaking me. "Ashley. ASHLEY! It's time for dinner. Geez, you sleep like a rock."

Kimmie walked over to the full-length mirror. She was stunning in a floor-length pale pink evening gown. Her wrists and neck were dripping with what I could only assume were real diamond and gold jewelry.

"You look beautiful," I said, pushing myself up to sitting.

"You look tired. Get dressed. You know dinner starts in fifteen minutes, right?"

"Fifteen minutes!" I flew out of bed and toward the closet. "Why didn't you wake me up earlier?"

Kimmie shrugged. "I'm not your mommy." I don't know

if I imagined it, but I thought I saw a smirk. Was this her competitive side?

"I'll meet you down there."

Kimmie walked out the door and shut it behind her. I tore through my clothes and looked for something that would even come close to the level of elegance my roommate had achieved.

I found a dark blue maxi dress. It would have to do. One of the good things about having held Aubrey 24/7 for the last ten months of my life was that I was used to doing everything with one hand. Finally having two, I was able to get my hair and makeup decent in five minutes.

After getting lost twice, I finally found the outdoor garden dining room where we'd be dining. Everyone was already sitting at several large round tables, including Emily's family. There they were: her husband and five perfect children in the flesh. Emily was wearing a plum three-quarter-sleeved, calf-length dress and black heels, and her husband was dashing in gray slacks and a crisp white dress shirt with a gray sport jacket. Her three boys were wearing white (WHITE) short-sleeved shirts and camel-colored shorts, and her girls were wearing the same outfit in jumper form. They looked like the cover of a fashion catalog.

"Ashley, over here!" I heard Lauren call. I glanced over and saw Janice and Lauren waving wildly from a table at the far end of the patio.

The last thing I needed was to spend the evening being re-ferred to as "tush girl." I waved politely and ducked behind a large plant.

I felt a hand touch my shoulder. "Ashley, would you like to sit with my family?"

I looked up. It was Emily. I stared into her blemish-free face for a full twenty seconds before sputtering out, "Yes."

I followed Emily to her table and noticed Kimmie glaring at me. Naturally, I beamed back at her.

"Ashley, I'd like to introduce you to my husband, Thomas."

I took in her husband's ruggedly handsome features and found myself staring. It was impossible not to get lost in his dreamy auburn eyes. I blushed. "Nice to meet you."

He nodded. "Likewise." He was holding Emily's youngest baby, eighteen-month-old Sage. He nuzzled up to his father. If Aubrey were here she'd be trying to pull down every table curtain in the joint.

"You met little Sage earlier today. These are my older children, three-year-old Willow, four-year old Henry, and my six-year-old twins, Eleanor and Gregory." All of her children smiled pleasantly at me. In the center of the round table were twinkling tea lights, and not a single child attempted to burn the place down.

Were they drugged, I wondered? I smiled. "Wow, you're all so well-behaved! And adorable!" I said, taking my seat beside Eleanor.

Emily sat down on my other side. "We actually try not to compliment them on their looks. It builds an unhealthy emphasis on the outer appearance."

"Yes, yes," I nodded, pretending to know what she was talking about.

Emily smiled. "It's best if children are raised knowing their true beauty comes from within."

I continued nodding, "Yes, the inside. Their internal… organs."

Emily cocked her head to the side. A member of the staff came by with a bottle of wine.

"Madame?"

Emily held up her hand. "No, thank you." She turned to me. "Breastfeeding. You know how it is."

I flushed. "Yes, but um…breastfeeding didn't really work out for us…" I said, trailing off.

"So your baby is on formula?" Eleanor asked. I was startled. What did a six-year-old know about formula?

I turned to the child. "Yes, she's on formula."

"Well, that's sad," said Eleanor, flatly.

"Eleanor," Emily interrupted sternly. "What did Mommy say about respecting the choices of others?"

Eleanor lowered her head slightly. "Know better, do better."

"That's right." Emily turned to me. "I wish I'd known. I would have introduced you to my naturopath. Have you considered donor milk at all?"

I motioned to the waiter for some wine.

"Not yet. There are so many preemies, you know. I wouldn't want to exhaust the supply."

The waiter filled my glass half full and I chugged the glass before motioning for a refill.

Emily eyed me. "That's so giving of you. You know what? I'm going to send you home with sixteen ounces of my own milk. How does that sound?"

"That sounds…amazing. Thank you," I said, trying not to choke.

Thomas grinned and took Emily's hand. "You're such a generous spirit," he said, gazing into his wife's eyes.

"And you are the love of my life," she said. They stared at each other ethereally.

I held my breath, not wanting to disturb whatever it was they were doing.

Kimmie popped up from out of nowhere.

"Oh, hi, Ashley! I just wanted to make sure you made it down alright." She was talking to me, but staring at Emily.

She went on. "Emily, Kimberly Reardon. From LA. I met you earlier. I just wanted to say how amazing and inspirational you are. The past few weeks have been incredible. My life has truly changed. Thank you." Kimmie held one hand to her heart.

Emily stood up and the two hugged. I tried to hold back my gag reflex.

"You are so welcome, Kimmie. Surely, there's space for one more. Would you like to join us?"

"Absolutely!" Before I could register what was happening, Kimmie was pushing her chair in between me and Emily.

When she was comfortably seated she gave me a tight smile. "Hi, roomie."

I shot venom at her with my eyes but smiled back. "Hi."

Within minutes Kimmie and Emily were lost in quiet whispering about the latest probiotic on the market.

"Ashley, what's your opinion on it?" Kimmie said to me, her eyes wide and innocent.

"I...uh, I love probiotics. I'm definitely pro-probiotic." I laughed, hoping other people would find my joke hilarious. Everyone at the table stared at me. Kimmie smirked.

The meal was halfway over when I saw Lauren and Janice make their way over to me. Oh, no.

"Ashley! Ashley, we just wanted to make sure we got this to you before the night was over."

Janice reached into her purse and pulled out a black T-shirt with the words Tush Girl emblazoned in pink rhinestones across the chest.

Kimmie covered her mouth and giggled. I saw Emily struggling to hold back a smile.

"What's a tush girl?" asked Eleanor.

"Oh, honey, it's for the tattoo on her tush," said Lauren, howling.

Eleanor's eyes grew wide. "You have a tattoo!" She burst into tears.

Emily rushed over to comfort her daughter. She looked up at me. "She's very sensitive. Unnatural body modifications upset her."

I took the T-shirt. "Thank you," I said without looking anyone in the eye.

Everyone was on their last cocktail when Emily tapped her water glass with her spoon.

"Before dessert comes out, I just want to say that I'm so glad all of you are here! I hope tomorrow you can experience the rest and relaxation you mama goddesses deserve! Have a wonderful evening!"

Everyone clapped politely. Despite the night turning out to be a royal mess, I was looking forward to getting pampered a little.

Waiters began placing large slices of a rich-looking chocolate cake with buttery chocolate cream frosting in front of every place setting.

"Mother," said Gregory. "Do we have any fruit salad?"

Emily grinned proudly and addressed the table. "The kids know they only eat refined sugar once every other month." To Gregory she said, "I can do even better than that!"

She turned toward Thomas. "Darling, will you ask the staff to bring out the date carob blueberry sweet potato tarts with the almond flour crust for the children?" She smiled at us, "I made them this afternoon."

Kimmie spoke up, "If it's okay, I'd love to try one of the tarts. I'm on a cleanse from refined sugars myself. Ashley, would you like one?"

I looked up from the piece of cake I was halfway through devouring and licked a glob of chocolate frosting from the corner of my mouth.

Before I could speak, Kimmie cut in. "Never mind. You look preoccupied."

Later, in our room, Kimmie couldn't stop raving about the night.

"Emily and I really hit it off," she gushed, sitting at the vanity, wiping makeup from her face with huge cloths. "I'd consider the night a win."

"Yeah, you really nailed it," I responded dryly, crawling under my sheets.

As I fell asleep I made a note to self: Don't trust Kimmie.

Thursday, March 7, 5:45 A.M.

My alarm beeped, waking me up with a start. It wasn't until I saw Kimmie standing in front of the mirror adjusting her top knot that I remembered where I was. I sat up. My body felt strange. I arched my back a little and tried to figure out what it was. It took me a minute to realize that what I was experiencing was…being rested. My mind was crystal clear. There was no pain behind my eyes. No sluggishness in my legs.

I felt rested. I hadn't felt like this since before Aubrey was born. I tried to wrap my head around the reality that some people feel like this every day.

"Good morning, sleepyhead," Kimmie sang. "Ready for yoga?"

I fake smiled in her direction and got out of bed. Rummaging through my suitcase I found a pair of sweats, sports bra and tank top. In two minutes I was dressed. As I leaned over the sink brushing my teeth, I heard Kimmie gasp.

I looked up. She was staring at me in abject horror. "Is that what you're wearing?"

I glanced downward at my blue-and-white tennis shoes, light gray sweats, black tank and blue zippered hoodie.

"Yes?" I asked.

Kimmie just scoffed before turning back to the mirror to perfect her cat-eye eyeliner. I took in her outfit.

Black and silver expensive-looking tennis shoes, skin-tight hot-pink Lycra leggings with black stripes going down the sides, a matching crop top that accentuated her perfectly flat stomach and a black headband. She looked like a fitness infomercial. I noticed the EW logo on the back of her pants.

"Is that from—"

"Emily Walker's line? Yes. I own every item. Ready to go?"

Next to Kimmie I was going to look like a garbageman making his weekly rounds, but we headed out anyway.

"No makeup?" Kimmie asked, as she shut our door.

"It's exercise."

"It's yoga," she corrected me.

It appeared Kimmie was right, because when we arrived at the South Lawn, there were only five other moms, and all of them were wearing makeup *and* Emily Walker's line of activewear.

"Good morning, ladies!" Emily was beautiful as always in a purple-and-white ensemble. "I'm tickled pink to see so many of you wearing my line!"

Her eyes settled on my hobo wear and she smiled sympathetically.

"I'd like to introduce you to Sven—if you read my blog, and I assume that you do, you already know he's my dirty little wellness secret." I heard one of the moms giggle.

Sven was six foot four of pure Greek male model. His dark brown hair accentuated his bright blue eyes. To the surprise (delight?) of many of the women, he was wearing only a small pair of black short shorts.

"Okay, everyone," Sven said with a deep Eastern European accent. "Grab a mat."

Sven and Emily led us through a variety of poses, each one more painful and impossible than the last.

"If you're a newbie to yoga, don't hesitate to take a break when you need one," Emily said, looking directly at me.

By the end I was a sweaty mess. I could see why everyone opted for synthetic materials. I had huge sweat stains in each armpit, a large one on my back, and to top it off, an embarrassingly large one in the crotch of my pants.

"Ashley, did you have an accident?" Kimmie asked in front of the entire class as we finished sitting cross-legged in deep meditation—a pose that exposed my swamp stain to the world.

Sven opened his eyes, looked at me and turned red.

"It's normal to experience these things during yoga, especially when your pelvic floor has weakened due to childbirth," said Emily calmly.

"I didn't pee. It's sweat," I said, humiliated, standing up.

"Yes," said Emily, obviously trying to preserve my dignity.

Kimmie snickered.

As we were stacking our mats, I placed mine on top of the pile.

"You can keep it," Sven whispered in my ear. I was mortified.

I assumed my nickname had morphed from Tush Girl to Pee Girl and ate my breakfast in my bedroom. Emily's assistant had been kind enough to grab me a muffin so I wouldn't have to face anyone.

I opened my computer and checked the time—7:15.

I had an email from David.

Hello supermom,
Everything's fine, don't worry. My mom is taking Aubrey to

the zoo today. I hope you're enjoying yourself. A Realtor came by and said we can probably get market value for the house. Have a good time.
Love, David

I'd almost forgotten about the house. Unless I won the grand prize tomorrow, and things weren't looking great, we'd be moving in with Gloria soon after I came home. I snapped my laptop shut and took a few deep breaths. It wouldn't be that bad. At least I'd always have help just an arm's reach away... and eyes watching me all day long. I guess roaming the house in my underwear eating chocolate-hazelnut spread right out of the jar was out of the question.

I thought *At least I have the La Lait moms*, but remembered that after telling the truth, I wouldn't. I'd be trapped in Gloria's house all day and night. There was no way around it. I had to win this contest. I grabbed the schedule off of the vanity.

8AM Basket and Dream Catcher Making in the Craft Room.

Oh, crap. Crafts.

Janice and Lauren were sitting on either side of Emily at the long wooden bench table when I arrived. I had showered and changed into dark blue jeans and a pink Emily Walker sweatshirt—David gave it to me the night before I left and I figured this was the perfect time to wear it.

"Hi, everyone!" I said cheerily. Almost everyone was at the workshop, including my roommate, who was seated directly across from Emily. I took my seat next to her.

"Hi, Kimmie!" I said, forcing cheerfulness.

"Hi, Ashley," she responded with an equally saccharine tone. "Missed you at breakfast!"

I flipped my hair over my shoulder. "After yoga I like to spend some time in quiet meditation in order to realign my—"

"Your mama chakra system," Emily finished for me, her

eyes bright with excitement. "Someone has been reading *Motherhood Better!*"

"Absolutely!" I said, ignoring Kimmie's mouth hanging open. "It's so important to clear yourself every morning. It has made the biggest difference in my life. My love tank is full." I clasped my hands together in silent prayer.

Janice and Lauren stared at me like I was from a different planet.

"That's absolutely wonderful!" Emily exclaimed.

"*Namaste.*" I bowed to her.

Kimmie glared at me.

Emily's assistant placed an enormous bundle of loose wicker in front of each woman.

"Ooh, goodie! Is everyone ready? I trust you read over the instructional materials for Basket Making 101 in your welcome packet?"

The only thing I remember about the welcome packet was that it contained a bar of expensive chocolate.

Everyone flew into craft mode and began twisting and winding the pieces of wicker around long pieces of wood to create a frame for their baskets.

I watched Emily out of the corner of my eye and copied every movement she made. To my surprise, I was actually keeping up.

"Good job, Ashley! You're really a pro at this," Emily said, grinning.

"I love crafts," I lied through my teeth. Turning to Kimmie, I eyed her progress. She was clearly struggling to manipulate the wicker. It wasn't easy, considering her long, acrylic nails. "Do you need some help, Kim?" I asked.

"I'm fine," she said through clenched teeth.

"Well, don't hesitate to ask. The key to success in motherhood and in life is to reach out when you need to." I'd memorized that quote from Emily's book during breakfast.

Emily looked up and absolutely beamed at me.

Kimmie was silent.

I started to really get into it and added my own personal flair to my basket by alternating different shades of wicker. *So this is what the big fuss about crafting is about?* I thought. It was actually pretty relaxing!

The craft was just wrapping up. To my utter surprise, I finished my basket first! It wasn't perfect, but it was done. My first successful craft was complete!

"Wow, Ashley! You're the first one done. Go ahead and use the paring knife to smooth out the splinters. Brava!"

"I'm also done!" shouted Kimmie. I looked at her basket. It appeared to have been run over by a truck.

"Good effort, Kimmie! I guess we have a tie!"

I stood up and rushed over to the knife station, determined to finish fine-tuning my basket before Kimmie. She must have sensed my intention because she jumped up at the same time. We walk-ran awkwardly over to the table and I picked up the small knife first.

"Shame, you'll just have to wait," I said, tightly.

Kimmie grabbed the knife out of my hand. "I guess you will," she hissed, out of Emily's earshot.

I tried to wrestle it away from her. "You know, you've been getting under my skin since we got here. What's your problem?"

Kimmie grabbed the knife back. "My problem is that you don't belong here. Look at you. Mellie the dog mom would have been a better contestant."

"Oh, yeah? At least I'm not a complete phony. I'd be surprised if you even had any kids." Kimmie's face fell. I went to grab the knife back but at the last second she lowered it, causing the blade to go directly into my palm.

A stream of blood spouted up and onto the front of my sweatshirt.

I screamed. Emily and several women rushed over.

"Oh, my!" Emily yelled. She grabbed an apron off of a wall hook and pressed it to my wound. "What happened?"

I looked over at Kimmie who had gone as white as a sheet. Her eyes were filled with tears.

"I slipped," I said.

"I'll take you to First Aid. We had a doctor stay for the week just in case something like this happened."

Kimmie stepped forward. "No, I'll take her. She's my roommate."

Kimmie and I were silent as we walked to the main house. It wasn't until the doctor had seen me and put some gauze over my palm (which turned out to have just a surface wound) and left the room that she burst into tears. Not tears—more like heaving sobs.

I was stunned. "Kimmie, it was an accident. I shouldn't have reached for the knife like that," I said, sitting across from her.

The tears continued to fall and snot poured out of her nose. I handed her a tissue.

She blew her nose. "It's not that. I'm so sorry for how I've been treating you, Ashley. You didn't deserve it."

I wanted to say, "No, I didn't," but this didn't seem the right time to rub it in.

"It's just that..." Kimmie blew her nose again and struggled to stop crying "... I know I'm not going to win the contest. I'm a crap mom. I can't cook. I can't craft. I lied on almost all of my journal entries. I'm a complete fraud. Compared to someone like you, I'm a complete mess."

Huh?

"Kimmie. Someone like me? Just what kind of mom do you think I am?"

Kimmie shot me an "oh, you know what I mean" look. "Come on, Ashley. I couldn't survive without my nanny and getting meals delivered daily. You do it all by yourself. You're probably so hands-on and patient all the time. You're the perfect mom."

I couldn't help it, I started to laugh. "Kimmie, I am not the perfect mom. I almost lit my entire house on fire during the craft challenge. I wear the same pants for three, four, seven days in a row. I'd do anything to have a body and sense of style like you."

Kimmie sniffled. "You think I have a nice body?"

I laughed. "Okay, let's go back to the group."

As we made our way back, things felt different. More relaxed. Not having Kimmie as my enemy was pretty awesome. Turns out she didn't know anything about probiotics and was totally talking out of her backside.

As we were walking, I decided to get some air.

"Kimmie, I'll meet up with you later. I'm going to take a walk."

"Are you sure?"

I nodded. She squeezed my shoulder. "Thanks…for understanding."

We parted ways and I followed a path through lush greenery and took in the view. Emily's house was slightly raised, making it possible to see the rows and rows of vineyards the area was famous for. The morning sun felt like heaven on my skin and a light breeze tickled the hair on the back on my neck. I felt like I was in paradise.

A twinge of guilt formed a knot in my stomach: Aubrey. I was sure she was fine, but felt a little bad enjoying myself so deeply. Then I remembered what was waiting for me when

I returned. It was almost a sure reality that we'd be moving. I'd known when David started his business that it was a risk, but I'd had so much faith that everything would magically turn out perfectly that I hadn't considered what would happen if it didn't. He must be feeling so bad right now. While I'd been worrying about finding friends and losing weight, he'd been quietly fighting his own battle for the financial security of his family.

I sat down on a charming wooden bench in front of a koi pond. A dozen big orange, black, white and red fish swam lazily among the water lilies and lotus flowers. I kicked a smooth white stone with my foot and it plopped into the water, creating a shockwave of circular ripples.

And there was still the matter of my La Lait friends back home. I'd procrastinated long enough. Maybe the best thing to do was send Nina an email to read to the group while I was here. Yes, that's what I'd do. The bit of geographical distance was just the courage I needed. At the same time, I'd email David and apologize for everything that had happened in the last few months. What he needed now was a strong wife who was by his side 100 percent.

I took a deep breath. It was time to face my problems. I stood up and was about to walk back to my room when a stunning red koi with black stripes down its back caught my eye. "Aubrey would love to see that," I thought to myself. Joy was always taking photos of interesting things to share with Ella and George. She called them "experience boosters." George did have the most amazing vocabulary for his age.

I pulled my phone out of my pocket and focused on the fish before snapping a quick pic. I examined my work. Too blurry. I needed to get closer.

Carefully, I made my way through the ankle-deep shrubbcry toward the edge of the pond and snapped another photo. Better, but it was hard to make out the details in his scales.

I planted one foot firmly on the ground, rested the other one against a smooth rock wedged in the corner of the pond for leverage and leaned in. My phone's camera clicked. I examined my work without moving. Absolutely perfect. It looked almost professional. I couldn't wait to post this one to Facebook. As I lowered my foot from the rock, it hit a wet patch, sending my body lurching forward, and before I could think, I was completely submerged in cold water.

My arms and legs flailed wildly as I struggled to stand. After a few moments of rising and then falling again on the slippery pond floor I found myself soaking wet in chest-high water, my phone nowhere to be found.

"This isn't happening," I muttered to myself, trying not to cry as I, with the elegance of a sea manatee, made my way out of the pond on my chest.

My jeans and tank top were stuck to my skin. My top, which was only meant to be worn under my Emily Walker sweatshirt, was completely see-through. I pulled the fabric away from my chest and looked around. The gauze on my hand was soaking wet and stung. Thankfully, there was no one in sight.

I was pushing strands of wet hair out of my face and trying to get my bearings back when I heard a woman's voice.

"Absolutely not!" she yelled. It was Emily Walker. I turned my head toward the sound. It was coming from the balcony above me. I had just enough time to run toward the wall and hide under the terrace before she stepped out onto it.

I froze.

"Thomas, you promised to be here tonight to help with the kids. I'm hosting a very important dinner!"

She paused.

"Okay, when will you be back? You can't expect me to do this all on my own. I need your support. Sage is teething—I can't stay up with him all night and be ready for taping tomorrow…" Emily's voice cracked.

A breeze swept over my already cold body, sending a chill down my arms. A sneeze began to build but I managed to squelch it before it erupted from my nose.

"Why is it that your work is always more important than mine?"

I looked right and left, trying to find a means of escape, but there was no way Emily wouldn't notice a soaking wet woman darting across the grass.

"Don't you dare throw the nanny in my face. I'm still their mother and I need you here! I'm exhausted. All of this is exhausting. I can't do everything by myself anymore, I just—"

Emily paused as if she'd been interrupted.

"Fine. Just do whatever you want."

I heard her sigh deeply and then sniff as if holding back tears.

I shivered. I felt another sneeze rising in the back of my nose and covered my mouth but it erupted before I could stop it. My heart skipped a beat.

"Hello?" Emily's voice cut through the silence. "Is someone there?"

I awkwardly walked out from under the balcony and tried to appear casual.

I waved. "Oh, hey, Emily! I was just passing by!"

Emily quickly wiped a tear from her eye. "Hi…Ashley. Um…are you wet?"

I looked down at my shirt and to my horror, the cold had affected much more than just my nose. I did my best to appear nonchalant.

"Oh, that, yes. I was swimming. I went on a swim."

Emily cocked her head to the side. "With your clothes on?"

I smiled like an idiot. "I'm shy."

Emily nodded, but it was clear from her expression that she thought I was mad.

"Well, I hope you're enjoying yourself. If you need anything don't hesitate to ask," she said, smiling tightly.

"Thanks so much!" I responded with too much enthusiasm before scurrying off.

It took me twice as long as it should have to get back to my room. I had to do plenty of ducking behind furniture and into stairwells to avoid running into anyone else with my pencil-pointed nipples.

When I finally closed the door behind me, I sank behind it to the floor. Thankfully Kimmie was nowhere to be found. Two thoughts ran through my head.

I'd just made a complete fool out of myself AGAIN in front of Emily. If the "tush girl" incident hadn't taken me out of the running, "swimming with my clothes on" certainly had.

Emily is far more normal than I realized. I must have had that exact conversation with David a million times. I knew her blog was supposed to be all rainbows and sunshine, but it was weird that she never talked about feeling overwhelmed.

I stood up and walked into the pristine bathroom to take off my clothes. As I undressed and hung my wet jeans on the shower rack, I felt a twinge in my chest. Aubrey. She had to be up from her nap by now. What time was it? I looked around for my phone for a moment before remembering it was at the bottom of a pond surrounded by majestic fish. Great. Just what I needed. Another bill.

6 P.M.

I stood in front of the bathroom mirror and studied my outfit. The black wrap dress I'd purchased for the date night that never happened looked great on me, paired with black pumps I'd borrowed from Joy. It was long-sleeved with a bit of a V-neck and hit perfectly at my upper calves, showing off a little leg. I had skipped the makeovers I'd been so looking forward to in favor of showering after my dip in the koi pond, but Kimmie had volunteered, or insisted, rather, that she do my makeup and the results were surprising. Every time I tried to pull off a smoky eye, it looked like I'd been hit in the face with a baseball bat, but she'd created the look flawlessly.

"You don't use lip liner?" Kimmie had asked while drawing on my lips.

"I pretty much only use lip gloss," I responded, trying to keep my mouth still.

She shook her head as if the information was too much to comprchcnd.

I twirled in the full-length mirror. I looked good. Amazing. I looked like the woman I was before Aubrey.

As much as I wanted to revel in my Cinderella moment, my heart was heavy.

An hour earlier I'd FaceCalled with Aubrey and David on my laptop, which had been bittersweet.

"Say hi to Mama!" David sang, while holding Aubrey up to the camera. Her sweet little face gazed innocently at me on the screen and it was all I could do to hold back the tears. I missed her so much. I wondered for a second if it had been a mistake to leave her. All I'd wished for the past ten months was a break, and now that I had one, I was dying to have her in my arms.

"I love you, baby!" I said, waving at her, and she broke out into a huge grin at the sound of my voice.

"So, how's Napa?" David asked, juggling Aubrey, who was wearing a pair of too-small yellow pajamas.

"It's good," I said. My mind flashed back to my accidental dip in the koi pond. "Really good."

"I'm glad," he said. I could tell his words were sincere, despite the solemn look in his eyes.

"David, are you sure this is what you want?" I asked gently. "I just can't believe this is happening. What about a business loan?"

David pursed his lips. "I've already tried, Ashley. We really needed the DentaFresh account."

I sighed. "So when do we move?"

Aubrey giggled.

"I found a Realtor who thinks that if we price it right, we'll have an offer in two weeks."

My heart sank. "How are Ross and Donnie doing?" Ross and Donnie were David's partners and both fathers with families. I figured they were as devastated as David. I tried not to cry.

He shrugged. "Nobody's happy, obviously, but they're young. They'll find work easily."

His voice tightened up. I knew this was hard for him.

"And Melissa?" I asked, trying to come off nonchalant.

David scowled. "I could care less."

I blinked. "What happened?"

"Oh, I didn't tell you? She's the reason we lost the DentaFresh account."

"What?"

"Yeah. An old buddy of mine on one of their accounts told me they passed on us because someone on our team sent them an email pretending to be a rival company to light a fire underneath them. She denied it, of course, but I checked up on it and the email definitely came from our server's network. What was she thinking?"

My body flushed with heat and I couldn't breathe.

"What...what are you going to do?" I managed to say, practically trembling.

"I fired her yesterday," he said, shaking his head. "I can't believe she'd do that to us."

"You can't," my voice said without permission from my brain.

"What?" David stared into the camera.

I moved backward on the bed, as if trying to create distance in addition to the thousands of miles already between us.

"You can't fire her. Not like this." I was shaking.

"Ashley, if—"

"It was me, David," I blurted out. "I sent the email."

David looked like he was going to faint as he took in my words.

"You? Ashley...why...when?"

I held my face with my hands. "I was trying to help, I knew you were worried, oh, my gosh, David, I'm so sorry. It's all my fault."

I covered my face and breathed deeply, waiting for him to speak.

He took a deep breath and his face relaxed. Relief washed over me. Then he spoke.

"Yeah. It is."

My breath caught in my throat. "What?"

"I can't believe you did this," he said, dryly. He stared at me as if trying to recognize a stranger.

Tears sprung into my eyes. "David, I said I was sorry..."

He stood up out of the frame. All I could see were Aubrey's feet dangling from his hip.

"I can't talk to you right now. I'll call you tomorrow."

"David."

"Bye."

The camera went black.

I sat there in shock. He had every right to be upset, but I wasn't expecting this.

What was I thinking? I sat on the bed, staring at my hands. I hadn't been thinking. I'd been in a sleep-deprived haze that day, but that was no excuse. I should have thought. I should have talked to him first. I was just scared for him, trying to help. He'd never forgive me for this. A tear slid down my cheek. I just wanted to be at home, not here in some mansion pretending to be someone I'm not.

I wiped my face. May as well let the other shoe drop.

I clicked on the email icon on my computer and without thinking composed a letter to Nina and Lola.

To: Nina Pikkering and Lola Vetter
From: Ashley Keller
Subject: The truth about me
Hello Nina, Lola and everyone at La Lait. I have something to confess that has been weighing heavily on me. I'm not who you think I am. I'm not breastfeeding and never was. What happened in the café when we first met was all a misunderstanding and then, because I was so desperate for friends, and you were all so wonderful to me, I led you to believe that I was one of you. Well, I'm not. I'm sorry for lying. I won't contact you again.
Ashley

I pressed Send before I could chicken out then clicked my computer shut. I took another deep breath. I didn't feel scared. I didn't feel sad. I didn't feel anything. I glanced around the room and noticed the welcome basket sitting on the dresser. Kimmie had already rifled through it and probably snagged all the good stuff, but a mini bottle of champagne remained. Not feeling the need for formalities like ice or glasses, I uncorked it and helped myself to a few long, bubbly sips. Within a few minutes I felt refreshingly peppy. When did I become such a lightweight?

I gazed at myself in the bathroom mirror. Two months ago I would have been thrilled to know I'd be standing right here, all dressed up, about to have dinner in Emily Walker's home. Two months ago this would have been my dream.

"Are you coming, Ashley?" I heard Kimmie call from the bedroom.

I walked toward the door and stumbled a little before catching my step.

"Note to self, don't fall over," I whispered, giggling. I hadn't drunk that much, but the tension from my call with David seemed to make the alcohol go straight to my head.

Kim raised an eyebrow at me as I walked toward her. She looked gorgeous in her red strapless minidress and matching red heels. Her makeup was even more dramatic than mine— from the cat eye to the bold, crimson lipstick, she looked like she'd jumped right out of a luxury car commercial. How did this person have children?

I stumbled again.

"Someone's been enjoying themselves a little too much! Wish you'd saved some of that good stuff for me!" she said, laughing.

I picked my purse up off of the bed and offered Kim my elbow. "Shall we?"

She hooked her elbow in mine. "We shall."

So what if I'd lost my house, my friends and my husband's trust? Tonight, I was determined to have one night of fun before facing the music that was waiting for me at home.

The large dining room had the air of a sophisticated French restaurant. Twinkling lights hung from the brick accent wall, which was draped with real ivy. The long, beautiful table was

set with glass vase centerpieces bursting with white hydran-
geas, and tall cream-colored candles adorned the silver run-
ner. The entire table was dotted with tea lights that flickered
against dimly lit walls. It was breathtakingly romantic.

Even in my state, I could appreciate how stunning the room
was. A butler, with a white tea towel on his arm, stood at attention by the door.

"May I help you ladies to your seats? Madame Keller and
Madame Reardon, yes?"

Kim and I looked at each other before bursting into laughter.

"How did you know our names?" I asked incredulously.

The butler didn't smile. "We have been briefed on all guests.
Please follow me."

We were led to seats at the head of the table. I picked up
the pink and gray folded name card on my salad plate. Ashley Keller.

Kimmie was seated beside me. She whispered in my ear,
"Ashley! You're sitting next to Emily! Lucky! Wanna switch?"
She tried to edge her way past me.

"Not on your life!" I yell-whispered back, sitting down
quickly.

A woman appeared on my right. "Champagne, madame?"

"Yes, please!" I answered.

The woman gently took my flute and filled it.

When Kimmie's glass was full we cheered and sipped. The
bubbly liquid was like a calming balm against my anxieties.

I turned to Kimmie and put a hand on her shoulder.

"I love this. I love you." A carefree laugh escaped out of
my mouth and became a snort.

Kimmie's eyes grew wide. She nudged me. "Well, you'd
better pull it together because here comes Queen Bee."

Everyone rose, as if a dignitary had just entered the room. I stood too quickly, causing my chair to fall backward. For some reason, I found it hilarious and dissolved into cheery laughter.

Janice, who was seated directly across from me, exchanged glances with Lauren.

"Whoops!" Emily bent down to help me right my chair. "Good evening, Ashley. How is your hand?"

I lifted up my palm. "As good as new. I can barely feel my hand. Or my face." I giggled.

"I'm…glad to hear it," she said, kindly ignoring the second half of my statement.

Emily looked stunning, as always, in a pale pink and lavender knee-length tea dress with white sling-backs. Her hair was pulled back into an elegant bun. She wore a pearl necklace and matching earrings. Her makeup was subtle but polished: a mauve lip, long dark lashes and charcoal shadow.

Emily took her place at the head of the table, to my right, and everyone took their seats.

"It's so nice to see all of you tonight. I can't tell you how excited I am about the Motherhood Better Bootcamp Finale tomorrow. Who's ready to find out who's going to be crowned as the Motherhood Better champion?"

Everyone clapped politely. I hooted. Janice coughed and gave me a disapproving look.

"Before we dig into this glorious meal that my chef, Lorenzo, put together, I just want to thank all of you for sharing so much of yourselves and being so willing to put yourselves out there. It means everything, not just to me, but to the thousands of women who will hear about your journeys tomorrow."

The women nodded politely. A chiseled Latin man wearing a chef's hat and black apron appeared behind Emily.

"Ah, Lorenzo! Everyone, this is the chef whose amazing

recipes grace the pages of EmilyWalker.com. He's been feeding my family since before my eldest could walk."

Lorenzo took off his hat, revealing a luscious head of black ear-length curls. It was as if the room suddenly grew warmer. I saw a few ladies shift in their seats.

"It's very nice to meet all of you. I hope you enjoy your meal. Bon appetit!" he said, nodding.

I raised my hand.

Emily looked at me, confused.

"Yes, Ashley?"

I heard myself speak. "Actually, I have a question for Lorenzo."

Emily laughed nervously. "Okay."

Lorenzo stared at me, curious.

I took a sip of my champagne and tried to look scholarly.

"Do you have any advice for mothers who hate cooking?"

The table burst out into laughter. Emily blinked, wide-eyed.

I glanced at Janice and noticed that her face was red with laughter.

Lorenzo chuckled and then placed his finger on his chin. "Takeout?"

Everyone burst into rowdy guffaws again. Even Emily had her napkin against her mouth to hide her chuckles.

Emily put her hands up. "Okay, okay, everyone. Very funny, Ashley. Who's ready to eat?"

Everyone clapped and hollered. I'm not sure if it was the promise of food, the champagne or my question, but the mood had relaxed significantly.

A flurry of waitstaff placed appetizers on everyone's plates.

Mine arrived—a set of three mini puff pastries, all stuffed with unique fillings. There was creamy chive, some sort of smoked fish and one overflowing with a fragrant relish.

Once everyone had been served, Emily raised her fork. "Dive in!"

And we did! Course after course continued to arrive. I lost count after five. The main dish was half a crispy, perfectly roasted duck with roasted garlic potatoes and asparagus. I hadn't eaten that well since my wedding.

"So, moms," Emily said, dabbing her lips with a linen napkin. "Before we go live tomorrow, I want to hear what your bootcamp experiences have really been like. Feel free to be perfectly honest."

A woman in her late twenties wearing a green cardigan and skirt set with black curly hair raised her hand. I recognized her as Lillian Pearson. She had three-year-old twin girls and had written the most thoughtful journal entry about starting a food drive in her city.

"Yes, Lillian!" Emily said, taking a most un-Emily-like swig from her wineglass. Was that her fourth glass?

Lillian stood. She smoothed the front of her sweater. "I just want to say that this has been the best experience of my life," she began shyly. "Usually, it's just me and the kids at home all day, not really talking to anyone. Since starting the Motherhood Better Bootcamp, I've felt like I have real friends and—" Her voice broke and she took a second to compose herself. "I feel like people understand me."

I could feel tears welling in my eyes. Glancing at Kimmie, I noticed her wipe the corner of her eye with her napkin. Even Janice was misting up.

Lillian continued. "I want to thank you, Emily, for putting this together. I've admired you for a long time and it has been an honor."

Emily stood up and, without saying a word, pushed out her chair, walked over to Lillian and gave her a long hug.

My heart swelled. *This is what it's all about*, I thought. *This is all I want and need in motherhood. People who get it.*

Emily made her way back to her seat, wiping her eyes with her fingers the whole way. She took another sip. "Does anyone else want to share?"

My hand shot up.

Emily smiled. "Ashley? The floor is all yours."

I stood up and felt myself get a little dizzy. My two glasses of champagne had gone right to my head. I used Kimmie's shoulder for balance. She laughed into her glass.

Once upright, I cleared my throat. "Everyone. Emily." I turned to face my host. "I'm not like all of you. I don't bake. Not anything very edible, anyway. I can't crochet my own baby clothes. I'd rather order pizza than make anything." I looked up and saw that everyone was staring at me, most with jaws dropped, but nothing was going to stop me now. "My house is always a mess and I'm genuinely surprised that a family of possums hasn't moved in." I paused, trying to find my words. My eyes met Emily's.

"I'm not like you. You're perfect, Emily. I've always wanted to be the kind of mom you are and I'll never be that. You make organic gluten-free apple butternut squash scones. I eat peanut butter off of a spoon in my underwear on the couch while my baby naps. You recycle old clothes into keepsake quilts. I sometimes buy new pants to avoid doing laundry. You make the most beautiful crafts out of mason jars and buttons. I don't know where my passport is."

I heard someone giggle.

"Point is, I know I shouldn't win tomorrow, because before me is a group of women—" I turned to Kimmie "—not you, Kimmie. You're just as messy as I am. Women who inspire me and make me feel insanely jealous and inadequate. I want to raise my glass to all of you."

I thrust my wineglass in the air, sending a stream of chardonnay directly into my face.

"Ow!" I screamed as the liquid burned my eyes.

Emily jumped up and put a napkin to my face, helping me back into my seat.

I blinked my eyes until everything came into focus.

Emily began to speak. "That was...quite the speech, Ashley, I—"

"I HATE MY HUSBAND," said a voice to my left.

It was Serena Hossfield, mother of four and bake-sale fundraising expert. Emily and I both stared.

She stood up, suddenly shy. "I mean, I love him, but I hate him at the same time. He doesn't understand my life at all. He pretends to take a crap and plays on his phone for hours at a time."

Other moms nodded enthusiastically and murmured. I exhaled sharply. Was this happening?

"I HATE CRAFTS!" a petite mousy brunette shouted, standing up. Tanya Gregory, mom of three. I'd recognize that face anywhere. She'd practically flooded the portal with photos of her creations: keepsake boxes, scrapbooking ideas and shadow boxes.

"I HATE THEM!" she screamed again. Her eyes were wide and wild. She took a long drink of the brown liquid on the rocks in her glass. "I only do them because they make me feel better than other moms who can't. It's my gift and my curse. But deep down, I'd like to douse my craft room and set it ablaze."

From her seat, Emily tried to regain control of the rapidly spiraling room. "Okay, okay, everyone," she said, pushing down with her hands.

"Breastfeeding sucks!" shouted a tall woman with a black

bob next to Janice. She stood up. Her sweater dress accentuated her slim build.

"I hated every minute of it, but my doula convinced me my baby would be a dumb-ass if I didn't do it. That's crazy. My nephew was breastfed for two years and he's the slowest kid I know."

Emily stood up. "That's quite enough, everyone. I know our lives aren't easy but..." Her voice trailed off and she stared at the empty seat directly across from hers. The one meant for her husband.

"You know what? Screw this." Emily threw her napkin down on the table and everyone stared at her like they would a mother who had finally snapped.

Emily picked up her drink. "I'm tired of being little miss perfect. Life is freaking hard sometimes. It's hard. Kids don't listen. Husbands act like jackasses and I do EVERYTHING! I do everything! I'm tired of making organic quinoa cakes when I just want to order a pizza. I love chocolate cake. I love gluten. I LOVE GLUTEN." Emily gestured toward her lower half.

Everyone cheered.

"To gluten!" she said, raising her wineglass. We all raised ours with her.

Emily put her other hand on the table and leaned forward. "Who wants to get crazy?"

Everyone hooted. Emily smiled. "Lorenzo! We're gonna need more wine!"

Friday, March 8,
6 A.M.

I woke up with a splitting headache. I put my hands on my head, trying to quell the throbbing coming from within my brain.

Opening my eyes, I noticed that I wasn't in my bed. I wasn't inside. I was lying in a pool chair next to the hot tub. Beside me was Janice, hunched over on a beach towel propped up against a table. I scanned the crime scene. Among the bottles, bags of chips, empty pizza boxes and wet bikinis were passed-out moms. Then I noticed Emily. She was fast asleep, curled up on a pile of robes under a patio table.

I sat up. Kimmie was on the next beach chair over.

I pushed her shoulder. "Kimmie. Kimmie, wake up." She grumbled and struggled to open her eyes.

"Kimmie, what time is it? Aren't we taping today?"

Kimmie's eyes flew open. She jumped up with the strength of a dozen toddlers. "You have got to be kidding me! I need my injections!" And with that she gathered her shoes and ran toward the main house.

"Emily! Emily!" I could see Anna running across the lawn toward us with her trademark clipboard in hand.

When she finally reached us, Anna stopped dead in her tracks, trying to take in the carnage.

"What. Happened. Here?" she whispered.

I stood up and wobbled a bit. "We got a little…um, wild last night after dinner."

"I can see that," Anna said through her teeth.

Anna stomped over to Emily and gently prodded her shoulder. "Emily. EMILY."

Emily woke up with a start and tried to rise, hitting her head on the bottom of the table.

"Oh, my, what time is it?" Emily said, rubbing her eyes.

"We're an hour from taping. The set is ready and the whole crew is here."

"No, no, no, no, no." Emily crawled out from under the table and wrapped a towel around herself. "Anna, why didn't you wake me earlier?"

"I couldn't find you! Hurry, you need to go to wardrobe. We don't have time for a rehearsal."

Emily stood up and faced the group of exhausted, half-sleeping, hungover women in various states of dress.

"Everyone! Wake up! We're going live in an hour! Go get dressed! Meet me in the main lobby in half an hour for makeup! Chop-chop!" she said, clapping her hands.

Women began to move, sliding off patio chairs and coming out from under tables. It was like a zombie invasion.

Emily and Anna were about to scurry off. I grabbed Emily by the arm.

"Emily, I'm so sorry, I—"

Emily raised a hand. "Ashley. Best. Night. Ever." She ran off and I stood there smiling.

It was showtime.

Back in the room, Kimmie was spinning around like a Tasmanian devil.

"I can't believe we partied last night! The night before we were supposed to go on live TV in front of millions of people!" she said frantically, throwing cosmetics and outfits in every direction.

"Relax, Kimmie," I said, removing last night's eye makeup with a baby wipe. "Just jump in the shower and get dressed."

Kimmie turned to face me. "I don't just 'jump in the shower and get dressed.' I had my routine all planned out and I'm about six hours behind on it."

She walked into the bathroom and slammed the door.

I'd planned to shower, but what was another day without one? Anyway, I was pretty sure I'd been in the hot tub at some point, which was as good as a shower.

My stomach fluttered. Tonight I'd see Aubrey and David. Hopefully he'd settled down a bit and wasn't still so angry with me.

I looked in the vanity mirror. The area under my eyes was streaked with dark makeup, my complexion was blotchy and my hair was a knotted mess, but I couldn't help but smile. I'd had fun. For the first time in a very long time, I'd had carefree fun. I hadn't even drunk that much, just gotten carried away with a group of women who were all having their first fun night in ages. I laughed as the night came back to me. I'm pretty sure Lorenzo brought out organic lychee Jell-O shots at one point, and Emily did a cannonball in the pool.

I wiped the rest of my makeup from my face and brushed out my hair.

Time to change. Thankfully, I'd already planned my outfit. I stood up and pulled a hanger out of the closet. The producers of *The Emily Walker Show* had emailed guidelines for what not to wear, which included blue (in case they used a blue screen), complicated patterns and wild colors. They hadn't said no to yoga pants and XXL T-shirts, but I assumed they were also discouraged.

I quickly changed into a slimming heather-gray skirt suit. I had plenty of these from my office days, but none of those fit, so I'd had to buy one the day before we took off. I knew we didn't have the money for new clothes but I considered it the last little splurge before we tightened up, and how often would I be on national TV? This moment would be frozen in history; I wanted to at least *look* pulled together.

I could still hear the shower running when I left the room. Kimmie was probably in there pumping her face full of a chemical cocktail.

The set was larger than life.

Large cameras and microphones on robotic arms, wires everywhere, men and women wearing all black hustling to and fro and staring at large monitors. How they'd managed to turn the room where we'd had brunch just two days prior into a real live set, I'd never know.

I tried to take it all in. At the front of the room were three large couches and Emily Walker's signature pink armchair. I presumed that was where we'd be sitting. My stomach flipped. I was going to be on live television. What if I threw up?

"Are you looking for makeup?" a college-aged man in thick horn-rimmed glasses asked me.

"Yes," I said, trying not to appear as flustered as I was.

"Right this way," he said, leading me through a tangle of thick black cords. As we made our way through the equipment jungle, I realized that today was the day. The winner of the Motherhood Better Bootcamp was going to be announced.

Before I knew it, we were in a corner of the room with several tall stools and women being painted by a crew of artists.

"Take a seat," a man with hair down to his lower back said to me, and I did.

I shifted. "I'm hoping for a natural look, I don't wear a lot of…"

He lifted his finger to his lips. "Shh. Fabio will take care of you."

I closed my eyes. I could feel him pressing a foam applicator to my face, then an eye pencil, lip liner, some type of tickly brush. I flinched as he tweezed my brows. After ten minutes I heard his voice.

"All done."

I opened my eyes, and saw him holding a round hand mirror to my face.

I took it and, with feelings of trepidation running through my veins, looked in.

I didn't recognize myself. I looked like me, but richer. Better. Beautiful. He'd used the contouring method I'd seen on several online videos and had tried once to emulate, which resulted in tiger stripes up and down my face.

I marveled at my reflection.

"Good, right?" Fabio said, grinning.

"Not good. Amazing. Thank you!"

"Ten minutes until we're live!" yelled a stagehand.

Out of nowhere, Kimmie ran into me. She was fully dressed in a stunning navy blue minidress and sky-high white heels. Her hair and makeup made her look like a Miss America contestant.

"Kimmie! When did you get your makeup done?" I didn't recall seeing her being made up.

She flipped her layered, bouncy hair. "I had my own makeup and hair team scheduled to meet me in the room. We barely had enough time."

Emily Walker appeared in the center of the room. She

looked flawless in a pink blazer, white skirt and pink heels. A hush fell over everyone.

"Hello, everyone! I know we had a...special night, but I'm so proud of all of you for making it here on time! This is the moment you've all been waiting for. In a few minutes, we'll be live on television to crown the Motherhood Better Bootcamp champion!"

Everyone cheered.

"And then we'll have breakfast."

A wave of nausea ran over me. I heard a woman say, "No, thanks."

I grabbed a bottle of water from a nearby basket.

"Five minutes until we're live!"

A man popped up next to me. "Ashley? Let's get you miked up," he said, affixing a microphone to the top collar of my blouse.

Kimmie grabbed my hand. "Are you ready?"

"Are you nervous, Kimmie?" I asked, teasing.

She took her hand back. "Absolutely not," she said, smiling sheepishly.

As a group, the women and I made our way up to the stage. Assistants directed us to specific seats. I was just one contestant away from Emily.

Emily sat down in her armchair with a handful of notes.

"Okay, everybody. We didn't have time for a rehearsal, so just act natural, answer the questions and don't be nervous."

Easy for her to say. She'd done this before!

I squirmed under the bright lights. This was the moment the last six weeks had been leading up to. I was a little sad it was all coming to an end, but excited, too. I knew my journey hadn't been as perfect as the others', but I still had a shot, right?

"Thirty seconds until we're live!" a woman shouted and I

felt my stomach flip-flop again. "Don't throw up," I willed my body.

"Ten, nine, eight, seven, six, five, four..." A man next to the largest camera motioned to Emily.

I felt a hot flash run through my body. This was happening.

Emily beamed her million-dollar smile at the camera. "Good morning, and welcome to *The Emily Walker Show*!"

A camera on a long metal arm panned over the three couches. I tried to smile naturally and not like I was being held hostage.

Emily went on. "As you know, this is the grand finale of the Motherhood Better Bootcamp! The moms you see before you spent the last six weeks being mentored by me on how to become the women they've always known they could be. I'd like to introduce you to these women."

Emily went down the line and, as the camera panned across the couches, introduced us by name. I was petrified. Millions of people were staring at us now. By the time she got to me, I was just doing my best not to visibly shake.

"Ashley Keller, mom of ten-month-old Aubrey!" I heard Emily's voice say. I stared like a deer in headlights at a large camera with a flashing red dot indicator. *Smile, Ashley, smile,* I heard my brain saying, and I managed a nervous grimace.

I could already see the Twitter hashtag. #WhatsWrong-WithAshley. It'd be trending before the day was over.

Emily leaned into the camera and smiled her perfect smile. "I'm SO proud of these incredible women! They've changed themselves, their homes and their communities in huge ways. Before I announce the grand prize winner, I have a little surprise for them."

A large, flat LCD screen was wheeled in by an assistant. The women began to murmur curiously. What was going on?

Emily stood next to the screen with a remote in hand. "Ladies, you're not the only ones proud of how far you've come. We have a little secret. We spoke to those who know you best and asked them to share their thoughts."

Emily pointed the remote at the screen and pushed a button.

The EW logo swirled across the screen in pink and white. Suddenly, a man in his forties with toddler twin girls in his lap was sitting on a couch in a modest living room. "Lillian has always inspired me to be better." Lillian covered her mouth and began to tear up.

"Watching her pour herself into this challenge just reminded me of how strong she truly is. I love you, Lil."

Lillian began to sob. "We wuv you, Mommy!" the girls said in unison. I noticed Kimmie quickly wipe a runaway tear from her cheek.

One by one, the women soaked up praise from their spouses and children. I wasn't surprised when a well-dressed man in designer glasses, sitting in what looked like a lavish mansion, turned out to be Kimmie's husband. "You're a winner, babe!" he said, winking.

Kimmie beamed and winked back at the screen. I coughed into my hand to hide my giggle.

When I looked back at the screen, there were David and Aubrey, sitting in our living room. They were on our old couch, which meant this was taped weeks ago. My breath caught in my throat. I missed that living room. I missed my life before I messed everything up and tried to become someone I'm not. I missed my family.

"Ashley is the most incredible, loving woman I know. She's an amazing mother and blows me away every day with her dedication to our daughter. If she didn't change a thing, she'd still be perfect. Perfect for us."

I felt a sob rise in my throat and, despite my best efforts, was in full ugly cry mode in less than five seconds. I couldn't stop. Sob after chest-racking sob consumed me. I had no idea David saw me like that.

A blurry woman handed me a box of tissues. It was Emily Walker, she was standing by my side.

"Beautiful, weren't they?" She spoke into the camera, with one hand on my shoulder. I blew into my tissue. The hashtag had probably changed to #GetAshleySomeHelp.

Emily continued. "When we get back from commercial, I'll announce the winner of the Motherhood Better Boot-camp challenge, live, right here on *The Emily Walker Show*. You won't want to miss it."

"Commercial!" someone yelled, and a flurry of makeup artists descended on the stage.

"Good emotion, Ashley!" Emily said, giving me a thumbs-up as someone dabbed at her eyelids.

I smiled weakly.

Kimmie touched my hand. "Are you going to be alright?"

I blew my nose again. "Yeah, I just…" I trailed off.

Kimmie waved the air in front of her. "No need to explain. When Max said, 'You're a winner, babe,' I would have lost it, too, but I remembered that we're on camera."

Kimmie side hugged me. I could tell she was trying to be sweet.

A makeup artist approached me. "Would you like me to, um…?"

"Yes. Yes, please," I said, bunching up my tissues.

A few moments later, besides slightly red eyes, I was TV ready.

"Twenty seconds!" someone yelled.

Anna appeared to my right.

"Ashley, we need you to move to the first couch."

"What?" My hands began shaking. I was moving closer to Emily? This had to be good!

I swapped seats with another mom and wound up right next to Emily Walker.

"Doing alright, Ashley?" she asked between powder poofs from the makeup crew.

"Absolutely," I said, still a little embarrassed.

Emily smiled kindly.

"We're back in five, four, three..." a man's voice boomed. The crew vanished as quickly as they'd arrived.

Emily flashed her pearly whites at the camera. "We're back live with the Motherhood Better Bootcamp contestants, ready to announce the winner of the $100,000 grand prize! Are you ready?"

Several of the women grabbed the hands of the people on either side of them. I wrung mine together and tried not to barf all over our host.

"The winner...of Motherhood Better Bootcamp is...."

I couldn't breathe. I felt like I was going to pass out. *Just say it!* I thought. Every second felt like an hour.

"Fiona Martin!" I heard the name being said and felt my heart shatter. I knew my chances were slim, but until that moment, hadn't let hope die.

Fiona, the mom of three who made hats for premature babies in NICU burst into tears. She and Emily stood and the two hugged before Fiona was presented with a huge check.

I forced myself to smile and clap politely. Glancing over at Kimmie, I saw that her smile was tight and her eyes narrowed. I stifled a laugh.

"Stay with us after the break!" Emily said.

"Commercial!" the voice boomed.

Emily turned to face all of us. "I'd like to formally present the winner of Motherhood Better Bootcamp, Fiona Martin!" Once again, everyone clapped. Fiona was beside herself.

Large tears streamed down her cheeks and a trickle of snot was threatening to make its way down her lip.

"You guys are all winners to me," Emily continued. "Which is why I'm giving you all the Emily Walker Home set, absolutely free. If you paid for it, you'll be reimbursed. I'm also treating you to a spa day in your city. I have loved getting to know each and every one of you, and I'm going to miss you terribly. Please stay in touch!"

With that, everyone rose and crowded around Emily for a group hug. I didn't even know who I was squeezing as I embraced my new sisters. I may not have won the grand prize, but I in no way felt like a loser.

"We're back in two minutes!" a voice yelled again.

"Okay, Anna will take you to breakfast! We have gift bags for everyone! Thank you, ladies!" Emily said, waving frantically.

I couldn't believe it was all over. I didn't want to go home to my real life where I'd be moving in with my mother-in-law, be friendless yet again and have to face my husband. I wanted to stay here in TV world.

I found my bag and began making my way over to the exit to have one last meal at the Emily Walker estate when Anna stopped me.

"You're not done. Emily needs you for the next segment."

"Next segment?" I repeated, confused.

"Follow me." Anna led me back toward the set where the couches had been replaced by another pink armchair facing Emily's.

I took the seat. Emily took hers and winked at me. What was going on?

"Five, four, three, two...!" the voice yelled.

"Hello, viewers! You just saw me announce the winner of

the Motherhood Better Bootcamp, but I wanted to introduce you to one very special contestant, Ashley Keller."

I tried my best not to appear as confused as I was.

I managed a weak wave.

"Ashley," Emily said, placing her hand on mine. "If you watch *The Emily Walker Show*, and I know you do, you know that every so often, we honor a mom who takes a stand for what she believes in. Today, you are that mom. Please watch the footage."

The room went dark, and behind us, a screen began to play a shaky video of the inside of an airplane. It looked oddly familiar.

A woman with crazy hair—me—was standing up and yelling. "Why don't you have the decency to let this mother tend to her baby in peace!" It was me! On the plane! Defending the mom!

At the end of my rambling speech the lights went back on.

"Someone filmed it?" I managed to sputter.

"Yes, Ashley. Not only did someone film your courageous act, they uploaded it to MyTube. The video of you standing up for a mom being poorly treated received 600,000 views in less than twenty-four hours. Now it's up to 1.5 million!"

"WHAT?" I yelled, forgetting I was on live television. Emily laughed.

"It's not easy being a mom today," she said. "There are so many expectations. You not only helped this one mom feel accepted in the world, but you helped all moms feel less alone when they watched that video."

I felt hot tears stream down my cheeks.

"For that, we'd like to present you with the Emily Walker Hero award and a check for $10,000."

I couldn't control myself any longer. I began to sob.

"I can't believe this. Thank you. Thank you," I sputtered. I leaned over and hugged Emily, crying even harder.

"No, thank you!" Emily said.

A crew member leaned in and handed Emily a box of tissues. She handed them to me and I dabbed at my face, unable to stop the flow of tears. Offstage, I saw all of the moms smiling proudly at us. A new flood opened up.

"When we come back, I'll show you three ways to upcycle used peanut butter containers!"

"Commercial!"

Emily and I stood up at the same time.

"Emily...this means so much. Thank you," I blubbered.

Emily put her hands on my shoulders.

"Ashley, you are an amazing person. Last night you helped remind me why I do this."

We hugged.

"I've got one more segment left—five baby arugula smoothies your toddler will love."

"Sounds delish," I said, and made my way to the group of moms waiting for me.

As soon as we were in the hallway and out of earshot of the set, they swarmed me.

"Go, Ashley!"

"Congratulations!"

Kimmie walked up to me. Her face was emotionless as she stood, her nose six inches away from mine.

"I'm so happy for you!" she said, and threw her arms around my neck, practically choking the life out of me.

To my surprise, I heard her sniffle. I hugged her back, shocked. "Thank you, Kimmie!"

She let go of my neck and wiped her eyes. "It's just that, I know how that woman on the plane felt. Every time I take the kids to the country club I feel so stressed out that they'll make too much noise. Everyone just glares." She flapped her hands emphatically. "But what am I supposed to do? Stay at home 24/7?"

I smiled, nodding. Kimmie's problems always sounded so glamorous.

Anna popped up with her trademark clipboard.

"Hello, ladies! It seems as if the overwhelming consensus is that a full breakfast isn't in the cards because of your...adventure last night." Anna looked up from her clipboard. "So we've taken the opportunity to pack each of you a lunch for your travel home."

Chef Lorenzo and his kitchen staff walked down the hall carrying cute pink bags with pink-ribbon handles.

"Good morning, ladies!" Lorenzo looked as dashing as ever in his pristine white chef's uniform with shiny silver buttons running down the front and a red apron. His crew began distributing the lunches.

"I've packed you all cold, slow-roasted, aged peppercorn beef sandwiches with our local buttery cheddar cheese," he began. Someone behind me dry heaved.

Lorenzo's eyes widened. "Perhaps I will not go into the details right now. You had some night."

Lorenzo leaned into my ear. "Lovely tattoo, by the way."

My body flushed. The skinny-dipping. I'd completely forgotten. He'd been there?

When I got back to my room I grabbed my computer and, typing faster than I ever have before, logged into Facebook to see if any of my new friends had posted incriminating photos from last night and to gauge the response to my televised tear fest. To my relief, there were only a few photos that included me. In all of them, I was smiling and fully clothed. Phew. And I wasn't trending on Twitter. What a relief.

I was just about to check Instagram when Kimmie walked into the room.

"Crazy morning, huh?" she said, throwing items into her bag. "You know..." She stopped packing and stared at me. "I'm going to miss you and all of the moms here. You're not the type of person I'd usually hang out with, or even notice, but I like you."

"Thank you?" I said, getting up to start packing myself.

The rest of the morning flew by. After packing we headed downstairs where all the contestants stood in the foyer, surrounded by bags.

After a few more hugs and exchanges of email addresses, it was time to go. You'd think I'd be sad to leave the gorgeous mansion, catered meals and excellent sleep, but all I could think about was seeing Aubrey and David. I couldn't wait to apologize for how nuts I'd been behaving and hold my baby in my arms.

It was already 11:30. My car was scheduled to arrive at noon to take me to the airport.

"My car's here!" Kimmie said, lowering her sunglasses. She stared at me as if trying to comprehend my entire existence. "You're a doll. It's been real, hun."

"It was great to meet you, Kimmie," I said, giving her a hug.

"Congrats again on the prize. You deserve it, Ashley. You're a good person."

I smiled. If only she knew about La Lait and the Denta-Fresh debacle. I still hadn't received an email back from Nina or Lola. Or anyone.

"Thanks, Kimmie."

"What are you going to do with the money?" she said. "If you're going to invest it in yourself, something I highly recommend, I know a great plastic surgeon."

I laughed.

Anna appeared before I could think of an answer. She was holding a ziplock bag that contained my cell phone covered in moss.

"The groundskeeper discovered this for you," she said flatly. "You do realize there are security cameras everywhere, right?"

I flushed red. "Sorry about that." I quickly took the phone.

"You also have a phone call."

"Oh, thank you."

I knew who it had to be. I quickly said goodbye to Kimmie and followed Anna to a waiting phone.

"Thanks," I said, cupping the receiver, but she didn't budge. I awkwardly turned my back to her.

"Hello?"

"Mama," a small voice said. My mouth hung open and I was speechless. Even though it was the first time I'd heard her say the word, I knew my daughter's voice. Tears began flowing down my face.

"Baby," I managed to choke out.

"Did you hear her?" David's voice was breathless with excitement. "She said *Mama*!"

"I know! It's amazing! When did she first say it?" I was shaking with emotion.

"She saw you on TV and pointed to you and just said Mama."

A fresh batch of tears cascaded down my cheeks and began to form a damp spot on my shirt.

I heard Anna take a few steps away from me to give me a bit of space, but she still remained close.

"I can't believe it. Tell her I love her so much!"

"She knows," David said softly.

The line was quiet for a few moments.

We started talking at the same time.

"David—"

"Ashley—"

We both stopped.

"I want to go first," I said, turning back to see how close Anna was to me. She'd given me a respectable distance of about six feet.

I leaned into the receiver and lowered my voice.

"I am so, so, so, so, sorry. What I did was wrong. I should have told you. I just need you to forgive me."

David sighed. "Ashley, you were trying to help. I know that. I made so many mistakes and the biggest one was making you think you were the only reason DentaFresh passed on us."

"What do you mean?"

"We're a young company. They wanted someone with more experience. I think I just used that email as an excuse to make me feel better. They wouldn't have gone with us, anyway."

"I'm sorry, David. Things will get better."

"No, Ashley. Folding the company is the right thing to do. I need to think about you and Aubrey."

As amazing as it would be to have David home at a normal hour and not be stressed out, I could hear the pain in his voice and knew I couldn't let him do this.

I clenched my fist.

"No. David, I won't let you do this. We'll use the prize money to help with bills until you get the company back on its feet. I know you can do this. This has been your dream forever. I believe in you."

As I said the words, I knew they were true. There was silence on the other end of the phone.

"What do you say?" I asked. "All in?"

After a few moments I heard David clear his throat, the way he does when he's trying not to cry. "All in. I'm all in. I love you, Ashley."

I smiled like a girl on prom night. "I love you, too, David. I can't wait to see both of you."

"You, too, babe."

When we hung up, Anna ran over to me quickly, her black adult-sized Mary Janes clicking on the marble.

"Before you go, Emily would like to speak to you."

She took my arm and we run-walked over to a small office just off of the foyer.

Emily was sitting in a makeup chair in front of a mirror framed by bright lights and wearing a pink robe. Her hair was in rollers.

"Ashleeeey!" she squealed. She hugged me, rocking me back and forth like a giant baby. "Were you surprised?"

I held my cheeks. "I almost fainted! I didn't even know anyone had filmed what happened on the plane! I was just speaking from my heart."

Emily sat back down on her chair and motioned for me to take a seat in the one beside her.

"That's exactly what I wanted to talk to you about."

I sat down.

"What do you mean?"

A woman began taking the curlers out of Emily's hair, sending her hair cascading down her neck like a mini waterfall.

Emily kept her face forward and talked to my reflection in the mirror.

"Ashley, you have a voice. A raw, honest voice that I think mothers everywhere would love. I want you to come work for me."

I laughed. "Me? Work for you? I can't cook, clean or make crafts…" I shook my head, confused.

Emily grinned. "I know. That's why I want you for this. You're real and messy…"

I cleared my throat, "Messy?"

Emily laughed diplomatically. "In the best possible way, of course. Moms relate to you. I want to add a more…relatable aspect to the blog. I want normal, everyday moms to feel part of the Emily Walker family. My marketing team thinks you're perfect and I agree."

I was stunned. I wasn't exactly thrilled to be such an obvious mess, but I totally got it. Emily wanted to inject a dose of reality into her scripted Insta-world.

"Emily, I—"

"Just say yes."

I stared at her, perfect Emily Walker in her robe with full makeup looking like a vision of everything I'd wanted to be. She didn't want me to change. I didn't need to be anyone other than who I already was. I never imagined that someone would want to pay me for that.

"Yes."

"Good. You start next week. Air kisses!" She pursed her lips in my direction and sucked twice.

"Your car is here, Mrs. Keller," said Anna, who had been waiting by the door.

"Bye, Emily…thank you…for everything."

Emily winked at me.

Before I lowered myself into the black Town Car, Anna handed me a white manila envelope.

"It's your check. Congratulations. I'll be in touch about the column." She smiled. I could sense that she was as shocked that I'd be working for Emily as I was.

"Thanks, Anna."

And we were off to the airport.

1 P.M.

I was sitting in first class again. The flight attendant had offered me a glass of champagne, but I passed. Somehow I'd managed to avoid a terrible hangover but my body still felt like I'd run a marathon on stilts.

There was another baby on the flight, this time accompanied by a mother and father in their early thirties. The toddler couldn't have been more than two and was raising absolute hell.

"WANT IPAD NOW!" he shrieked as his father unsuccessfully tried to get him to doze off.

"Sammy, the iPad is dead. Would you like to color?"

His high-pitched growl sounded only partially human. Sammy didn't want to color.

I glanced back and saw his mother trying to buy his silence with a pack of gummy bears.

The passengers around him looked like they were trying to will themselves onto another plane. I smiled. *Note to self: If I ever fly with Aubrey when she's a toddler, bring a charged iPad*, I thought before turning around.

Aubrey. I couldn't wait to see her face. Two months ago I was bored to tears every single day, but now, all I wanted to do was spend a long afternoon on the floor playing blocks.

I looked out the window at the clouds. Everything just felt *better* somehow, and nothing had really changed. Well, except my phone was dead. I wondered if anyone tried to get in touch with me since the show aired.

I fished my laptop out from under the seat in front of me and fired up my email. Forty-three new messages! Most of them were old coworkers and friends saying they saw me on TV.

There was one from Nina. She'd sent it last night.

To: Ashley Keller
From: Nina Pikkering
Subject: Re: The truth about me
Ashley, we know. We've known for some time now. It's not every day someone thinks "nipple confusion" means a baby

can't decide which breast to feed from first. We love you. Can't wait to see you at the next meeting.

PS. You can stop feeding Aubrey in the bathroom now. We don't care. Why should you?

For the second time that day, I was crying. Thank you was all I could write. There was so much to say. I'd say it the next time I saw them.

I saw an email from Joy and clicked on it.

We all watched you on TV together! Congratulations! You were beautiful. You looked a little tired and puffy though— what did I say about making sure you got enough sleep the night before? Check Instagram when you get a minute. When did you get a tattoo?

No. No. No. No.

I'd deal with that later, too. I closed my laptop and placed it in my bag under the seat.

My hand hit a paper bag. It was the pink lunch bag that Lorenzo had packed. I was starting to get a little hungry.

I put my tray down and set the gorgeous pink-and-white checked bag in front of me.

Inside a mesh cooler was a plastic container. Through the lid I could see a delicious-looking artisanal sandwich and some kind of potato salad, separated by dividers. Yum!

I opened the plastic and BAM: the scent hit me like a punch to the face. A wave of nausea rolled through my insides and quickly rose in me like a snake. I closed the container and jumped over the empty seat next to me before sprinting down the aisle.

Once inside the bathroom, my entire guts spilled out into the toilet. I didn't even have time to lock the door. I held it closed with the back of my foot.

I took a deep breath. Maybe I was more hungover than I thought. I tried to make sense of this. I'd been feeling okay a minute ago.

Another wave came and I heaved into the toilet.

After a few moments I flushed, pulled myself up to the sink and washed my hands and face. I looked into the mirror. My eyes were bloodshot and my face ashen, but I felt better.

I opened the door.

A flight attendant was standing in the small hallway of the plane. He looked at me, concerned.

"Ma'am, are you okay?"

I tried to not look like I'd just left all of my internal organs in the flying porta-potty.

"Yes," I said, steadying myself against some turbulence with the wall. "Just a bit sick from a long night."

He smiled knowingly.

"That's not it," said the elderly woman in a green pleated skirt and matching argyle sweater seated in A1.

"Excuse me?" I replied, confused.

The woman looked up from a ball of peach-colored yarn and two quickly moving knitting needles. She wasn't a day under eighty-five. She stared at my face as if she were studying every cell.

"I said, that's not it. You're pregnant." She pointed a needle at my abdomen.

The flight attendant laughed.

"What? I'm sorry, ma'am, but…" My voice trailed off.

My period. It was late.

My eyes widened in abject terror and I looked down at the woman. She smiled, as if taking delight in my realization.

"I'm pregnant."

★ ★ ★ ★ ★

Acknowledgments

Thank you to my agent, Holly Bemiss at the Susan Rabiner Literary Agency. You made this possible. To my editor, Emily Ohanjanians at MIRA Books, thank you for saying yes.